HIGH COUNTRY JUSTICE

HIGH COUNTRY JUSTICE

NIK JAMES

THORNDIKE PRESS
A part of Gale, a Cengage Company

GALE
A Cengage Company

**LIBRARY OF CONGRESS CIP DATA ON FILE.
CATALOGUING IN PUBLICATION FOR THIS BOOK
IS AVAILABLE FROM THE LIBRARY OF CONGRESS.**

ISBN-13: 978-1-4328-9069-8 (hardcover alk. paper)

Published in 2021 by arrangement with Sourcebooks, Inc.

Printed in Mexico
Print Number: 02   Print Year: 2022

To George and Iraj

CHAPTER ONE

Elkhorn, Colorado, May 1878

Caleb Marlowe watched the embers of the fire throw flickering shadows on his new cabin walls. Outside, a muffled sound drew his attention, and Caleb focused on the door at the same time Bear lifted his great head. The thick, golden fur on the neck of the dog rose, and the low growl told Caleb that his own instincts were not wrong.

In an instant, both man and dog were on their feet.

Caleb signaled for the big, yellow animal to stay and reached for his Winchester '73. The .44-caliber rifle was leaning, dark and deadly, against the new pine boards he'd nailed up not two hours before. If he'd had time to hang the door, whoever was out there might have gotten the drop on him.

Moving with the stealth of a cougar, Caleb crossed quickly to one side of the door and looked out, holding his gun. The broad fields gleamed like undulating waves of silver under the May moon between the wooded ridges that formed the east and west boundaries of his property. Down the slope from the cabin, by a bend in the shallow river, he could see the newly purchased cattle settled for the night. From this distance, the herd looked black as a pool of dried blood in the wide meadow.

He could see nothing amiss there. Nice and quiet. No wolves or mountain lions harrying the herd and stirring them up. The only sound was a pair of hunting owls hooting at each other in the distant pines. Still, something was wrong. His instincts were rarely off, and he had a prickling feeling on the back of his neck. He levered a cartridge into the chamber.

Caleb slipped outside into the cool, mountain air and moved silently along the wall of the nearly finished cabin. Bear moved ahead of him and disappeared into the shadow cast by the building blocking moonlight. The crisp breeze was light and coming out of the north, from the direction of Elkhorn, three miles away as the crow flies.

When Caleb peered around the corner, he was aware of the large, yellow smudge of dog standing alert at his feet. Bear was focused on the dark edge of the woods a couple hundred yards beyond Caleb's wagon and the staked areas where the barn, corral, and Henry's house would eventually set. Bear growled low again.

Caleb smelled them before he saw them. Six riders came out of the tall pines, moving slowly along the eastern edge of the meadow, and he felt six pairs of eyes fixed on the cabin.

He had no doubt as to their intentions. They were rustlers, and they were after his cattle. But this was his property — his and Henry's — and that included those steers.

If they'd been smart enough to come down from Elkhorn on the southwestern road, these dolts could have forded the river far below here and had a damn good chance of making off with the herd. It must have surprised the shit out of them, seeing the cabin.

"Bad luck, fellas," Caleb murmured, assessing the situation.

He needed to get a little closer to these snakes. Standing a couple of inches over six feet, with broad shoulders and solid muscles, he was hardly an insignificant target, even at night. His wagon was fifty yards nearer to them, but with this moon, they'd spot him and come at him before he got halfway there. It'd take a damn good shot on horseback from a hundred and fifty yards, but they could close that distance in a hurry. And Caleb would have no cover at all. Beyond the wagon, there were half a dozen stone outcroppings, but nothing else to stop a bullet.

Just then, the cattle must have smelled them too, because they started grunting and moving restlessly. That was all the distraction he needed.

Staying low, Caleb ran hard, angling his path to get the wagon between him and the rustlers as quickly as he could.

He nearly made it.

The flash from the lead rider's rifle was accompanied by the crack of wood and an explosion of splinters above the sideboard of the wagon. A second shot thudded dead into the ground a few yards to Caleb's right. Immediately, with shouts and guns blazing, they were all coming hard.

If Caleb had entertained even a fleeting thought that this might have been a neighborly visit — which he hadn't — the idea was shot to hell now.

He raised his Winchester and fired, quickly levering and firing again. The second shot caught the leader. He jerked back off his saddle and dropped to the ground like a stone.

Caleb wasn't watching. As he turned his sights on the next rider, a bullet ripped a hot line across Caleb's gut just a few inches above his belt, spinning him back a step. Big mistake. Now he was really angry.

They were not a hundred yards away, close enough that he could see the moon lighting their features.

And close enough that he wouldn't miss.

Setting his feet, he put a bullet square in the face of the nearest man, taking off the rider's hat and half his head.

That was enough to give the other four second thoughts. Reining in sharp, two swung out of their saddles and dove for cover behind a pair of boulders. The other two turned tail, digging in their spurs and riding hard for the pines.

Shots rang out from the stone outcroppings, and the sound of bullets whizzing through the air and thudding into the ground around him sent Caleb scurrying toward the wagon.

Both of the rustlers stopped firing almost simultaneously, and Caleb knew they were loading fifteen more into their rifles. The man on the right seemed to be the better marksman. His bullets had been doing serious damage to the wagon.

Going down on one knee between the

front and back axles, Caleb slid the barrel of his rifle across the wagon's reach. Aiming for the spot on the edge of the boulder where he'd last seen the better shooter positioned, he waited.

He didn't have long to wait. The gleaming barrel of the rustler's rifle appeared, immediately followed by a hatless head. Caleb squeezed the trigger of the weapon Buffalo Bill himself called the *Boss*. The shooter's head disappeared, and the rifle dropped into the grass beside the boulder.

Before Caleb could swing his gun around, the other fellow gave up the cover of his boulder and started running for the pines, stopping only once to turn and fire a round. That was his final mistake. A flash of golden fur streaked across the field, and Bear's teeth were in his shoulder even as he bowled the desperado to the ground. Managing to throw the dog off him as he staggered to his feet, the rustler was drawing his revolver from its holster when Caleb's bullet ripped into him, folding him like an old Barlow knife before he fell.

Caleb called off Bear and strode quickly across the field toward the pines, loading cartridges into his Winchester as he moved. He knew the place where the other two entered the forest had put a deep gulch

12

between them and Elkhorn. So, unless they planned to ride their horses straight up the side of the ridge to the east, they'd boxed themselves in.

Caleb entered the pines, listening for any sound of horse or rider. It was dark as a church here, with only a few openings where the moonlight broke through the boughs. The cool smell of pine filled his senses, and he saw Bear disappear off to the right.

Since the dog was following them, he decided to track to the left.

A few minutes later, his foot caught air, and he nearly went over the edge of the gulch. Caleb caught himself and peered into the blackness of the ravine. The spring melt was long over, and there was no sound of running water. And no sound of any riders that might have gone over the ledge either.

No such luck, he thought.

Working his way along the edge, Caleb soon heard the sound of low voices.

". . . got to go back down there. Ain't no other way."

"I ain't heard no shots for a while."

Caleb moved closer until he saw them standing with their horses in a small clearing illuminated by the blue light of the moon.

"Maybe they killed the sumbitch."

13

"Maybe they did, and maybe they didn't."

They froze when their horses both raised their heads in alarm.

"What's that?"

On the far side of the clearing, Bear crept into view, head lowered and teeth bared.

Before either one could draw, Caleb stepped in behind them. "Throw 'em down."

Unfortunately, some fellows never know when to fold a losing hand.

One of them drew his revolver as he whirled toward the voice. Caleb's Winchester barked, dropping the man where he stood.

The other swung his rifle but never got the shot off. Bear leaped, biting down on the hand holding the gunstock. Locking his viselike jaws, the dog shook his head fiercely, eliciting a scream.

Trying to yank his hand and the weapon free, the rustler stumbled and fell backward into the shadow of the tall pines, pulling the yellow dog with him. As Caleb ran toward them, he fired his rifle. The intruder twitched once and lay still.

Even in the dim light, he could see the life go out of the man's eyes. The bullet had caught him under the chin and gone straight up.

"Leave him, Bear," he ordered.

The black-faced dog backed away, shook his golden fur, and stood looking expectantly at his master.

"Done good, boy."

Caleb straightened up and, for the first time, felt the stinging burn from the bullet that had grazed his stomach. Pulling open the rent in his shirt, he examined the wound as well as he could. Some bleeding had occurred, but it had mostly stopped.

Could have been a lot worse, he thought.

A few minutes later, with the two dead men tethered across their saddles, Caleb led the horses single file back down through the pine forest. As they drew near the open meadow, Bear stopped short and raised his nose before focusing on something ahead.

Caleb looped the reins of the lead horse over a low branch and moved stealthily forward.

In the darkness at the edge of the forest, another rider — wearing a bowler and a canvas duster — was peering out at the unfinished cabin and the four saddled horses grazing in the silvery field. Caleb raised his rifle and took dead aim.

"All right. Raise your hands where I can see them."

Slowly, the hands lifted into the air as Bear

15

trotted over and sniffed at the intruder's boot.

"Start talking," Caleb demanded.

As the rider turned in the saddle, a spear of moonlight illuminated her face. A woman's face, and a damn pretty one, at that.

Caleb nearly fell over in surprise.

"I was coming after you, Mr. Marlowe. But the fellows who were riding those horses beat me to it."

CHAPTER TWO

Caleb approached the woman cautiously. Right now, he was trying to ignore the empty feeling that always came after killing. And even though his instincts told him this rider had no intention of doing him any harm, he had no assurance she wasn't packing a firearm beneath that duster.

"You are Mr. Marlowe, aren't you?"

"I am. What's your connection with those fellas, ma'am?"

The rider tilted her head slightly as she considered the question. "Oh! I have no connection with them whatsoever. I was coming to find you when I saw them leaving Elkhorn ahead of me."

"And you followed?" His tone was sharp. Following six unfamiliar men in the middle of the night. She was evidently not too smart.

"I heard one of them mention your name." She matched his tone. "I figured following them would be the easiest way to get here. They did look like a rough bunch, however, so I was careful and stayed well behind them."

He wasn't feeling any better about what she'd done but decided to let her talk. The woman wasn't really his concern, but the sooner she had her say, the sooner he could go about his own business. He had more bodies to collect while the moon was still high.

"I must admit, when they turned off the road into the pine forest some ways after leaving town, I got a bit lost. But I heard gunshots and followed the sound. I hope there was no trouble."

Depends on who you ask, he thought. Caleb eyed her horse. "Ain't that Doc Burnett's gelding?"

"Yes, it is."

"Who are you, ma'am, and what are you doing with his horse?"

She took off the bowler, and a thick braid fell down her back. "I'm Sheila Burnett. My father is Dr. Burnett. I know from his letters that he's a friend of yours."

Caleb was taken aback by her words. Doc was indeed a friend of his, about the only one he'd claim as such in Elkhorn. But he'd had the impression that Doc's daughter was

18

a young girl living with his in-laws back East somewhere. This was a grown and confident woman.

Maybe a bit overconfident.

"Why the devil is your father sending you out here in the dark of night, Miss Burnett?" Perhaps his tone was too sharp still, because Bear gave him a look and then trotted off into the pines.

"That's the problem, Mr. Marlowe. He didn't send me. I arrived on the coach from Denver yesterday to find he's gone missing. I need your help finding him."

Caleb had seen Doc only two days ago, and he was just fine. This daughter of his couldn't know it, of course, but the doctor often traveled away from town to look after miners and other folks who needed him. He might be on the road. Curious that the man had said nothing about the imminent arrival of his daughter, though.

Caleb cradled his rifle in the crook of his arm. "Your father can take care of himself, Miss Burnett. But tell me, are you armed?"

"Of course not."

She had the false confidence of a greenhorn.

"Was Doc expecting you?"

"In our recent correspondence, I mentioned my interest in paying him a visit."

19

"Was your father expecting you?" he repeated.

"Not exactly. Once I decided to come, a letter would have been too slow in arriving. And as you know, the telegraph lines haven't reached Elkhorn as yet."

Caleb shook his head slightly. An overly confident greenhorn with an impetuous disposition. A dangerous combination in these wild Rockies. Someone needed to explain a few things to this young woman about the dangers she'd exposed herself to, but he had six dead blackguards who'd be attracting wolves and coyotes and all kinds of undesirables before sunup.

"If you wouldn't mind moving out into the field there a ways, I'll follow you directly. After I finish up a chore or two, I'll take you back to Elkhorn and —"

"But what about finding my father?"

"We'll talk about that after I deliver you back to town." This woman was trouble he didn't need.

As Caleb turned to retrieve the horses and the dead men lashed to their saddles, he saw his dog trot out ahead of Doc's daughter.

"And what's your name, fellow?"

"That good boy is Bear," Caleb called after her. "But usually he ain't one to offer up his name to folks he don't know."

A few minutes later, he led the two mounts out into the field to find Miss Burnett standing by her horse with Bear sitting and leaning against her leg. Not his dog's customary response to strangers, though maybe it was because she was wearing Doc's bowler and duster, Caleb decided.

She stopped petting the dog's head, and he heard her sharp intake of breath the moment she saw what the horses were carrying.

"These men are dead?" she asked, her voice wavering.

"Yes, Miss Burnett. They are." Not an uncommon outcome for fellows like these.

"You killed them?"

"I did, ma'am," Caleb replied, stopping as he reached her. "Though it could have turned out different. And that would not have been good for either you or me."

"You took their lives."

That was the same as killing, but he didn't feel it was worth dwelling on. "They came to take mine."

"Are you sure that was what they intended? Did you speak to them before . . . before . . . ?" She waved a hand toward the dead bodies.

"There's no *before* in that situation," he

21

said, now irritated.

"You couldn't shoot them in the leg? Or in the arm? You couldn't stop them?" She shook her head in frustration. "*Why* did you have to kill them?"

When someone opens fire on you in the dead of night, Caleb thought, you react or you're dead. He bit back the lecture he was ready to deliver, reminding himself it wasn't his job to make this woman understand the realities of frontier life.

"Take a step back, ma'am, so I can finish what I have to do here."

As he led the horses bearing the corpses past her, she drew back in silent but obvious aversion. Welcome to Colorado.

Four bodies lay in the field between the pine forest and the cabin. When Caleb reached the closest one, he heard a low moan coming from the inert shape. The yellow dog stood beside him, a growl emitting from his throat.

"It's all right, boy," he said quietly. "He can't hurt nobody."

The rustler was lying on his side, his hat and rifle strewn in the grass nearby. To be safe, Caleb knelt and moved the man's fallen Colt .44 away from his body.

"He's alive." The soft voice came from right behind him.

For the moment, anyway. The bullet had caught the fool in the gut and doubled him over. He heard her footsteps move toward the nearby corpses.

"But these men are dead," she called out, standing over one. "You killed them. Every one of them. Five lives. Assuming this man lives."

"Would you mind helping here, Miss Burnett? Where you could be of some use?"

"Of course," she said, immediately coming to him. "How can I help? What can I do?"

For a moment, the tone of hostility was gone. There was some of the Doc's spirit in the woman, to be sure.

"This moonlight ain't quite bright enough for tending to this one. Could you fetch the lantern hanging by the hearth in the cabin? If you'd light it and bring it here, I'd be much obliged."

She ran off across the field, and Caleb gently turned the rustler over. Even in the dim light, it was obvious the bullet had struck him beneath the ribs and had done a great deal of damage. The man's woolen vest was black with blood.

"I'm sorry for coming after you," the wounded man gasped, drawing Caleb's gaze to his face. "We only planned to take the cattle."

Good thing Miss Burnett wasn't hearing this, or she would tell him he should have handed over his herd and hidden under the wagon to avoid bloodshed.

"Save your strength, fella."

"Nothing to save it for now. I know I'm a goner."

Caleb figured they were about the same age. Late twenties. "Don't get ahead of yourself. We're gonna patch you up as best we can and then get you to town."

"Listen." The man's hand reached out and clutched at Caleb's sleeve. "I ain't made much of my life, but I still got a ma back home . . . Michigan . . ." He winced with pain and then coughed. Blood speckled his lip and chin.

"And you'll see her again."

The man was fading fast. "Inside pocket of my coat . . . a letter . . . for her. If you could send it. And let her know . . ."

He gazed at the rustler's face. Doc's daughter was coming across the field, holding up the lit lantern. "I'll do that. You just lie quiet."

The man's face twisted, and then the light went out of his eyes. He'd be lying quiet for a long time.

Caleb reached into the dead man's coat and found the letter. Holding it up to the moonlight, he could see it was addressed and sealed. He frowned, slipped it inside his elk-skin vest, and stood up.

Sheila Burnett came close, holding the lantern high. "Is he . . . ?"

"Gone."

"Six. You killed six people tonight."

She drew back, and Caleb took the lantern from her. He watched her look around and wondered if, before tonight, she'd ever seen anyone dead, never mind six who'd bought eternity so suddenly and violently. That would be a lot for anyone to take in.

"If you could help gather those horses, I'll hoist up the bodies, and we can take them back to town."

"I'll gather the horses for you, but I take back what I said before."

Finally, she was regaining some sense. He waited for her apology.

"I think you're a barbarian, Mr. Marlowe. And for the life of me, I can't understand how it is that my father — a doctor, a man dedicated to saving lives — could befriend someone who takes them with no feeling of regret whatsoever."

This woman was definitely testing his patience. Not Caleb's long suit.

"You don't know what you're talking about."

"I'm simply stating facts."

"And they're taking you down a slippery trail. You know nothing about me."

"So be it, Mr. Marlowe. I shall not need your assistance. I'll find my father on my own." She gave him a curt nod. "Good day to you."

"Considering the hour, miss, and the unfamiliar terrain, I'll be taking you back to Doc's house in Elkhorn, whether you like it or not."

His tone was hard enough to leave her no choice.

"As you please." She turned on her heel in a huff and stomped toward the horses.

Caleb shook his head and prayed that his patience would hold out until they reached town. And for Doc's sake, he hoped this daughter of his would keep her visit here brief.

CHAPTER THREE

Doc Burnett carefully peeled away the surgical gauze he'd used to cover the woman's wound. The operation had gone well enough, all things considered. He held the lantern up to look at the injury. The hole where the bullet entered the shoulder above the right breast was red and swollen, but it hadn't festered yet. Still, she was not out of the woods. It had only been a few hours since he closed the wound.

If her luck held, she'd live. For now. But with these killers holding Doc's and the woman's fates in their hands, he didn't know for how long. The odds weren't too good that he'd survive this either.

He had a pretty fair idea what was going on. Two open Wells Fargo strongboxes sat in a corner of the one-room shack, and unwanted bundles of letters lay scattered around them. Whatever gold or valuables had been in the strongboxes was gone.

27

Doc had heard and read plenty of stories about road agents holding passengers of quality for ransom. Occasionally, the kidnap victims were even returned alive. But not often.

Smith, a miner he'd only known by sight, had come after him yesterday morning with a confusing story about an accident. The man had been twitchy as a cat in a downpour, but Doc was well aware of the dangers surrounding the search for silver. Digging in the earth made men a mite strange sometimes. He didn't hesitate. Grabbing his medical valise, he went to get his horse from the livery.

Riding east, they were barely out of Elkhorn when two grim-faced gunslingers came out from behind a clump of pines. Their clothes showed the grime of long use, and their boots were scuffed and worn from the brush and brambles of the Colorado terrain. Each wore a brace of Remingtons on his gun belt. One man had a Winchester in his rifle scabbard. The other, a Henry.

Their appearance didn't come as a great surprise to Doc. There were always reports of road agents operating in the hills, and he never carried anything of great value, other than his pocket watch and a few dollars in his billfold. The real surprise came when, not a half hour later, one of them shot Smith dead, sending the miner tumbling into a ravine at the edge of the road.

Stone-cold killers.

Roughly an hour later, they left the Denver road and made their way up through the pine forests and cottonwood groves, sometimes following a rushing river or a ridge of lichen-covered rock. Several times, they passed solitary shacks by mountain streams and the ghostly gray remains of cabins clustered around the collapsed entrance of an abandoned mine.

Eventually emerging from a forest of fir, Doc spotted the tall peak called Devil's Claw. The mountain was aptly named, stretching clawlike into the blue Colorado sky.

Doc knew there had been mining camps beyond the pass that led north of the Claw. Gold, mostly. But the word was that they were all pretty much deserted. He never ventured this far from Elkhorn.

They rode on silently for an endless stretch.

Checking his watch, he reckoned it took over eight hours for them to reach their destination, the ruins of a deserted mining camp with nearly a dozen tumbledown shacks. This camp, unlike the others he'd seen, had a makeshift corral holding a number of horses.

And a well-dressed, unconscious woman, shot in the upper chest.

Doc stretched his tired back and shoulders. Outside, night had fallen, and a cooking fire crackled and threw flickering light through the open door.

The shack looked like someone had been living here. Sacks of flour and salt and dried beans in the corner. A rough bed, a scarred table, an ancient potbellied stove, and barrels for chairs completed the furnishings.

Doc glanced at the outlaw leaning against the jamb. One of the other men called him Lucas. Lean and tough as buffalo tendon, he was staring at him, his dark eyes hard as coal. Including this one, Doc had seen four gang members. So far.

The patient stirred, drawing his attention. She was a mature woman of quality, based on her clothing, and she was still unconscious. He held the back of his hand to her forehead. She was warm, but not dangerously so. When he first laid eyes on her, all his training and experience told him that he had one course of action. He needed to operate and get that bullet out. She'd lost a lot of blood even before he arrived, and she looked as gray as the blanket she lay on.

In his medical practice in New York prior to the war, he never once treated a gunshot wound. After joining the Union Army Medical Corps back in 1861, however, he'd dug more bullets out of human flesh than he could count.

By the time he was discharged, the war had destroyed the decorous sham of everyday life. Nightmares of crying men and piles of amputated limbs plagued the darkness. The carnage he saw changed him forever.

Back in New York, he saw streets filled with crippled men, victims of the fighting. They were a constant reminder of the horrors of the war. In the end, it had been too much for him to bear. Secure in the knowledge that his growing daughter would be safe in the bosom of his late wife's family, he headed west to get away from it all.

But frontier life was by nature violent, and it had its own generous share of killers. These road agents were perfect examples of it.

Doc reached down into his open medical valise. Pulling out his stethoscope, he proceeded to insert the ear pieces and position the bell-shaped head to her chest. Her heart was strong, and he could hear no fluid in the lungs. It was still early, but so far, so good.

The steady footfalls of an approaching horse drew Doc's gaze to the small window cut in the rough plank wall.

"So much as a peep out of you, and you're a dead man." The outlaw already had his revolver out, and he positioned himself to one side of the door.

Whoever was coming, he was in for an unpleasant surprise. And there was nothing Doc could do about it.

"Howdy," a voice called out from a distance. "Traveling through and seen your fire. Thought to stop. Heard there was a town down here somewheres, but ain't found it afore the sun dropped."

Outside by the fire, one of them answered, "Don't know nothing about no town, but you're welcome to stop here."

"I'm grateful. Be good to get out of this saddle and stretch my —"

Doc winced as two shots rang out in the darkness outside the shack.

A horse whinnied and then quieted down, and then only the sound of the crackling fire could be heard.

Lucas holstered his gun. That made two dead in less than two days.

"When is she gonna wake up?"

Doc Burnett ignored the question.

"I ain't gonna ask you ag—"

"The answer is no different than the last time you asked," Doc snapped. "I don't know."

He adjusted the spectacles on the bridge of his nose, trying to keep his temper from boiling over. He'd seen too much death to be afraid of dying. But he had a patient to protect.

Doc had already decided what the outlaws wanted. If ransom was their goal, they clearly wanted this woman conscious so they could glean whatever information they needed. She must be extremely wealthy or important to someone who was, he decided. Or at least, *they* thought so.

"Lucas, come out here," a voice called.

The road agent scowled and went out the door. It was the chance Doc had been waiting for. He snatched a vial of morphine from his valise and quickly measured out a strong dose of the liquid.

Before he could give it to her, though, the woman opened her eyes for the first time. Seeing the dropper descending to her lips, she raised a wavering hand to stop him.

"No," she murmured.

"It's all right," he told her, administering the sedative. "Trust me, this is the only way to keep you alive. Sleep a while."

CHAPTER FOUR

Caleb climbed down from Pirate, his buckskin-colored gelding, and glanced up at the new sign, smartly painted and telling the world — or Elkhorn, anyway — that MALACHI ROGERS LIVERY. HORSES BOUGHT, SOLD, AND BOARDED was a moneymaking concern.

The place of business itself was sound and well-kept. It was a large, wood-plank barn with a good-sized loft space for hay. Under the beams of the loft, the left side of the building consisted of a small office space with a cot, and beyond that was a row of enclosures for oats storage. The back wall had stalls for horses, and on the right, doors opened out to a large fenced area. The owner was known in town to be a skilled blacksmith, and his forge and anvil sat under wide, overhanging eaves facing the corral.

The son of Malachi Rogers himself trotted out into the moonlight, trailed by a member of the passel of cats that lived and hunted in the barn. The young man's sleepy face brightened when he saw who it was. He occasionally helped Caleb on the ranch when he could use an extra hand. "Hullo, Mr. Marlowe."

"Gabriel." Caleb nodded and handed him the reins of his and Doc Burnett's mounts, then gestured to the other six horses laden with dead bodies. "Need to turn these over to the sheriff. Could you run and fetch him for me?"

Gabe Rogers, tall and strong and trustworthy for his fourteen years, looked wide-eyed at the corpses, at Doc's riderless gelding, then back at Caleb. "Hope nothing bad happened to Doc's daughter."

"Just delivered the lady to his house."

"I was a little worried about giving her his horse, it being after dark and all." The boy shrugged. "She don't seem like a woman too willing to take no for an answer."

"Stiff-necked, some might call it."

During the entire three-mile ride into town, Sheila Burnett had barely said two words, which suited Caleb perfectly fine. You could have froze a glass of whiskey solid with the looks she shot at him from time to time.

35

"Gabe, do you recall when Doc last fetched his horse?"

"Sure. He came in yesterday morning at dawn. Pa was set to put a new shoe on this one in the morning, so Doc took his dun."

"Was he alone?"

"He had a miner with him."

"Know him?"

The kid shook his head. "Seen him before, but I don't recall his name. He don't bring his horse here when he comes to Elkhorn. He must do business with them fellas at the other end of town."

Doc had been gone less than a full day. Riding out to some of the claims in the hills, seeing to a broken bone or a cut or whatever needing tending, and then riding back to Elkhorn could take at least a day. Caleb decided Miss Burnett was worrying for nothing. Hell, Doc could show up anytime.

The yips and howls of coyotes hunting in the hills above the town reminded him why he was here. The sheriff. Three buildings farther along, at the corner of Main Street and an alley, lamplight spilled out the front window of the jail. He ran a tired hand on the back of his neck.

"Fetch Horner. I'll wait here for you."

Gabriel ran off to do as he was told, and Caleb tried to turn his mind to other things

36

and not let his history with Elkhorn's new sheriff further ruin what had already been a dismal night.

His gaze wandered to the lot between the hardware store and the butcher shop. Stacks of new lumber glowed white in the light of the moon dropping low in the west. Elkhorn was growing by leaps and bounds. Buildings were springing up faster than corn in June.

Looking down Main Street, he noted the town now had two hotels for overnight visitors and one taking guests solely on an hourly basis. They all seemed to be doing brisk trade.

Across the way, a handful of men were standing around jawing in front of the Belle Saloon. With the front doors wide open, he could see the whiskey and the brandy were flowing, the card tables were full, and the dice tables were crowded with miners falling over themselves looking for a reason to be back working their claims in the morning. He knew most of them would wake up with empty pockets, a pounding head, and a sick feeling that they'd surrendered the rewards of all their digging without so much as a fight.

With the silver mines producing nearly instant fortunes, the men working them were looking for any way they could find to blow off steam, as the riverboat fellas say. And there were people arriving in town on a daily basis. Bounty hunters, outlaws, traveling salesmen, and folks just looking for whatever job they could get their hands on. Between them and the miners and the wagons pushing west toward Mormon country and far off California, Elkhorn's streets were constantly filled with the worn, the tired, and the hopeful.

Caleb's attention fixed for a moment on a building across from the jail. It too had a smart, important-looking sign, illuminated by a flaring streetlamp in front. H. D. PATTERSON, JUSTICE OF THE PEACE, and below it in smaller letters, LAND AND MINE SALES, SIDE DOOR. Here, Judge Patterson's clerks handled all of the local area's legal business. And this was where, four months ago, Caleb had bought his spread outside of town.

Caleb knew he should be grateful that Elkhorn was doing so well. He and Henry planned on raising their cattle to feed these hungry miners and townsfolk. Already, though, he was feeling the hot breath of civilization on his neck. Three miles downriver might not be far enough.

Shaking off those dark thoughts, he

glanced at the dead rustlers he'd brought in. He hadn't recognized any of them, but now that the weather was good, there were plenty of drifters in the area, too ornery to prospect and too lazy to find honest work.

Caleb looked at the fellow who'd given him the letter. He'd have to come back into town to mail it when Red Annie O'Neal was due to come through. She was the only star route carrier for the postal service that he'd trust with a letter. He'd heard too many stories of mail and parcels getting lost with Wells Fargo and the other overland stagecoach lines.

He figured this knothead surely wouldn't begrudge him a few days to send it off.

The sound of ragged coughing drew his attention back toward the jail. Sheriff Grat Horner was still strapping on his Remingtons as he came out onto the street.

Unfortunately, he'd known Horner in an earlier life, and the man barreling toward him hadn't changed much since the last time they met. Beneath the same droopy, chaw-stained moustache, those wobbling bulldog jowls hung a little lower, maybe. Nearly as tall as Caleb, he was twenty pounds heavier, at least. And the blackguard loved to throw that weight around.

Horner hadn't been wearing the tin star

back then. Like too many men of his ilk, though, he knew that being the law in a town flowing with silver or gold gave a clever man plenty of opportunities for putting some of it in his own pocket. And it appeared this miserable bastard was living high off the hog here. To be sure, he was dressing better. But those fancy new boots, gold brocade waistcoat, and new black suit didn't add a lick of value to him.

The burly lawman cleared his throat and spat without breaking stride. Two of Horner's no-account deputies followed close in his wake. Gabriel trailed them, and he seemed to be looking a little anxious.

This was not gonna be pretty, Caleb thought. He unfastened the leather thongs securing his twin Colts.

A couple of years ago, it had been Caleb wearing the star, and Horner had been working as muscle for a rancher up near Greeley. The man talked himself up for being quick on the draw, but he was one of those fellows who'd sooner shoot you in the back as try you in a fair fight.

Though he couldn't prove it, Caleb knew of at least one homesteader up there who found that out the hard way. The farmer made the fatal error of putting down stakes on land claimed by Horner's employer. Caleb found the unarmed man facedown in his newly tilled field, his mule also shot dead in his harness for good measure.

He tracked the gunmen right to the ranch, and he and Horner came near to shooting it out. But the rancher intervened. The man's defense and the fifteen hired guns pointing at Caleb convinced him that, if he pushed it any further, there was little likelihood of getting out of there alive. When he got back to town and suggested pursuing the matter with a posse of deputies, he was met with a marked lack of enthusiasm. That was the day he decided it was time to take up a different line of work.

When Caleb eventually found his way to Elkhorn, he heard right off that the town was looking to establish some semblance of order. There was no law officer, and the miners were raising hell in town. Somehow, they needed to contain the chaos.

Caleb had different plans and wanted no part of it. But not long after, he was surprised to see Grat Horner tipped back in a chair in front of the jail, a star on his lapel and his feet up on a barrel. The fact that this low-down, poor excuse of a hound dog was their newly minted sheriff only proved that Elkhorn was desperate.

Watching Horner now, Caleb was already

sorry he hadn't left the rustlers up in the ravine for the wolves. Of course, it would have been a little difficult with Doc's daughter harping at him. But the last thing a man wanted was to give a snake like Horner a chance to get at him.

"Busy night, Marlowe?" the sheriff said, gesturing toward the bodies.

"Not *my* choice."

"Who are they?"

"Just six upstanding citizens out for a moonlit ride, I guess."

Horner glared and spat in the dirt again. "You don't know 'em?"

Caleb shook his head. "Came for my cattle. Didn't expect to see me out there, I'd say."

"Didn't expect to end up dead, neither . . . *I'd* say."

"We all end up dead, sooner or later, Sheriff. You should know that."

Horner's eyes narrowed and then flicked for a moment to the two gleaming pistols holstered at Caleb's hips.

These were new guns. Colt Frontiers. Caleb was not one to change with every newfangled thing that came along. But a gun dealer in Denver had convinced him that the action and balance and precision of the weapons were as good or better than his old

Peacemakers. And it used the same .44–40 bullet as his Winchester rifle; carrying only one type of ammunition was a convenience he'd appreciate. Caleb had tried them out, and they were smooth and accurate. So he bought them.

So far, he hadn't killed anyone with them. But the night was still young.

"I hear you own a stake a few miles out."

Caleb said nothing in response. It wasn't a question.

For the past few months, they'd been two mountain rams circling each other. Each one knew the other was around, encroaching on his territory. Each keeping his distance, knowing it was inevitable they'd be locking horns.

Horner spat, wiped tobacco juice from his chin with a big hand, and waved at the dead rustlers. "So you hold that it was self-defense. Any witnesses?"

Caleb decided to keep Doc's daughter out of it, not that she'd be much help. "My dog."

"You ain't wearing a star no more, Marlowe."

"And that one you're wearing don't mean nothing to me, Horner."

The sheriff's eyes narrowed. "You'd best get used to it. Cuz like it or not, I'm the law in this town."

"And there's a snake in every woodpile."

Behind Horner, the two deputies edged away from the sheriff, making room for any gunplay that might develop.

"You keep poking that woodpile," Horner growled, "and you're gonna find there's a rattler in it."

As the two men stared hard at each other, Caleb knew he could drop all three. From the Badlands to the Black Hills and beyond, it was known how fast and how deadly he was. Then the sheriff blinked.

"Lucky for you I don't rile easy, Marlowe."

"Blessed," he said dryly.

Horner turned his head and barked at his deputies, "See what those boys have on 'em. The judge'll want something to put on them death certificates."

The two men moved around Caleb toward the dead men.

"Well then, I'll leave you to it."

"Not so fast. That don't mean this is over. I can't just turn you loose."

Caleb frowned. "Why?"

"I don't decide who's at fault."

"Who decides?"

"Judge Patterson."

"Then I'll come back in the morning and talk to the judge."

"Nope. You ain't going nowhere, Marlowe,

44

until he says you can go."

Without looking, Caleb knew the deputies had their pistols trained on his back.

If he drew, he'd be painting Main Street with their blood. But Gabriel Rogers was standing too close to the line of fire behind Horner.

"I'll be at the Belle," he growled.

"No, you won't. You'll be enjoying the hospitality of my jail tonight. Now, slowly unbuckle them Colts."

CHAPTER FIVE

By the time the sun had risen to midmorning outside the small, barred window, Caleb was ready to kick down the door of that cell. He didn't like waiting, and he definitely didn't care to be at the beck and call of anyone in this town.

This wasn't the first time he'd spent the night in a jail cell. Far from it. As a very young man, before he got his head on straight, he'd done more than his share of drinking, fighting, and general carousing. It was more than looking for a good time, though. More like trying to forget where he'd come from and what he'd done. Guilt and anger can bore a hole deep inside a man that's difficult to fill, no matter how much brandy he pours into it.

When one of the sheriff's deputies unlocked the door, Caleb had to hold himself back from knocking him on his scrawny tail. He stepped onto the threshold, and the

46

deputy backed away, his eyes open wide and one hand on the Remington holstered at his hip.

"Where's Horner?" Caleb had it in the back of his mind that he had a score to settle.

The deputy shrugged. "Ain't seen him. I just come on."

"How much longer?" he barked.

"I'm to let you out. Judge Patterson is waiting for you. Right across the way."

Caleb stalked past him. A table with a chair on either side sat by the front door, where a score of WANTED posters had been tacked up and probably forgotten. Another desk, Horner's, sat by a rack with four rifles and hooks for a half dozen old Colt Dragoons. Except for a cabinet no doubt filled with ammunition, a pair of lamps, and a couple of spittoons that showed some very negligent aim, that was all there was.

Caleb gestured to the rack and the hooks. "Where are my weapons?"

"Sheriff took 'em last night." The deputy sat in a chair and put up his feet on the table, keeping his hand on his revolver. "Judge has 'em now, I s'pose."

Caleb considered kicking the chair out from under his lazy ass, but he didn't think that would do anything to ease his temper.

47

It was his fist in Horner's ugly face that would do that.

"Better go. The judge ain't one to be kept waiting."

As he strode across busy Main Street, he thought more about last night and got more wound up. Horner had just thrown him in that cell to show him who was in charge. There'd been no reason to keep him. He wasn't some drifter passing through. It was a pissing contest, nothing more. Even so, Caleb was ready to do some damage.

Under a clear Colorado sky, the town was bustling with activity, reminding him that he belonged back at his ranch. All along the streets and alleys, miners and range riders in various states of sobriety milled about on foot or horseback. Men wandered in and out of storefronts and saloons and brothels. Through the open doors of the Belle, Caleb could hear the efforts of someone who clearly hadn't seen a piano in years hammering out a tune on the saloon's tinny instrument. And down by the bath house, a rowdy crowd was egging on a pair of chuckleheads who were already battered and bloody and ready to give up the ghost.

Three boys ran by Caleb with a dog chasing after them, barking and nipping at their bare feet. Along the wooden sidewalks, women moved in pairs, clutching their purchases and keeping a wary eye on the men they passed. In front of the hardware store, a wagon filled with crates was being unloaded.

One thing about Elkhorn, he thought as he reached the other side, was you could find men of every size and color and quality. Black men and Chinese. Dandified greenhorns from the East and itinerant salesmen from the devil knows where. Tough-eyed cowhands and sharpers looking for a gull. And homesteaders by the dozens, all wearing the same mildly dazed expression, no doubt wondering when they'd finally reach that promised farmland.

There were even a few Indians — Crow mostly — almost all of them wearing battered blue jackets and insignia that showed their army service as scouts. Not that the insignia helped them escape the more-than-occasional gibes and abuse.

Why they came to town, Caleb couldn't fathom. He only came to Elkhorn when he needed to. When he did, he had a destination in mind. Get in and get out. The hardware store for nails or tools or rope. The butcher shop where he planned to sell his cattle. The general store for food supplies. And he'd been to the Belle Saloon on those occasions when he felt the urge for female companionship.

Climbing the wooden steps to the porch beneath the H. D. PATTERSON, JUSTICE OF THE PEACE sign, he stopped to scrape the street off his boots. As he did, the door swung open, and he came face-to-face with Doc's daughter.

Sheila Burnett was dressed differently this morning than she'd been last night. Doc's duster had given way to a long-waisted, form-fitting dress of dark blue that was finer than any woman owned within a hundred miles of Elkhorn. The bowler had been replaced with a ridiculous little hat sporting white silk flowers and sitting on top of a pile of knots and braids of golden-brown hair. She would, without a doubt, be a glorious sight on the sidewalk of any fancy city back East, but in this Colorado mining town filled with too many roughnecks to count, she was . . . well, something else.

He tipped his hat. "Miss Burnett."

She nodded. "Mr. Marlowe."

She was easy on the eye, all right, so long as a man decided to overlook her disposition.

"Did you stay the night in Elkhorn?" Her eyes wandered toward the Belle Saloon.

"Matter of fact, I visited an old friend

50

across the way."

She moved slightly around him to see what he meant. As her gaze lit on the jail, one of her gloved hands rose to her lips. She glanced quickly to see if he was wearing his revolvers. He pulled one side of his jacket open to show her he was unarmed.

"Consequences, Mr. Marlowe?"

"Nothing to it, miss."

"Well, if you need someone to testify on your behalf . . ."

He doubted she would make a very good witness, considering how she'd expressed her views last night. "I don't think so."

"I had a conversation with Judge Patterson only a few minutes ago. He appears to be a very reasonable man."

"Not a barbarian, then?"

Her eyes narrowed. "Not at first glance."

"I'll take your word for it."

Caleb had yet to meet the man, but no one on the frontier got to be as rich and powerful as Patterson without *some* willingness to use a heavy stick on occasion. When a fellow like the judge appeared "reasonable," that usually meant he had other men to do the dirty work. Men like Grat Horner.

"The judge assured me he'll do everything in his power to facilitate my father's safe return."

51

"Very obliging."

"You sound skeptical." Her brow furrowed, but not with annoyance. Caleb read worry in her eyes, and he reminded himself that this was a young woman concerned about her father.

"I suspect Doc'll be back, safe and sound, in a day or two. And with no assistance from the judge."

Three rowdy cowpunchers raced by, whooping and hollering and raising a cloud of dust. They reined in their mounts in front of the Belle.

"I hope so," she breathed.

Sheila Burnett had spunk. Caleb had to give her that. Riding out to his ranch to find him in the dark was proof of it. But she didn't look or act like any other woman he'd met here in Elkhorn, not that he'd met many. She was a fish out of water. And that wouldn't change when her father got back to town.

Doc lived a bachelor's life. He worked and read and drank and gambled and lived as he pleased. He had a woman who came in and cooked and cleaned regular. Caleb knew nothing about having a family, but he couldn't imagine Doc having any need for a grown daughter chirping at him if he scattered cigar ash in his own house.

"If you hear anything before I do, Mr. Marlowe, I'll be at my father's house."

He nodded and then gestured down the street. "You might stop in at the hardware store over there. Mr. Lewis'll be working behind the counter. Ask him to have his wife pay you a visit. She's Doc's housekeeper. If you'd like company, she might stay at the house with you until your father gets back."

Immediately, her eyes flashed fire, and her cheeks turned a deep shade of red. "I don't need *company*, Mr. Marlowe. And I'm perfectly capable of taking care of myself."

He tipped his hat again. Another reminder that he needed to stay out of the way of people.

"Good day to you, ma'am." Caleb stepped around her, opened the door, and went in.

The lobby was three times as wide as a railroad car and about half again as long. Behind a railing on the right side, two bespectacled clerks working at high desks were eyeing him, pens poised in their hands and matching sour looks on their faces.

Caleb nodded curtly, and they went back to work.

Behind them, there was a closed door that probably led to the land-sales office where he'd done business. On the left side of the lobby, a set of double doors stood open, displaying the insides of a courtroom. The judge's bench lorded over everything else, in front of a picture of Rutherford B. Hayes, flanked by Washington and Lincoln.

As he started toward the wide stairs at the far end of the lobby, Caleb chewed over the arrival of Sheila Burnett in Elkhorn. Doc hadn't said anything to make him think the daughter was thinking of making the long trip to Colorado.

From what Caleb gathered from conversations with Doc, there wasn't much to the relationship between the father and daughter. He'd left New York when she was very young, and his letters didn't do much to tighten the bond. It wasn't that he didn't love her — Doc had said one night over a game of chess — he just didn't know her well enough.

Caleb couldn't blame Doc for leaving her back East with her mother's kin. The West was no place for raising a girl without a mother. He paused at a turn in the stairs and looked back at the front door. He only hoped she'd be smart enough to stay safe in Doc's house until her father returned and shipped her home.

At the landing at the top, a black-suited guard about the size of an ox stood by a closed door that had to be the judge's office. He had his thumbs tucked into his waistcoat pocket, displaying a brace of short-barreled Colts in cross-draw holsters. He had an unexpectedly squeaky voice, the blotchy white face of a sick pig, and the sorriest excuse for whiskers Caleb had seen on any man over the age of twenty.

And he was talking to the sheriff. The hackles on Caleb's neck immediately rose.

"Sleep well, Marlowe?" Horner smirked at the mountain standing next to him. "We've had a problem with rats over there in my office lately."

"The kind with four legs or two?" Caleb replied.

Horner bristled, and his smirk disappeared.

"Cuz I got a good idea which."

The sheriff's eyes narrowed, and his hand drifted to the iron at his hip. "Keep it up, slick."

"We both know you ain't above shooting an unarmed man." Caleb opened his jacket. "Here's another chance for you, killer."

The air was as still as death. About ten feet separated them, but Caleb knew he could cut that distance in half or better before Horner cleared leather. If the sheriff hesitated a split second, Caleb would drive his shoulder into the burly bastard. Once

55

they hit the door behind him, it'd be every man for himself.

Caleb waited for him to make his move.

Pig Face let go a stream of tobacco juice into the spittoon next to the door, breaking the tension. Horner made an effort to laugh off the taunt, but the sound that came out was more like a strangled bark.

Caleb turned his gaze to the big man. "The judge is expecting me."

"He's right inside," Horner answered. He wiped his moustache with the back of his hand, and the smirk returned. "Oh, you just missed the prettiest piece of calico, Marlowe. Doc's daughter was here, looking for her father."

"Saw her outside. What of it?"

"I'm thinking of paying her a call."

Caleb felt his temperature rising.

"I reckon your friend would be mighty appreciative of an officer of the law keeping an eye on her till he gets back to town. What do you think?"

"I think you should do just that, Horner."

"Do you?"

"Cuz I'm sure Doc will cut out the heart of any man who looks twice at his daughter. And I'd pay money to see that."

The sheriff stiffened again as the hulking presence beside him snorted. Still fighting

the desire to plant a fist in Horner's face,
Caleb looked up at the guard. The man had
to be half a head taller than him.

"You gonna announce me, Virgil? Or do I
just waltz in there on my own?"

The man's black button eyes went dead
as he tried to decide if Caleb was mocking
him or not. Without a word, he turned and
knocked once. A voice within answered, and
Pig Face opened the door.

The two men separated to make way for
Caleb to enter. But as he went by, the big
man took hold of his arm with a hand the
size of a saddlebag.

"Take care," he said in that squeaky voice
that did not go with his size. "Cuz I'll rip
your damn head off."

"Well, I wear it right up here on my
shoulders, any time you're feeling the urge."

Caleb looked coolly into those dead eyes.
The face got even blotchier. Wrenching his
arm out of the man's grip, Caleb went in,
and the door shut firmly behind him. Another friend made.

He found himself in a small outer room
where a harried secretary sat at a desk piled
high with papers. The man lifted his balding
head and gestured to the open door beyond.
Caleb went through and paused inside to
take in the sight.

Doing some quick figuring, he decided the judge's office could easily house an entire cavalry unit *and* their horses. One end of the dark, wood-paneled room contained a long, heavy table and matching chairs of carved oak. A chandelier of gleaming brass and crystal hung above it. Wine-colored velvet drapes were held back by gold ropes, and the entire floor was covered by a half dozen carpets that looked like they came right out of some Ali Baba story.

It was the fanciest room Caleb had ever seen, outside of a whorehouse.

Horace Patterson, Justice of the Peace, sat at a desk the size of a small Indiana farm. Behind him: a locked cabinet was topped with three handsomely bound law books. In front of him, a pair of oil lamps, a desk set of pen and ink, a writing blotter, and a large, bronze sculpture of Napoleon with his hand resting on the head of a whipped-looking lion.

The judge stood. A man of medium height, he had a solid build and graying hair. He wore no moustache or beard, but thick side whiskers spread like wings from his face. The man knew how to dress, Caleb thought. In that charcoal suit, silver-gray waistcoat, white silk shirt and black tie, he could dine with President Hayes himself.

Patterson nodded and slid his hand into his waistcoat. There would be no shaking of hands.

This was the first time they'd met. When Caleb bought his land, he dealt with one of the clerks in the land office downstairs and around the side.

"Mr. Marlowe, thank you for coming by to see me."

"Didn't have much choice, Judge," Caleb replied. "As you know."

Patterson eyed him, taking his measure, and Caleb did the same.

The judge had a kind of suppressed energy to him, like a timepiece wound too tight or an unbroken stallion waiting for his chance to either bolt or stomp you. He had a sense that the man before him did more stomping than bolting. And he had a look in his eyes that Caleb had seen too many times before. It was the cold, hard look of a seasoned gunhawk. Even if his business required that he kill you before breakfast, he wouldn't remember you at all come suppertime.

The judge waved him into a chair by the desk and sat down himself. "Drink, Marlowe? Or too early for you?"

"Never too early," Caleb replied. "But I have cattle that need looking after."

"Just a few questions before you go. Our

59

good sheriff neglected to seek out some of the relevant details last night."

He sensed from the judge's tone that he was not entirely happy with Horner. Well, he hired him. He could live with him. "Go ahead and ask."

"Why don't *you* tell me the facts?"

Patterson sat back and steepled his fingers, looking intently as Caleb told him in about three sentences what happened.

"And you didn't recognize any of the riders?"

"No," Caleb replied shortly.

"The sheriff has implied that you shot first. Without cause."

"He wasn't there."

The judge gazed at him for a long moment. "I believe you, Mr. Marlowe."

"Then I'll be going."

Caleb planted his hands on his knees and searched around him for his weapons. It would definitely get ugly if he had to face Horner or Pig Face outside in order to get them.

"First, you should collect what you've earned."

"What would that be?" He'd spent a night in jail for no reason. He'd come here this morning without making a fuss. But his patience was about pinched out.

"Two of those men had bounties on their heads. You're a hundred dollars richer."

Chapter Six

Patterson unlocked a drawer and pulled out a stack of bills. Caleb waited to feel the hook set. There had to be a catch.

As the man counted out the money, Caleb was thinking of that snake of a sheriff. Horner knew about the bounties but said nothing of them outside. His fists were itching to knock a few of the sheriff's teeth loose. Maybe Caleb would pay him a visit before leaving town. If he could find the woodpile Horner had slithered into.

The cash slid across the desk. A hundred dollars was a hundred dollars. He stuffed the money inside his coat, snugging it up against the dead rustler's letter to his mother. Caleb wondered if he was one who had a bounty on his head.

"Where do you hail from, Mr. Marlowe?" The judge leaned back in his seat.

"Here and there. Been everywhere." Caleb pushed to his feet. "My weapons?"

Patterson gestured to a table in the corner, and Caleb strode across the room, picked up his belt with the twin Colts, and strapped them on.

"No. Originally, I mean. Where were you born? Who were your folks? What did your father do?"

No one in Elkhorn knew the answers to those questions and never would. Everywhere he'd been, folks asked the same thing, but Caleb felt no need to satisfy idle curiosity.

"Born under a rock and raised by wolves, they tell me."

The older man's face hardened for a moment, and then his features relaxed somewhat. "Ha! Well, a fellow has a right to keep his history to himself."

"My knife?" Caleb asked, picking up his rifle.

The judge watched him approach before taking the knife out of a drawer and laying it on the desk in front of him.

"It's a beauty. I was hoping you'd forget about it."

"Not likely."

"It belonged to Jacob Bell, didn't it?" Almost reverently, Patterson picked up the massive, wood-handled hunting knife, its twelve-inch blade sheathed in buffalo leather.

Caleb wondered how he knew.

"I've heard so much about this weapon. I'd hoped to see it for myself one day."

"Well, now you have."

"In these parts, Jacob Bell is more legend than man. But you should know that better than anyone."

"I know the man. Legends are just made-up stories mostly, I've found."

Mountain man, trapper, wilderness guide, Jake was sixty years old when he found a half-frozen nineteen-year-old on the snowy banks of the Keya Paha River up in the Dakota Territory. Beaten, robbed, and left for dead, Caleb had reached the bitter end. Looking back, he had nothing much to be proud of in those early years. They were times better off forgotten.

But he didn't die on that riverbank. The old man picked him up and tucked him under his wing. In their time traveling together, the two of them crossed the frontier from Missouri to the Wind River and from the Bighorn Mountains to the Calabasas.

"Is it true that you rode with Jacob Bell when he opened the new route to the Montana gold fields?"

Caleb was fine sharing that piece of his history. "I was with him."

"And you were with him up north during the Indian Wars? They say you saved more men's lives with your scouting than you can count. Is that legend or true?"

It seemed to Caleb that the judge had done a little more scratching into the past than was called for. And he didn't particularly like it.

What *was* true was that his time traveling with Old Jake had made a man of him. Jake taught Caleb to hunt and track and shoot as well as any man alive. By the time they were done, he could find a lamb in a Montana blizzard or follow a rattlesnake across solid rock. Together, they guided expeditions, worked in the gold fields, traded amicably with different native peoples, and got conscripted into scouting for the army. Jake had been married to a Shoshone woman when he was a young man, and through him, Caleb learned to understand the character, peculiarities, superstitions, and beliefs of many tribes. And he found out along the way that those stories in the papers back East only told one side of things.

All that aside, Caleb didn't feel too comfortable singing his own praises. "You know what you know, Judge."

And *he* wanted to know exactly what the man was after. Caleb was pretty good at reading fellas, and Patterson didn't strike him as one to waste his own time.

"How is it you've come to have Old Jake's knife?"

"A parting gift when he went back to his farm in Missouri." The frontier life had gotten to be too much for his creaky, old bones. This knife had been lucky for him for over thirty years, he said, and he wanted Caleb to have it.

"I'll pay you five hundred dollars for it."

He took the sheathed knife out of the judge's hand and slid it into his boot.

"It ain't for sale."

The judge shrugged. "Pretty much what I expected. You strike me as a man who knows the value of what he's got."

And right now, he had a ranch to get back to. "Are we done here?"

"Almost."

Patterson sat back in his chair and folded his hands over his waistcoat. "I heard you wore a badge up by Greeley."

He'd read the man right after all. The knife wasn't what interested him. It was Caleb himself.

Whatever Elkhorn's snake of a sheriff had

66

told the judge about Caleb, it looked like it had backfired.

"I'm a mite surprised Horner shared that with you."

"He didn't. I have other sources of information."

Of course he would.

From what Caleb had seen since he bought his land, the judge ran everything in Elkhorn. He and a few men who followed his lead. This was nothing new or different. He'd seen the same thing across the frontier. As soon as news spread of gold or silver being discovered, men like Patterson arrived. Ordinary fellas might pan or dig for it, but businessmen and politicians like the judge wanted to make sure they had a piece of every dollar. And to make that happen, they needed control. So they brought law and order where none had existed. Their *own* version of law and order.

"The town put the word out that we were looking for a sheriff. You didn't apply."

"Wasn't interested then. Ain't interested now."

"You've been here four months, Mr. Marlowe. You've seen what's happening in this town."

He'd seen plenty, and he was happy to be three miles or so downriver.

67

"Elkhorn is growing. New streets are being laid out. We have a church and a schoolhouse now. Right here on Main Street, hardware and mercantile stores are busy all the time. The mail and freight businesses connect us to the outside world. As does the newspaper. We've got several butchers and green grocers, a general store, and even a new restaurant."

Caleb had tried out the restaurant that claimed to have the "best steaks in town." He planned on selling his beef to them.

"We even received a letter just last week from an acting troupe in Denver. We'll have our own opera house soon."

Caleb figured the judge had been working hard on this speech, and there'd be no walking out of here until he was done delivering it.

"Yes, indeed, sir. Elkhorn is the city with a future. It is the place to be."

So long as the silver held out, Caleb thought.

"But to keep what we have and to grow, we need the law."

It was a long way around the barn, but Patterson finally got to it.

"You have a sheriff."

Patterson sent him a look that let Caleb know exactly what he thought of the current lawman.

"I ain't interested," he repeated.

"But you haven't heard my proposition, Mr. Marlowe."

"Judge, I ain't selling Jacob Bell's knife, and I ain't interested in being sheriff . . . in Elkhorn or anywhere else."

"I hear you loud and clear. My proposal for you is something far more important." He leaned forward. "You help me, and I help you. Quid pro quo, as we say in the legal profession."

There was sure as hell no way of cutting this conversation short.

"Don't think I need any help, Judge." Caleb shook his head. "Unless, while I was hanging about here this morning, a few more fellas decided to ride out to my ranch and help themselves to my cattle."

"Don't sell me short." The civic leader spouting off was gone. Patterson was all business now, and the hard edge in his tone matched the look in his eyes. "I'm not a man to be used lightly."

"Then how about if you tell me straight exactly how I can help you," Caleb said coolly.

The judge slid open a drawer and placed a sheet of paper on the desk. It appeared to be a letter. Unsigned.

"First, I want to be sure you know I wield a certain amount of influence . . . power in this state. I can help my friends, Marlowe, when it suits me."

"I'd be a fool to doubt it."

The older man tapped the letter with his fingers.

"Your partner, Henry Jordan, is serving time right now in the Arapahoe County Jail for some difficulty he got involved in up there."

Caleb was suddenly interested.

His partner had an unfortunate combination of good looks and a quick temper that had been the cause of trouble for him for as long as Caleb knew him. Up north in the Indian Territories, Henry was a sergeant in a cavalry unit that Caleb was scouting for, and they became good friends then. Henry loved poker, whiskey, and women — in no particular order — but he was as fierce and solid as Pike's Peak when he needed to be.

The fight he'd won in a fancy saloon in Denver had landed him in the pokey for six months. The timing was bad, considering their partnership and the purchase of the ranch and cattle, but he was due to be released in a couple of months. Caleb was looking forward to him getting here and doing his part to make their investment pay.

"I understand that there were witnesses who testified Mr. Jordan was not the instigator, but I've learned recently that one of the men involved has been lingering for all this time," the judge told him. "If he doesn't survive, your partner may be facing charges of manslaughter. He could spend more time in jail than either of you expects."

Damn.

"What can you do for him?"

"I will send this letter to the governor. I *can* get your partner released."

Buying a ranch and putting down roots — building something solid — had been Henry's idea. Elkhorn had been Caleb's. His partner had liked the possibility of striking it rich with a silver claim on their own land. That was their future, he'd said. Caleb liked the feeling of having a place of his own. But if it weren't for his friend, he was sure he would still be exploring new frontiers and wandering along new trails until he was too old to climb onto his horse.

For Henry's sake — hell, for both of their sakes — this was worth listening to.

"What do you need from me?"

Patterson got up and went to the cabinet behind him. Taking out two glasses, he poured out some brandy and set one in front of Caleb before sitting again.

"The Wells Fargo Overland from Denver to Elkhorn has fallen prey of late to a band of vicious road agents. Six attacks since the beginning of the year. Over fifty thousand dollars in silver and currency has been lost. They struck again two days ago. They're up in the hills, possibly somewhere around Devil's Claw. I want you to put on a tin star and go after them."

"You already have a sheriff."

"I need him here where I can keep an eye on him."

"How about your own men?" The judge had a spread, mines, and men at his disposal.

"They're out there already. But they don't have your expertise. No one around here has your tracking skills."

Caleb stared at the glass of brandy for a moment, considering his options. He had no interest in this business, but if he refused, Henry's future was looking grim.

"There's something else you should know."

"What's that?"

"Your friend . . . Doctor Burnett." The judge set down his empty glass with a resounding click. "They have him."

CHAPTER SEVEN

The news was a mule kick in the gut.

If what the judge said was correct, Sheila Burnett had been right to worry about her father.

"How do you know they have Doc?"

"Yesterday morning, a miner named Smith came to town. He's got a claim about ten miles east of here, not far from the Denver road. He's been scratching out silver by himself for a couple of years. Some folks saw him riding out early with Doc."

Caleb figured that was the miner Gabriel Rogers had seen at the livery stable.

"Not far outside of town, a pair of gun-slingers were waiting for them." The judge got up and poured himself another drink.

"What makes you think these were the same fellas you're looking for?"

"It makes sense. When the Wells Fargo stage was held up two days ago, it was the bloodiest attack yet. The driver and the

73

stage guard were killed. There was blood inside the coach as well. We don't know the identity of the passenger yet, but it appears he was wounded and taken. Probably for ransom. Smith's claim is not a mile from where the stagecoach was found. Do I need to say more?"

Doc Burnett was the only sawbones within a hundred miles of Elkhorn. If the passenger was hurt and the outlaws wanted him alive, they'd come for Doc.

But when they didn't need him anymore, his life wouldn't be worth a Reb dollar.

"Anyone gone up to Smith's cabin?" Caleb asked.

"My men were out there yesterday. No sign of him or anyone else."

Damn. Caleb had been telling Sheila Burnett that Doc was fine, but he was wrong.

"What did you say to the daughter this morning?"

"Nothing of what I'm telling you. She's better off not knowing."

"I agree." Caleb nodded to the judge. "I'll go after them."

"I thought you would."

Patterson reached inside his desk again and produced a WANTED flyer. "This is a state-issued notice. The governor is offering

74

a reward of a thousand dollars for the arrest and delivery of the leader of these outlaws and a hundred dollars for any gang member."

"Them folks over at Wells Fargo must be leaning pretty heavy on him."

"I'm sure you're correct." Patterson handed over the flyer. "But holdups across the state have become bloodier of late, and the governor wants people to feel safe traveling in Colorado. As do I."

Caleb looked at the proclamation. It contained no sketches of the road agents. No names or descriptions.

"How could any bounty hunter prove he had the right fellas?"

"Recovering stolen property would be proof enough."

"Do they even know how many men are riding with this gang?"

The judge shook his head. "Not with any certainty. Could be four. Could be a dozen or more. Each time, some of them stay in the woods. During a recent robbery, one of them was wounded, but the outlaws still escaped into the hills with the strong boxes. They seem to be very careful about concealing their identities."

"But it's definitely the same fellas?"

"That seems to be the case."

"And you think they're holed up somewhere near Devil's Claw?"

"That's as far as my men have tracked them. Beyond that . . ." Patterson shrugged. "That's why I need you. A real tracker. Someone who can follow the scent and run them to ground."

That was rugged country up there beyond Devil's Claw. Thick pine forests that suddenly ended at walls of rock that rose straight up a hundred feet or more. Ravines and gulches that had snow and ice ten months of the year and flooding rivers the other two. Trails that disappeared under ice or rock slides.

There were few better places to go if a man or a gang didn't want to be found.

"And you want to get Doc back."

"Absolutely. We need him in Elkhorn." The judge motioned to the flyer in Caleb's hand. "Bring Doc *and* the leader of those road agents, and I'll give you thousand dollars of my own money as reward. And I have no preference how you bring that outlaw in."

"Dead or alive?"

"I have no desire to hamstring you, Marlowe. You might not have a chance to negotiate. Last night, with those six rustlers, I know it was killed or be killed. You did what you had to do. Now, I don't know how many are up there, but you will undoubtedly find yourself outnumbered and outgunned."

This wasn't the first time.

"These are desperate men, and they are not just hiding themselves. They're hiding all their ill-gotten gains. So I want you to know you have a free hand. And I'll stand by that."

Caleb was no bounty hunter. He didn't care so much about the money. But if doing this job saved Doc's hide as well as helping get the ranch up and running smoothly, then he was just fine with the arrangements.

"And that letter for Henry Jordan?"

"I'll sign it now." Patterson picked up his pen and scratched his name at the bottom. As he sealed it, he called to his secretary, who came running. "This goes to the governor in the next mail pouch."

The judge held out his hand, and Caleb shook it.

"We have a bargain, and I trust you, Mr. Marlowe. I believe you will do right for me, for Doc, and for Elkhorn."

Caleb strode out of the judge's office, looking for the sheriff. Pig Face was standing by himself. Neither man spoke, but the big guard spat contemptuously in the general direction of the spittoon. He wasn't finished with either one of them, Caleb thought as he descended the stairs and went out onto the street. But he had more important things to take care of.

He crossed the busy street toward the livery stable, waiting as a wagon filled with sacks of flour lumbered past. Caleb considered all he had to do. He needed to go back to the ranch for provisions and ammunition. And while he was getting his horse, he also had to arrange for Gabriel to go out there and look after his dog and the cattle while he was away.

Caleb stopped in front of the livery and gazed up at the mountain peaks to the east. Doc was his friend and in real danger. He wasn't making less of that. But the thought of going out on the trail again made the blood pulse in his veins.

It was months since he'd been alone in the mountains, surrounded only by the tall trees and the cool breeze. He missed the cold, clean taste of spring-fed water. The smells of the pine forest. Of silence broken only by the chittering of birds and the rhythmic thudding of his horse's hooves. And the night sounds of wolves and owls and a crackling fire.

Staying in one place and ranching was a

responsible thing for a man. But that other life — simple and pure and solitary — called to him still.

Shaking off these thoughts, he went through the open doors of the livery stable and called out for Gabriel. There was no sign of him or his father. Caleb's buckskin gelding was tied in a stall next to a small paint, and he leaned his Winchester against the wall of the enclosure. A sound behind him drew his attention. It wasn't Gabe.

Out of the shadows came a young fellow, little more than a boy. He was wearing a battered old hat and wool coat that were both too big for him.

So was the Colt Dragoon in his hand. But he was having no trouble leveling it at Caleb's chest.

"You killed my brother, mister."

CHAPTER EIGHT

The boy wasn't alone. The shadow of another spilled across the packed dirt floor from the open doors leading to the corral.

Caleb instantly judged that the wheezing breaths coming from behind him were about three paces back and from someone less than five feet tall. It was the sound of a child's breathing, and nervous, at that. From the shadow, Caleb could tell there was something in his hand — an iron rod, a baling hook, a horse shoe. Whatever it was, it wasn't a gun. He never took his eyes off the young fella with the old long-barreled revolver, but he knew he was dealing with two children.

The boy in front of him was on the edge of tears, and the gun shook a little in his hand. He was clearly angry and hurting in a way that only came with grieving. His brown felt hat, far too big and hanging over his ears, had to be twenty years old if it was a day. It was missing a big chunk out of the brim on the left side and had a bullet hole in the crown near the top. The worn wool coat must have been of a definable color when it was new, but that would have been back when this fella's grandpappy was a boy. Now, it was the color of scorched prairie with a smattering of mud and straw clinging to the shredded sleeves. From what Caleb could see of the cotton shirt, it was little more than a rag, and beneath the boy's tattered woolen trousers, bare toes stuck out of broken shoes.

Caleb considered his two choices. First, he could take that old Dragoon away from the kid right now and kick him and his half-pint friend in the doorway halfway across Main Street. That wouldn't be difficult. A simple distraction, two steps, and this confrontation — if you wanted to call it that — was over. Or, second, he could find out what they wanted and deal with it. Maybe the would-be gunslick would learn something.

"What's your name, fella?"

"Why you wanna know? You're gonna be dead."

"The Code of the Gunslinger requires that — as a courtesy — a man knows who shot him."

The young face darkened as he ran that through his mind. "What Code of the Gunslinger?"

Caleb saw the puzzled eyes flicker toward the twin Colts at his hips.

He raised his eyebrows in a look of surprise. "I thought all gunhawks knew the Code."

"Of course I know it." The gun dipped a little. "My name is Paddy."

"Good to meet you, Paddy. I'm Caleb Marlowe."

"I know who you are."

"Paddy, tell your friend behind me," he said casually, "that according to the Code, only a coward shoots a man in the back."

"I ain't no coward," the wheezy back-up cried. "And I got no gun. But I'm Dusty."

Caleb was right. Dusty couldn't be more than eight years old.

"How old are you, Paddy?" he asked sharply.

"Twelve." From the look on his face, it was clear he was angry he'd answered so quickly. "It don't matter none if I'm twenty. You're still about to die."

Dusty moved slightly around to the side, and Caleb turned his head a little until he caught sight of the baling hook he was holding.

"Dusty, if that hook is getting heavy," he said, "you don't need to be holding it up like that. I ain't going to make a run for it." From the corner of his eye, he saw the tool being lowered.

"And even though you ain't no coward, you'd best get out of the line of fire of your friend here. Cuz, being this close, that bullet will tear clear through me and more 'n likely hit you. If he don't miss me, that is."

"I ain't gonna miss."

"You won't miss because that old cannon you're carrying will more likely misfire."

"It won't misfire."

"Pretty sure of yourself." Caleb nodded toward the Dragoon. "But those cartridges are notorious for not firing once they get wet. You been out in the rain at all?"

A shadow of doubt flickered across Paddy's dirty face.

"But let's get things straight between you and me before the shooting starts."

"Whaddya mean?"

"What makes you think I killed your brother?"

"I seen him laid out by the undertaker's. They was making boxes for him and his . . . well, for them other fellas." Paddy ran a quick sleeve across his face and then pointed at a mount in a stall. "And that there's our horse. Right there. The dun."

Caleb thought again about the best way to proceed. He was not about to throw down on this young fella. He'd already had four separate opportunities to draw and shoot, but he'd decided right off that he wasn't going to hurt him. The best thing would be to get Paddy to decide for himself that shooting wouldn't be the best way to go.

"Why do you think it was me that killed him?"

"I heard the deputy tell the undertaker that Marlowe done 'em all, and they had you in the pokey. That's you. Don't deny it."

"I ain't going to deny it, Paddy, but I got a few things to say about that." Caleb glanced over at Dusty. "Are you another brother?"

"Uh-uh." He shook his head slowly. "A friend."

"Good to know. You two been friends a long time?"

"Since last night."

Caleb looked back at Paddy. "You and your brother just passing through Elkhorn?"

"Going to Montana. My brother says there's gold fields there where folks can still strike it rich. We're gonna do just that. And then we're gonna get ourselves a ranch and raise cattle. We're gonna have it made . . ."

His words tapered off, and a tear ran a streak through the dirt on his cheek.

The boy was talking about his brother as if he were still alive. Caleb knew how that went. He'd been there. It took a long time to sort out losing someone. You kept hearing their voice, but when you looked around, it was someone else. You thought you saw them down the road, so you hurried. But when you got there, it was some stranger who turned and stared.

It was a bad feeling.

"We had a plan. Him and me. But we ran out of money. When them other fellas talked to him, they made it sound easy. Cattle just sitting there and waiting to get took. But you stopped 'em. And now he's gone."

Caleb heard the pain of the loss in every word. He was sixteen when he ran away from his home. And he'd had nothing. No brother. No plan. There had been so many nights when he was out on the prairie, miles from any other person. And when he was around others, he was too afraid of getting caught.

Sometimes, even now, when he looked up at the flickering stars glowing in a blue-black sky, that lost and empty feeling came trailing back. Like a nightmare that wouldn't quit. He never forgot being so bone-tired and lonesome and ripped up inside.

Twelve years old was a mite young to be facing the world on your own. The place was big and cold and as unconcerned as the stars in the night sky. And a frontier town was an especially hard and dangerous place.

"I ain't gonna ask you the name of your brother."

"Why not?"

Caleb knew from the way the muzzle of that old Colt Dragoon kept dipping lower and lower that the iron was getting heavy. If he kept Paddy talking, pretty soon that gun was going to be pointed right at the ground between them. He wasn't worried. He knew men, and he knew there was no way this boy was going to shoot him. If he were going to do it, he'd have opened fire before they exchanged even one word.

But he still wanted Paddy to talk himself down.

"Cuz he and his friends could not be bothered to introduce themselves before trying to put a hole in me." Caleb tapped his chest in the general proximity of his heart.

"But you killed Billy, and I gotta vengeance him."

Billy. Caleb heard no names spoken, but he doubted the boy's brother was the one who'd entrusted him with the letter to his mother. The one he was still carrying. He'd made no mention of Paddy.

"Getting revenge ain't something a man jumps into. You got to think it through."

"I don't see that there's no thinking that needs doing."

"Was he a good brother?"

"He was my kin. My only kin."

The boy's eyes were wide and misting, his hand shaking. It was tough enough being alone in the world, but having bad kin didn't make things any easier.

He wasn't going sit in judgment on that brother, though. True, he'd shot Billy dead in the act of rustling his cattle. But when he himself was not much older than Paddy, he'd done bad things. Still, Caleb never had any kid brother relying on him.

His instincts already told him that this young fella had better sense than his brother.

"How come he didn't bring you along with him to my spread when he and his fellas went out there?"

"He wanted me to go."

"Why didn't you?"

"Cuz . . . cuz I had things to do."

"What things?"

He glanced at the boy with the baling hook. The tool was hanging loose as his side. He was more interested in hearing the conversation.

"Just . . . things."

Caleb turned his attention back to Paddy. "You knew they were up to no good, didn't you?"

There was a slight shrug.

"I'd be willing to bet you told him not to go, but he went anyway."

Another shrug.

"Tell me this, Paddy. If I corner you in an alleyway and start shooting, what do you do?"

"I shoot back."

"But what if I have a brother? A wife? A couple of kids? Will that give you pause?"

"You started it."

"Your brother and his friends started that trouble on my ranch. They shot first."

Paddy's face was pale under the dirt, and his thin shoulders shook.

"You got no call for vengeance. I didn't go looking to kill your brother or any of them other fellas. They made a bad choice. You made the right choice not going with them. So what are you going to do now?"

"I don't know!" he cried.

This boy was lost and hurting. But he was facing the same thing that a lot of young folks faced. People lost their kin. Found themselves with nothing. Their dreams shattered. A lot of them, like this waif standing here with a gun in his shaking hand, would cling to the edge of a cliff.

Paddy was at a fork in the road. He had good sense. Caleb wanted to give him the chance to use it. It would make all the difference.

He looked hard into the boy's face. "All folks make mistakes. But if they learn from them, they're better for it. Is that gonna be you, Paddy? Is this a mistake? Or do you still think you need to do for me?"

"I don't wanna shoot nobody. But what am I gonna do?" he wailed. The gun dropped to his side. "I got no kin left. No place to go. I got nothing. And Billy's gone."

Just then, a gate creaked open in the fenced enclosure outside, and the voices of Gabriel and his father could be heard.

When the boy turned his head, Caleb stepped toward him and took the pistol from his hand. Paddy gave it up willingly.

As he decocked the hammer of the Dragoon and slid the weapon into the pocket of his coat, he saw that the baling hook lay on the ground. Dusty was just disappearing through the doors to the street and moving faster than a cougar with his tail on fire.

Malachi Rogers and his son came into the stable, and the livery owner smiled in recognition.

"Gabriel told me you had some trouble out at your place last night. We're keeping those fellows' horses and saddles here for the time being." He glanced at Caleb's ragged companion. "Brought a friend along, Mr. Marlowe?"

The elder Rogers was a sharp-eyed, dark-skinned man of medium height with the broad shoulders and massive arms of a man who'd put in his years muscling livestock and hammering hot iron into horseshoes and other necessities. He was wearing a well-brushed black stovepipe hat and a gray wool coat over a black waistcoat and black cotton shirt, open at the neck. He'd retired his pants with the army stripes down the side a few months ago — a nod to his increasing prosperity — and wore heavy wool pants of a darker gray tucked into well-worn boots.

Malachi Rogers was a former Buffalo Soldier. When Caleb first brought his horse in to be boarded, he spotted the blue cap of the 9th Cavalry hanging from a nail above the desk in the livery office. When the man noticed him eyeing it, they had a short but interesting conversation about the Indian Wars. Malachi had served as a corporal in a unit stationed at Fort Stockton. While he was there, he'd seen more action than he cared to remember. When his regiment was sent to Fort Union in New Mexico in '75, he'd decided it was time to hang up his spurs and settle in Colorado. At the time, Elkhorn was little more than a ragtag community of tents, log cabins, and knee-deep mud. The son of a blacksmith himself, Malachi knew his trade, and the fledgling town needed him.

"We're a new acquaintance," Caleb replied somberly, putting one hand on the boy's shoulder. "Lost his brother last night."

The stable owner's eyes widened as the meaning sank in. He nodded, a frown creasing his face. "So what now?"

"That's what we were just chewing over."

Malachi glanced at his son and then back at Paddy. "You got any place to sleep, young fella?"

Paddy shook his head.

"Well, there's room in that loft. You'll be warm and snug up there." He and Caleb exchanged glances. "When's the last time you ate?"

A shrug.

91

"If that means you can't recall, it's been too long," the stable owner said. "Gabriel and me are about to go in for our noon dinner. I'm sure Mrs. Rogers has enough for another. How does that sound to you?"

"Much obliged, sir," Paddy murmured.

"Look at that, Mr. Marlowe. Manners and all. If your friend could bring himself to scrape some of that dirt off his face and hands, I think Mrs. Rogers will be well pleased having him at our table."

This was working out better than Caleb hoped.

He addressed Malachi and his son. "I need to go out of town. I can't say for sure how long. Think you could spare Gabe for a few days to watch over things at my ranch and take care of Bear? I'll pay him same as last time."

Gabriel tried to suppress his excitement, unsuccessfully. Malachi looked doubtful.

"If you're worried about trouble," Caleb said with a quick side look at Paddy, "after last night, I don't think any fellas will be going out there anytime soon."

Gabe's father put a big callused hand on his son's shoulder. "Who's gonna help me in the livery? We got a shipment of oats coming tomorrow and a full stable of horses to tend to."

92

"I can work the stable," Paddy chirped up. "I know horses good. And . . . and I owe you."

Malachi Rogers thought about it for a moment. "Then I guess that'll work out."

Ten minutes later, after smoothing out the details, Caleb mounted his horse in front of the livery. Paddy had taken off his hat to wash his face and hands. Having handed over the reins, the boy stood patting the buckskin's neck. For the first time, with his ginger-colored hair slicked down and darkened by the water, he looked his age.

"When I get back, maybe we can set and talk about the future. I'm gonna need help on the ranch, at least until my partner gets here."

As Caleb rode out, Paddy's bright face stayed with him. He wasn't too sure why he'd said that. Taking on responsibility for a kid was no small thing. And, considering his own upbringing, he had no example to look to as far as how it should be done. Even so, someone had to step up for this boy.

He thought about how many street rats he'd seen in his travels. Towns seemed to breed them.

CHAPTER NINE

Doc woke up with a start, instantly alert, his pulse racing. On the blurred edge of a dream, a sound or a movement — some threat of danger — jarred his defenses. He was unaware that he'd fallen asleep.

He sat rigidly still, leaning against the wall by the bed, listening for a repeat of the sound, trying to identify what had awakened him. It was a hiss. Or a growl. Or a light footfall. Something.

For two days he hadn't slept at all. He hadn't intended to today either. His neck was stiff. His butt was asleep. Doc pressed a hand to his chest. His heart was still pounding, and every nerve in his body hummed. From the light in the shack, he guessed it was still afternoon. He shot a glance across the room. The door to the outside was closed. The road agent called Lucas was not in his usual place, watching every move he made.

Perhaps he'd been awakened when the young outlaw went out. Maybe the sound of the door closing had startled him from his nap.

He turned his head slowly and looked up at his patient. Her head was moving restlessly in the cot, mumbling incoherent words under her breath. She was due to have the dressing on the wound changed again.

A low, raspy, hissing growl from beneath the cot fired a bolt of white-hot lightning through Doc and sent him scuttling backward.

"What the blazes!"

He stared at the shadows beneath the bed for the source of the sound. Black, gleaming eyes stared back at him.

"Get!"

It didn't move.

He leaned down to get a better look at what was hiding there.

The creature had a tapered snout. A fox? No, the ears were round and close to the head, giving it the look of a miniature bear's face. The fur was thick and golden-brown, too dark and with no raccoon's mask. If it were a weasel, it was the largest he'd ever seen. From one side of its mouth, the head of a fat, lifeless rat dangled, and the rodent's

95

long tail hung out the other side.

"Get. Go!"

The unwelcome visitor let out a scratchy piercing snarl as it pulled back its lips and showed more of the rat along with vicious fangs and teeth. The animal made a quick, aggressive movement forward. Instinctively, Doc kicked out at it, but he was too far away.

The creature dropped the rat and emitted another screechy snarl, louder and longer than before. Doc reached back, and his hand found an empty medicine bottle. He flung it, but the bottle glanced off the thick fur and skittered harmlessly past.

The thing turned slightly on short nimble legs. The body was at least three feet long and the furry tail twitched nervously. Even glimpsing it in the shadowy recesses beneath the cot, Doc realized what it was. A fisher.

He was suddenly on his feet and across the room without realizing he'd moved. His legs were stiff, but there was plenty of blood roaring in his head.

Doc had only seen one of these before, when he was traveling to see a friend in the Berkshires. Up there, they called it a fisher cat. Out walking one morning, they'd run into a trapper who had just taken one. The animal had still been alive when the young

96

hunter went to check his lines, and the bite marks and torn flesh the fisher inflicted on the trapper's arms were a clear testament to its fearlessness and its ferocious temperament.

And this beast was larger than that one, by far.

Doc didn't have many options. There was no way he'd go for help and leave his patient alone with the animal.

By the stove, a barrel held a few sticks of wood, and he grabbed the largest one. It was only a couple of feet long and thinner than his wrist, but it was the best weapon he had at hand.

Picking up his medical valise, he approached the cot, suddenly feeling like some ridiculous Don Quixote with a leather bag for a shield and a branch as a sword.

He went down on one knee and stabbed at the fisher. The animal sank its sharp, powerful claws into the stick, and Doc was hardly inclined to pull the thing toward him.

He jabbed again, and suddenly, the creature released the stick. Snatching up the treasured rat in its teeth, it turned and darted toward a far corner of the shack. In an instant, it disappeared behind a pair of barrels in the corner. Doc pursued with the upraised stick and cautiously peered over them. The fisher was gone, having escaped through a hole in floor.

Doc dropped his makeshift weapon and shoved one of the barrels over the hole, effectively sealing off the entry.

He backed away, expelling a long breath as his heart took its time and finally slowed. He stretched his back muscles, bent his neck from side to side, feeling as if he'd fought a battle.

He was only glad no one had been around to see his moment of panic.

There wasn't enough air in the shack, and Doc went and opened the door, welcoming the cool rush. Outside, one man was standing by the fire, looking across the wide opening of the camp at the corral, where his buddies seemed to be working to settle the horses in the corral. He couldn't see Lucas, but Doc assumed he must be over there.

His patient's voice grew louder, and Doc grabbed some washed strips of bandage and went back to the cot. Her face was flushed. She seemed more agitated than before. The utterances before were mostly gibberish, but he could make out some of it now.

"Get them . . . Dark . . . She's scared."

"Who's scared?"

"Hold her hand . . . Don't let go."

He touched her brow. She was burning with fever.

"Don't let go of what?" Doc asked.

"No . . . My daughters . . . Get them . . . Get them!" The anguish was clear in her tone.

Standing there, Doc thought of Sheila, his own daughter.

Where was she? What was she doing? He couldn't recall how long it had been since she'd written to him. He was always fairly dutiful in writing back to her as soon as her letters arrived. But why did he think he needed to wait? He chided himself for that now. In fact, why hadn't he planned a trip to New York to see her? She'd asked more times than he cared to remember. And in return, he'd promised so often to go, but he never saw it through.

From the tenor of her most recent letters, he sensed she was no longer very happy living with her grandparents. Sheila was so much like her mother. She had been from the time she could talk. Smart and strong-willed. His beautiful Anne. She'd shown such strength of character when she rebelled against her parents and married him. Doc knew it was only a matter of time before Sheila did the same thing as her mother.

He walked to where Lucas had brought in

a pitcher of water earlier and poured some into a bowl. He carried it back to the cot.

His father-in-law — J. T. Spencer — could be narrow and overbearing, to be sure, but it had been the right thing to do, leaving her in New York. She was reasonably safe there, much more than she'd ever be in the West. Even so, her letters of late led him to believe she was trying to decide for herself what her future would be. He didn't blame her, at all. Hell, he wouldn't be surprised to hear any day now that she'd run off and married some artist or writer.

After dipping the cloth in the water, he washed his patient's face.

Doc kicked himself again for not being closer to Sheila as she got older. He wished that, just once, he'd told her — in spite of having spent so much time apart — that he was still her father. She could always reach out to him if she needed help.

"Save them. Please. Save my girls." Tears ran from the corners of the woman's eyes and disappeared in her hairline.

Doc patted her tears and prayed to the Lord above that he'd see Sheila again.

Damn. Nothing like seeing the shadow of the Grim Reaper to bring out a man's regrets.

CHAPTER TEN

"You stay here, Bear." Caleb patted the massive head of his yellow dog. The brown eyes in his black face were attentive and responsive. "I am relying on you to help Gabriel run the ranch. We don't want nobody sneaking up on this young fella."

The dog cocked his head, turned and looked at Gabe, and then trotted over and flopped down next to him. Caleb had had a number of dogs travel with him over the years, but this golden-furred creature was, without a doubt, the smartest. The animal understood every word spoken to him, and Caleb suspected he could find his way home from a hundred miles off. But he never tested him on it. It didn't pay to give a dog too big a head.

The shadows were growing long, and he clapped on his broad-brimmed black hat as he strode to his horse. Beneath his dark oilskin duster, he wore a plain, brown woolen shirt, an elk-leather vest, and buckskin pants tucked into his boots. While he'd been waiting for Gabe to arrive, he'd packed up his trail gear. Rolled up with his bedding was a bearskin coat he'd made from a grizzly he shot while riding with Jacob Bell. It could get cold in the high mountains, even at this time of year.

Caleb wanted to be prepared for spending some time up there. That wild country beyond the Devil's Claw had never been tamed, despite the few hardy gold seekers throwing up shacks there, digging their yellow treasure, and carrying it out. The land was rugged and vast. He'd hunted up there with Old Jake eight or ten years ago, but trails changed and disappeared. It was a place that challenged even a man who knew what he was doing.

Still, these gangs of road agents wouldn't want to be so far out that they couldn't get to the Denver road in a day or two of traveling. That would limit the area he'd need to search, but not by much. Even though Caleb had no doubt he could find them, there were dozens of deserted mining camps where they could be holed up. And they'd surely pick one where they could see anyone coming and defend themselves without a great deal of trouble.

He picked up his saddlebags and slung them over the gelding's back. He'd taken the time to clean his Winchester and his pistols and run a stone over the long blade of his knife till it could shave the whiskers off a baby rattler. He made sure the leather thongs were fastened over the hammers of the Colts at his hips, and he double-checked his ammunition. He had enough to take down a whole company of desperados, if need be.

He swung up onto the saddle. "Your father will be checking on you if I am not back in a few days."

"We'll be fine, Mr. Marlowe," Gabriel called, standing tall and looking as serious as he could muster. "Don't you worry."

"I ain't worried." Caleb could see the young man was proud to be given the responsibility. "But don't forget what I told you. If any unsavory types show up looking to put their hands on that cattle, you throw a rope around that dog's neck and skedaddle into the pine forest. I don't want nothing happening to either of you."

"I won't forget."

"Even if someone drives off that whole herd, I can track them down when I get back."

And even if his cattle were long gone, Caleb thought as he rode off, he'd earn enough bringing in these outlaws to replace the herd with twice the number he lost.

Dusk was giving way to night by the time he reached the place where the road agents had hit the Wells Fargo stagecoach.

Caleb had no trouble finding it. Even in the waning light, chunks of splintered wood showed white on the ground. At the edge of the road, bark had been blasted off a couple of trees by errant shots.

Whoever was running the gang had a working brain and showed cunning in choosing this spot. The road here descended for at least a quarter mile until it reached this gulley, where it made a slight bend and then ran up the next hill. The way Caleb saw it, the driver would have had to slow way down to navigate the turn safely before starting up the slope. The outlaws simply waited around the bend where the pines and low brush provided good additional cover.

Those fellows riding on top never stood a chance.

Caleb crouched in the near darkness and frowned at the piles of shit in the road. After the attack, the road agents had left a perfectly good team of horses for hours, by the looks of things. He didn't particularly like that. It was one thing fighting other men,

104

but leaving harnessed horses to the violence of wolves and other predators was another. It was fortunate that someone had come upon the coach and the dead men.

But a passenger inside the coach had been shot and taken, the judge said, possibly for ransom. Whoever it was, they needed a doctor to keep him alive. So they cleared out quickly, taking only the wounded passenger and the strongboxes. And then they escorted that miner into Elkhorn to fetch Doc Burnett.

It was too dark to track the killers into the hills. But Smith's claim was nearby. Somehow, the road agents must have known about it.

Caleb swung up onto his mount. He'd spend the night there, see if he could find anything of the gunslingers who took the miner to town, and start out at first light.

A light breeze was drifting out of the northwest, and he caught no scent of any cooking fire. So he rode east. The stars were appearing in the black velvet sky, and a soft bulge of white was forming above the ridge of mountains ahead of him. A few minutes later, the moon showed her face.

He could have found the trail leading off the main road even without the light of the rising moon. The judge told him his men

105

had been out here already and found nothing of Smith or the road agents. They'd come through like a troop of cavalry, a half dozen sets of hooves obliterating any telltale signs of the outlaws.

He dismounted and led his Pirate along the trail. From the wear of the brush on either side, he could see the miner had once used a wagon, but not lately. The forest pines grew higher as he made his way along, with occasional groves of cottonwood, and the darkness was vast and deep. He moved silently and carefully, wary and attentive. He didn't expect to find any of the road agents, but if they turned Smith loose after fetching Doc, he could be back here.

The trail followed a creek for some time before entering a gulch. Here, the moon barely filtered through the sighing boughs of the trees. A mile or so from the Denver road, he reached a stump-filled clearing surrounding a log cabin.

Caleb paused, studying the place. With the exception of the burbling sound of water running fast and smooth in the nearby creek, a stern and heavy silence weighed down the cool air. There was no movement that he could see. No smoke rose from a stovepipe above the cabin.

The side of the cabin in front of him was

facing north, with no door and no windows showing. Beyond it, he could see a grassy meadow and a gradual slope down toward the creek.

Tying his mount to a branch at the edge of the clearing, he shrugged out of his duster, unfastened the thongs over his Colts, and loosened the iron in their holsters.

"I'll be back and tend to you shortly," he murmured, running his hand over the buckskin's neck.

He knew Smith had been working this claim for a couple of years — a long time for a single miner to work it alone. If a place was profitable, it would pay off fairly quickly, and the prospector would expand the effort to mine it properly. Hire extra hands. Bring in machinery. But if it wasn't profitable or the vein pinched out, a miner would leave everything and move on.

As Caleb treaded softly toward the south side of the cabin, it seemed to him that neither of those things applied. Most miners went to town for provisions rather than take the time and effort of growing anything. But in the moonlit meadow beyond the cabin, a good-sized garden had been planted. A weave of pine branches formed a perimeter border fence, and neat raised rows ran side by side. Smith had an established garden, and it wasn't the first year he'd raised crops in it.

Halfway along the cabin, a small window had been cut into the timber wall. Caleb carefully peered in, but the inside was dark as the grave. There was no movement. No fire showing. The hackles on his neck rose, however, and his instincts told him he wasn't alone.

Near the corner of the building, an axe, a maul, and a cross-cut saw leaned against a half year's stack of firewood. By it, the ground was soft, covered with sawdust, and a fresh footprint caught his eye. Beside it, there were black spots that trailed toward the south side. He crouched and pressed his fingers to it, rubbing it between thumb and fingertips before raising it to his nose.

It was blood, but not human blood. Maybe rabbit or squirrel, but more likely grouse. And from the scent and texture, he knew it was fresh. No more than an hour or two old.

It would be someone's supper. And that someone wasn't too far away.

He slid one of his pistols from its holster, moved stealthily to the corner, and peeked around it. The moon was nearly full and high enough to light everything clearly. Two more windows had been cut on this side, but they were shuttered. A door sat between them, but it too was shut.

Caleb scanned the blackness beneath the line of trees bordering the meadow. Everything was quiet, but again he couldn't shake the feeling that he was being watched. Whoever or whatever it was, they were either waiting to see what he intended, or they were waiting to get a clear shot at him.

Out here, he decided, he was too exposed. Moving in a low crouch, he ran to the cabin door and eased it open.

As the light of the moon spilled across the floor, Caleb saw two things. First, a native woman standing as poised and still as a cougar on the hunt. Second, the gleaming barrel of the shotgun in her hands pointed directly at his chest.

CHAPTER ELEVEN

Caleb stared at her over the thirty-inch barrels of the 12-gauge Greener. The woman had the shotgun's walnut stock comfortably nestled against her side, and both hammers were cocked and ready. One barrel at this range would put a hole in the front of him the size of his hand. Both barrels would send him off in two pieces to the Promised Land.

He had his Colt Frontier trained on her as well. Because she hadn't blasted him as he came onto the threshold, they appeared to be at a standoff. Dark eyes, shining in the spill of moonlight, watched him intently. They each knew that if those guns started blazing, they'd both be dead.

Fringed buckskin, cinched at the waist with a belt of dark leather, hung to below her knees, where a brown-and-yellow wool skirt was visible above elk-hide shoes. Long, thick, black braids had been thrown back

110

over her shoulders. A modest string of elk teeth lay on her breast, and silver earrings glinted in the light of the moon.

"My name is Caleb Marlowe. I mean you no harm," he said in Cheyenne.

From her clothing, he thought she might be Arapaho, but he knew there were strong similarities between her language and Cheyenne. He hoped she'd realize he was making a peaceful effort to communicate.

He slowly lowered his weapon. She didn't move a muscle.

His eyes were growing accustomed to the darkness inside the cabin. He was surprised by the orderliness and comfort of the place. He'd seen plenty of mining claims, and the men who worked them generally had little interest in the civilized upkeep of their living quarters. Prospecting was a rough life, and all their energy was directed at one thing: drawing gold or silver from the ground and streams.

Smith's cabin was different. The place was . . . well, homelike. A big bed, raised off the ground. Bearskin covered it, and elk skins had been tacked up on the walls to keep the winter winds out. Baskets hung from the beams, alongside dried meat and herbs. There was a potbellied stove and a rustic table fashioned from split pine and cottonwood. Two stumps served as chairs. There was no fire going, but inside the cabin, the smell of stew hung in the air.

She lived here with Smith.

Caleb understood why the fire was out. Being here alone, she didn't want the smell of it to draw attention.

Never mind that she was a woman; she was a native. It wasn't even two years since the Lakota and Cheyenne wiped out that fool Custer near the Little Bighorn River. It didn't matter to most of the white folks pushing west that Indians had been living on the land they wanted. To them, they were all savage and barbaric and deserved to be wiped out.

Ugly words from Caleb's childhood echoed in his mind. The words of the missionary. *For those who are spared, kill the Indian in them and save the man.* He bristled at the memory of the man who said it.

Caleb forced back the recollection and focused on the woman pointing the gun at his chest. She had to be cautious. Unless she was married and protected by her white husband, men could abuse and even murder her, and no law would provide justice.

"I mean you no harm," he repeated in Cheyenne.

"What are you doing here? What do you

want?" she responded in English. She spoke the language with the ease of someone who had been using it for years.

Caleb didn't blame her for not trusting him. A few words in Cheyenne weren't enough. "Looking for Smith, the miner who owns this claim."

"Why?"

He had no problem answering her question if it would put the woman's mind at ease. She still hadn't moved at all. She was standing, feet braced, finger on the trigger.

"He came to Elkhorn two days ago. He left there with my friend, Doc Burnett. The doctor has not returned, and people suspect foul play."

"Smith is guilty of no foul play."

"I believe you are correct in that, ma'am. But I need to find him."

"Slowly, put your gun in the holster, Marlowe."

Caleb pouched his iron and felt the woman immediately relax. She had no way of knowing, but there had been many times in the past where men thought themselves in a position of power just because his pistols were holstered. On more than a few occasions, those men had paid dearly for their error. He could still cut her down if he had to.

"I know of you, Marlowe."

Caleb was surprised.

"My people knew and respected the one they call Old Jake. I saw him once when I was very young. He came and traded in my village. People say you are like a son to him."

"I rode with him for a long time."

She lowered the shotgun but didn't decock the hammers. She still hadn't decided to completely trust him. Knowing of a man only goes so far.

"What are you to Smith?" he asked.

"I am his wife. My name is Imala."

He was not taken aback by her answer. Many men out here, including Jacob Bell, were known to take a native wife. It was curious, though, that the judge didn't seem to know about her. Unlike other miners and settlers who had an Indian wife, Smith apparently wasn't one to parade her around like some peculiar possession.

The way Imala dressed, however, told Caleb she was not one to abandon her ways. Maybe that was why Smith kept her out of Elkhorn.

"You are mining now, Marlowe?" she asked.

"I have a silver claim and a ranch I bought with a partner a few miles south of Elkhorn.

So far, I ain't worked it, though. I raise cattle."

She stood for a moment, watching him and considering until she reached a decision. She uncocked the shotgun and crossed the room. Rows of pegs had been driven into the logs above a line of barrels, and she set the Greener up with three other rifles.

They were quite a collection for a miner. A Springfield .45-caliber single shot that made Caleb think Smith had served in the Indian Wars. An old .50-caliber Hawken that could bring down a charging grizzly. Above them all was a .47-caliber Lancaster flintlock with a gleaming maple stock. Old Jake always held that the Lancaster was the best rifle he ever carried.

"Are you hungry?"

"I don't want to cause you any bother, ma'am."

"Sit there." She gestured to the table and then lit a fire in the stove.

He removed his wide-brimmed hat, hung it on a peg by the door, and sat at the table. She lit a candle and placed it in front of him.

Caleb watched her go wordlessly to the line of barrels along the wall and come back carrying an iron pot that she put on the stove. When she lifted the lid to stir it, he

115

smelled stewed pheasant, and his stomach rumbled.

"I apologize for busting in through the door and surprising you like that."

She put a basket of biscuits and a spoon on the table for him. "You didn't surprise me. I knew you were coming from the time you left the main road."

Of course she did. She was waiting with a shotgun aimed at his chest the moment he walked in.

"I was told Smith lived alone. I didn't expect to find him or anyone. But coming up to the cabin, I knew someone else was here. I just didn't know who."

"You are more alert than the six men who came looking yesterday."

Caleb figured she was speaking about the judge's men.

"You didn't show yourself to them."

He didn't mean it as a question, but the side look she sent him reminded Caleb of the dangers she faced. A native woman alone in an isolated cabin. It was best to hide.

"Sorry. I shouldn't have said that. You were right."

She stood by the table. "Smith does not drink spirits, but there is a jug filled with water from the creek. And I can make cof-

116

fee for you, if you want it."

"Thank you. I wasn't expecting any of this, but I'd love coffee, if it's not too much trouble."

"No trouble. Smith drinks coffee morning and night."

She took a tin bowl down from a shelf by the stove and filled it with stew. She placed it in front of him. "Eat, Marlowe."

"How about you? Ain't you eating?"

"I ate before."

The stew had large pieces of pheasant, potatoes, parsnips, and herbs he couldn't identify. The food was savory and filling. He finished it quicker than was polite. She filled his bowl a second time, and he sopped up the gravy with the biscuits. It was a better meal than any other he'd had in the four months since he arrived in Elkhorn. And that included several of the "best steaks in town."

When he told her so, she made no response.

As she went back to the stove for his coffee, he decided he should get down to business.

"When did you last see your husband, Imala?"

"Three nights ago. They came and took him away."

117

"How many men?"

"Two."

She sat across the table from him. In the candlelight, Caleb could see the web of lines spreading out from the corners of Imala's eyes. Gray strands were beginning to streak the black hair. He guessed her to be in her thirties, maybe older. It was tough to judge the age of some women, and those who lived out on the frontier tended to age faster than the women he recollected from back East. Except for Caleb's mother. He believed that she began aging the day she married.

"Tell me what happened when they came for him," he said.

She looked toward the door, remembering. "The moon was still high enough that the light was good. I woke Smith when I heard them. He pulled on his coat and boots and was waiting outside for them. They rode up to the cabin like they owned it."

"Where were you?" he asked.

"I was inside. I had the shotgun, but I am to use it only when it is necessary to kill. Smith says it is better to stay out of sight. He doesn't want anyone knowing I am here."

"Could you hear what they wanted?"

"The men wanted to know where they could find the nearest doctor. My husband told them Elkhorn was the only place."

"Either of them wounded?"

"No. They sat straight in their saddles."

Caleb considered. However many road agents were in this gang, they only sent two to get help. These fellas had to be the same ones who'd been spotted waiting for Doc and Smith at the edge of town. The rest of the gang, or at least some of them, had taken the wounded passenger somewhere else. Possibly to a hideout up past Devil's Claw, as the judge said. They must have been concerned about being caught here, so close to the holdup.

"Why did your husband go with them?"

"He had no choice. He was in the army in Wyoming, but he was no killer. He had his pistol, but it did not frighten them. They drew their guns and made him drop his in the dirt. Then they told him to fetch his horse."

They were in a hurry, Caleb thought.

"I think they are the kind who fear nothing, Marlowe."

Caleb knew men like that. The frontier was full of them. Men who had endured the hardships that this life threw at them and came to believe they were invincible. Tough, hard, clever. Many were just lucky. Until they weren't.

Gunslicks were the worst of the breed. Always thinking they had the fastest draw, the steadiest hand, the best shot. Always striving to prove it. Always looking to build their reputation by gunning down some other gunslinger who'd been around longer, whose fame had spread wider. And then, eventually, their luck ran dry, and they called out the wrong man.

He knew exactly the kind of men Imala was talking about. He'd had to kill more than a few.

"That's the last time you saw him?"

"The last." She stood and went to the stove, busying herself there.

Caleb figured that come daylight, he'd search the tracks along the trail and see if there was anything distinctive about the horses those men rode in on.

"Anything else you can tell me about them? Anything that stood out with you?"

"One was called Dodger," she said. "He was young, big, angry. He drew his pistol first. I think the other one thought he would kill my husband. I heard him say, 'Easy, Dodger. Let the man get his horse.' "

"What were they wearing?"

"They both wore dark coats, not dusters.

The young one wore a dark bandana. One wore a stovepipe hat and the other's hat had a wide brim, like yours. I could not see their faces clearly."

She went on to describe the horses they were riding.

Caleb decided this was the most anyone seemed to know about the members of this outlaw gang. He had a name. Dodger.

"Are you the sheriff in Elkhorn?" she asked, startling him.

She was looking at his chest. He'd pinned the tin star the judge had given him to his brown wool shirt. It was showing from under his leather vest.

"No. A special deputy, I guess. Only wearing this thing till I find Doc and your husband and the outlaws who took them."

"You're doing it alone?"

"That's my way."

"I know you are a tracker."

"Spent a few years working at it."

"When my husband was in the army, before we were together, he worked with the Indian scouts. That was long before we came here."

"You've known him a long time?" As he asked it, Caleb realized he was prying. But this claim and the cabin were not a situation he ran into every day, and she seemed to want to talk.

"When I was young and still living among my people, I had a husband. We lived east of here on the plains near the river you call the Arkansas. We lived in peace and followed the buffalo. It was a good life."

Imala looked at the door, and Caleb knew her mind was far away. The Arapaho lived the life of nomads, traveling where the food was plentiful. With the Lakota keeping to the lands farther north and the Cheyenne to the west, her people found themselves facing the hard push of settlers sooner than those other tribes. And they paid a heavy price.

"My family was all killed at Sand Creek. My parents and grandparents. My husband."

Damn. Everyone knew about Sand Creek. When it happened, most folks back East at the time were sick of bloodshed. The soldiers of the Union and the Confederacy had gone home, bone-tired from fighting. Lincoln was dead. The rebel states were still smoldering, and everywhere, mothers were still grieving. And then word spread of the massacre of women and children and old people.

The army said what happened was a disgrace. The colonel — a dog named

Chivington — was relieved of his duties. He'd led his troops against a camp of friendly Arapaho and Cheyenne people down by Fort Lyons. Cannon fire and a cavalry charge. The butchery that followed was sheer madness.

"Soon after the attack started, our chief, Left Hand, sent me and some others off with as many horses as we could drive away. If not, I would be dead too. Many times at night, I think of everyone that I left behind, of all those people who were left behind."

Her face was grim. She was trying to keep her emotions in check, but he saw her clenched fist pressing hard against the table-top.

"The soldiers attacking our camp were pure evil." Her voice was strained. "Afterward, I went back and saw what they did. The whites call us savages, but what they did was true savagery. Old women and men. Young women with their babies beside them. Children scalped. Mutilated. Cut to pieces. No one was left. All dead and left in their blood and gore."

Her eyes flashed at him, and she pounded her fist once on the table.

"The white man is my enemy. I will never forget what they did to my people."

Fourteen years had not eased the memory

or the burning emotion. How could it, Caleb thought. The pain of that loss had carved great slashes deep into Imala's heart, into her soul. A hundred years would not erase it.

He understood exactly why Smith kept her from town. It was not so much to protect *her* as to protect some fool who thought the color of his skin made him better.

Caleb knew he was very fortunate he hadn't taken both barrels of that Greener the moment he pushed that door open.

They sat in silence for a while as she made a visible effort to compose herself. Finally, she turned her dark eyes to him.

"But you asked about me and Smith."

Just saying her husband's name had a gentling effect on her. Softness replaced the tension of her jaw.

"We have been together almost ten years. I went to Wyoming with the survivors of my people. A few years later, when the prospectors came for gold, Smith was among them. He was finished with the army and went to the gold fields but lost his claim when he became sick."

"What was wrong with him?"

She shrugged. "Sometimes, bad things in life drive out a person's spirit. The two of us were very much the same."

She took his cup and went for more coffee.

"I helped him. I made him think he needed to take care of me. In truth, I took care of him. Each of us needed a purpose. Someone else to worry about."

She brought the cup back and put it in front of him.

War left too many damaged people in its wake. Like Imala. Like Smith. Like Doc Burnett.

"We married. And when silver was discovered in Colorado, we came. For two years, we have been here."

Caleb gestured to the cabin. "You've made a fine home here."

Imala looked around her. "It pleases him. I still find it strange to stay in one place. There is very little silver, but I don't think he minds. I work the garden, he works the claim, and we hunt together. It is a different life, but a good one."

Caleb finished his coffee and thanked her for his supper.

"I'll take my horse down by the creek there and camp for the night. But tomorrow I'll go and find him."

Her gaze was steady when she replied, "When he rode out with them, he did not look back. Smith always worried about me."

"He sounds like a good man."

She got up, took his cup, and went to the wash bucket without another word.

Caleb went out and led his mount to the creek where he could keep an eye on the cabin. When he was settled for the night, he leaned back against his saddle and listened to the running water. In the distance, a pack of coyotes were talking over their hunting plans, and an owl occasionally put in his two cents.

As Caleb watched the moon crouch on a peak to the west and then drop behind it, he had a bad feeling that Smith was never coming back here.

CHAPTER TWELVE

Through the branches of the cottonwood above him, Caleb opened his eyes to see that the black night sky was lightening to a deep blue. The sun would soon be climbing above the mountains to the east, and he needed to get himself going. Devil's Claw wouldn't be coming to him.

He went down to the creek to clean up. The water was ice-cold, and as he stood in the shallows looking, a speckled trout that had to be two feet long wandered by to see what Caleb was doing. A friend joined him, and they moseyed on together up the creek, following the deeper channels.

No one needed to go hungry in this part of the world, he thought.

When he came up to the cabin leading his buckskin, saddled and ready to go, Imala was already digging around in the big garden. She looked up, pushed a stray wisp of hair off her forehead, and pointed to a nearby stump. Caleb spied the pot of coffee, a cup, and a covered basket she'd put there.

He went over and poured himself some coffee. The basket held biscuits that were still warm.

"I'm obliged to you for your hospitality, ma'am," he said, going to the edge of the garden. Most of it was still in the morning shadow, but sunlight would soon warm the turned earth.

"Thank you for looking for my husband."

He said nothing and watched her work for a moment. "Is there anything I can do for you before I go?"

"No, I'll get on well enough," she told him, sinking the blade of the shovel into the soil and putting a foot up on the shoulder of the long-handled tool. "While Smith digs for silver, I spend most of my time alone here, anyway."

"Between the garden and the hunting, you must eat fairly well, I'd guess. I saw some trout in that creek that could feed a half dozen people."

"That's true. And the grouse and pheasant and rabbits are plentiful here. We only go and hunt larger game when one of us fancies venison. When autumn comes, Smith likes geese the best."

"Well, I need to be going. Thank you again for the food."

"Be careful as you search. These men are killers. Watch out for the one called Dodger, especially."

He hadn't talked about the stagecoach robbery with her, but she was correct about them being murderers. The driver and the guard that rode with him were dead — quite possibly the passenger was, as well. Caleb didn't want to say it, but he had little hope of bringing Smith back alive. The miner would have been of little use to the outlaws once he'd fetched Doc for them.

"Do not worry, Marlowe," she said, as if reading his thoughts. "I will survive if Smith is gone."

He held her gaze. He wouldn't share his doubts with Imala, but this was not a woman to be coddled or lied to.

"How'll you make do?"

She drove the shovel deeper into the dirt. "Maybe I'll carry things from my garden down into Elkhorn. Or catch fish to bring to the town. They could fetch a good price."

"You're right. Your fish and your produce would pay steadier than prospecting."

But even as he said the words, his thoughts were already running to how Smith felt about her safety. A passel of decent folks lived in Elkhorn, Caleb supposed, but there was also plenty of low-life scum.

"Before you start developing a market trade in town, will you wait to hear word of your husband?"

"Who will bring me word?"

"I'll do it."

Imala left her shovel and came out of the garden. "You worry."

Damn right, he worried. Here on the frontier, it took a strong person to live alone. He needed no one, but he knew other men who had been beaten down and broken by the solitary life. It was a choice they made, mostly, and they were free to make it. But he'd worry about any woman out here alone. What if she got hurt or fell sick? What if some knothead decided he wanted an unworked claim with a comfortable cabin? She'd be out here on her own, fighting for her life.

Caleb thought about his mother. She had him to protect her, and he still hadn't been able to keep her from harm. He felt the old familiar ache. Some guilt never went away. What would have happened if he'd stayed at the house that day? How would life have been different if he'd come back in from the barn sooner?

"I am Arapaho, Marlowe."

Imala's words yanked away the iron fist squeezing his windpipe.

"My connections with the earth and the sky are strong. Smith thinks he protects me — I let him think it — but it is not that way." She pointed at the garden. "I grow roots and vegetables and herbs that my people have gathered for all time. I take what the trees and bushes provide. I hunt for meat. I cook and feed him. Who takes care of who?"

Caleb nodded in respect. He knew every word she spoke was the truth.

"I'll be going, then."

She walked to the cabin and picked up some things by the door. She handed him the larger bundle. It was buckskin tied with a leather thong.

"Food for your journey," she said.

She held out a second bag, smaller and stitched together from buffalo hide.

"A medicine pouch. Do you know what it is?"

"I know what it is." He didn't need to open it. It contained items representing sacred animal spirits. It would bring him good luck, protection, and strength in battle.

"I will carry it with me."

After securing her gifts in his saddlebags, Caleb led his horse down the trail toward the Denver road. She was still watching him as he made his way around a bend and out of sight of the cabin.

Before he reached the main road, he found signs of the visitors. It had been about a week since they had rain here. Now, in broad daylight, it was easy to see the tracks of the six who rode in and rode out together. He found the single track of Smith's horse going out from the cabin. Eliminating all of those, he distinguished which hoofprints belonged to the road agents' horses. The shoes were badly worn from being ridden over rocky terrain, and one had a particularly distinctive gash on the right side of the front shoe.

Caleb mounted up and soon found the trail that would lead from the Denver road up toward Devil's Claw and the land beyond.

He'd been riding for hours, and the sun was high and hot on his back as he made his way along a narrow trail that resembled the path of a monstrous snake. He kept his eyes open for signs of riders coming through. There were occasional prints, but none had the distinctive gash on the right horseshoe. For the most part, the prints were of deer and elk as well as bear, cougar, and bobcat. These lands teemed with game.

As Caleb rode deeper into the mountains, fir-covered slopes rose on either side of him, with patches of loose, jagged rock and shale that protruded and hung menacingly over the trail. The path wound steadily upward, and a deep, trackless chasm of a valley dropped away on the left. In some places, one misstep by Pirate would send them both tumbling to certain death.

The gelding was as fine a mount as a man could want, though. He could go all day and was always attentive and agreeable to what Caleb wanted. Sure-footed as a mule, Pirate was also so quick and agile that cutting a rambunctious calf out of a herd was no chore. Between that horse and his dog, Bear, the hard work of muscling cattle was damn near enjoyable.

The trail dropped steeply down into a ravine and forded a creek that ran through a rock-studded meadow bordered by thick forests of fir. To his left, the running water fell away in a series of small waterfalls until it disappeared from view. He stopped to let Pirate drink and rest for a few minutes.

The buckskin suddenly raised his head, his attention focused on the meadow above them, not far from where the creek emerged from a grove of cottonwoods. From the line of trees, two bear cubs wandered out into the stretch of grass and rocks. Young grizzlies no more than a few months old, from the size of them. Their shaggy coats were dark brown, nearly black, and each of them had patches of white fur near the shoulders and neck. They were upwind and heading toward the creek, unaware of the human and equine intruders watching them.

They were damn cute to look at, tumbling and wrestling as they moved along, but nothing panicked a horse quicker than a bear.

Pirate had good reason to be spooked. The mother bear lumbered out of the woods, and when her big head swung around toward her cubs, she stopped and rose up slightly onto her two hind legs. The grizzly was upwind, about a hundred and fifty paces away. Far too close.

"Never mind me," he whispered.

Her nose sniffed the air. She couldn't pick up his scent, but Caleb could smell her just fine. It was difficult to tell how big she was under that shaggy brown coat, but he judged she had to run close to four hundred pounds. Even so, he knew she could cover ground in a hurry.

In an open field, Pirate could outrun the bear easily, once he got going. But if the trail ahead looked like what he'd been following, it would be twisting and uneven. The gelding wouldn't have much of a chance to show his speed.

Caleb slowly slid his Winchester from its scabbard. He didn't want to kill the mother if he didn't have to. This was her place, and those two cubs were still too young to survive on their own. But if she decided to charge, there'd be no help for it.

She was still undecided. The low growl reached him. He cocked the hammer and raised the rifle to his shoulder. He sighted along the barrel, aiming for her lower jaw. If she came hard across the meadow, he'd at least hit her in the chest or shoulder. That would slow her down.

Suddenly, her great head swung away from him. Caleb followed her gaze. A lone coyote stood in the shadow of the pines at the far edge of the meadow. His tongue was hanging as he stared at the cubs.

That threat was the more imminent, and she bolted, moving with astonishing speed toward her offspring. Her feet thundered across the meadow, and she let out a roar as she ran. The two cubs had picked up the scent of the predator and were bawling loudly as they looked at the coyote.

In a moment, the grizzly was between the

cubs and the coyote, on her back legs and roaring.

That was all the distraction Caleb needed. The confrontation between mother and predator could last some time, but unless the coyote had help, he wasn't going to be eating any bear cubs today.

He nudged Pirate, and the gelding carried him up the trail and into the forest.

When they reached a wide bluff of bald rock, Caleb reined in and pulled a brandy bottle filled with water from his saddlebag. As he drank, he looked down at the mist rising above a frothing river that thrashed and battered its way past shimmering boulders and fallen timber.

To his right, ridgelines and depressions in the mountain terrain rose and fell, each one as deep and wide as the river valley that held his entire ranch. But the land here was steep and rugged and filled with pine and fir that stood straight as sentinels. And above it all, Devil's Claw reached for the sky, an open hand of rock ready to pluck down and crush in its grasp any cloud foolish enough to stray too close.

On the westerly side of the river, Caleb spotted another trail winding in and out among the trees and rock. There was more than one way through here, and miles ahead, beyond this narrow pass, Caleb knew that the land opened up into high mountain forests and meadows, rock canyons, and crystal-clear rivers and lakes. But it was a hard, unforgiving place, unfit for the faint-hearted. Over the years, more prospectors and hunters went in there than returned.

The shadows were growing long when he heard the sound of rifle fire ahead. Twilight had gathered under the walls of rock and forest on the western face. Caleb dismounted and led his horse along the trail. Before he could get close enough to see who was going at it so fiercely, he realized he would not be able to pass by without getting caught in the crossfire.

After tying his mount in a protected grove off the trail, he slid his Winchester from its scabbard, unfastened the thongs from his twin Colts, and moved stealthily along the shadowy trail.

CHAPTER THIRTEEN

Doc Burnett withdrew his hand from the patient's forehead and sat back. It was late afternoon, and the fever that had started yesterday was worsening. He needed to act soon, or this woman would surely die.

Doc pulled open his valise on the odd chance he'd missed something. It was a waste of time. He knew perfectly well what he'd brought, and the bottles he carried in the bag were sitting on the floor beside the bed. He picked up each one, hopeful there was a drop left. They were empty.

This old, abandoned mining camp the road agents were using as a hideout lacked the provisions that he'd need if he was to save this woman's life. Still, he wasn't about to do nothing while she suffered an increasingly unpleasant end.

Since Doc arrived three days ago, the outlaw called Lucas had been the one who spent the most time in here, watching him.

138

He'd made no mention to the young man of the fisher that came calling yesterday. There was no point in doing so, and the animal hadn't made another appearance, anyway.

Through the window and open door, Doc could hear the others, though their conversation was often just a dull blur in the background of his mind. Even so, he had learned a few things.

He couldn't quite determine the exact number of men in the gang, but they were using one or two of the other shacks for sleeping. They seemed to argue almost all the time — about the food, the remoteness of the camp, the quality of one horse over another, the boredom of waiting, the lack of women. None of them liked taking a turn going out and watching the trail for unwanted visitors. That task seemed to have begun after the appearance of the traveler who was shot dead the night Doc got here.

The lean one, Lucas, was something of a lone wolf. He didn't take a turn standing guard, which made Doc think he was in charge. He didn't appear to give the others orders, even though they often called him outside to get his input on something they were arguing about.

But if he was their leader, his hold on

them was not a strong one. Silent and morose, he lacked the bullying bravado one would expect of an outlaw leader. Mostly, he just sat on a crate in the corner of the shack, watching Doc and the patient while the others spent their time elsewhere.

It seemed to him that the young gunslinger showed more concern about the condition of the ransom victim than any of the other road agents. He guessed that Lucas may have been the one who shot her.

Doc took the bottle of morphine out of his bag and inspected the few drops that were left. The woman moaned in pain, but he placed the precious bottle back in the bag instead of administering a dose. He had to stretch what was left.

Half an hour ago, he'd had Lucas replace the water in the tin bowl he carried in his valise. He dipped the wet cloth he was using as a compress into the bowl and wrung it out. Patting it over her face, he wiped away the beads of sweat standing out on her heated skin.

She had a familiar face, though he was fairly sure she wasn't someone from Elkhorn. She had fine symmetry to her features. A high forehead beneath thick, auburn hair. A straight nose between high cheekbones. Thin, pallid lips, slightly parted as she took shallow breaths.

Though she was probably in her forties, she had not gained the weight often added in one's middle years. Her eyes, when she'd opened them, were deep brown.

Before being shot, she had to be enjoying general good health, otherwise she couldn't stand the extreme strain on her system now. She'd need every ounce of her strength to pull through.

Rinsing and wringing out the excess water from the compress again, Doc laid it across her fevered forehead.

Her eyelashes fluttered, her lips moved, and another moan escaped her throat. She was fighting a battle while she slept.

Carefully pulling back the collar of the dress, he lifted the dressing away from the wound. The flesh around the incision he'd made when he dug out the bullet was gray and shot through with red. The wound itself was oozing, and the fluid emitted a faintly fetid smell.

He called Lucas and waited until the young man came over.

"Do you see this pus?"

The road agent nodded. "What of it?"

"This fluid would be classified as *vile,* as opposed to *laudable.*"

Lucas was staring at the woman's face,

rather than at the damage he'd inflicted. His eyes flicked back to Doc.

"I ain't no sawbones. Speak English."

"Laudable pus is considered a sign that the wound should heal. It means that nature is putting up a bold fight against infection. It isn't festering."

"But . . . ?"

"But that's not what we're looking at."

The young man's eyes were troubled, and a pair of furrowed lines creased his brow. "What are we looking at?"

"This fluid is watery and tinged with blood. You can see it if you look closely. And there's a hint of a foul smell that is going to get worse," Doc told him. "If that wound has not already become malignant, it will be soon. And that will kill her."

"So you're saying she's a goner?" The outlaw's voice had taken on a steely edge.

"Not necessarily."

Lucas stood up straight. "All right. You're a doctor. Fix her."

"To *fix* her, I have to open the wound again."

"But you said you took the bullet out already."

"There may be something else in there that is causing it to fester."

"Why the blazes didn't you take it out the

142

first time?"

Doc heard the anger in the outlaw's voice, but he was feeling his own temper heat up.

"It was an emergency situation. I extracted the bullet that I saw, using what I had."

"What you *had*?" Lucas snapped. There was murder in his eyes. "You had your damn bag with you. What else did you need?"

"My surgical instruments."

In one motion the outlaw picked up Doc Burnett's bag and dumped the contents on the floor. Scissors and clamps and tweezers, two scalpels, and a saw clattered out. Doc quickly snatched up the bottle of morphine, relieved that it didn't break.

"What are these, then?"

"Not what I need, imbecile," Doc barked back at him. "You don't use a bullwhip to cut your bread, do you? I need different tools, depending on the surgery I need to perform."

"Why didn't you bring what you needed when you left Elkhorn?"

"I don't carry all of my surgical instruments every time I'm called out."

Doc picked up his things one by one, piling them on a cloth under the cot. The instruments glinted in the light, reminding him that he could inflict a mortal wound on this outlaw with half of them.

He softened his tone. "When that fellow came to me, he told me there'd been an accident. He said nothing about any bullet wound. I rode up here with the medicines that were in my bag. But I had no way of knowing what I was facing, who I was seeing, or what the injuries were."

Lucas ran a hand down his face, glanced at the woman, and then turned his glare back at Doc.

The woman groaned, and her pain was evident. Doc wasn't surprised. He'd had to cut back the amount of laudanum he was giving her to make the medicine last longer. Lucas's attention focused on her face again.

"I am trying to save her life."

"Are you?"

"I am a *doctor*. That's my job." Doc's voice was sharp, his eyes reprimanding as he glared at Lucas.

The young man let out a frustrated breath. "If you cut her open again, what do you think you'll find in there?"

Doc shook his head. He was glad to be past the outlaw's temper. "Hard to tell. There may be shreds of her clothing that were embedded when the bullet entered the body. There may be dead skin that is putrefying inside the wound. There could be a tiny fragment of bone. In any case, the bullet that I dug out was complete. There were no pieces that broke off. But for all I know, there could possibly be another bullet in there. I *won't* know until I'm in there."

Wound infections were always a serious problem. During the war, he and other doctors working close to the battle lines were constantly improving operating protocol and sharing successful techniques with one another. Despite what the newspapers printed, the first choice of the surgeon, notwithstanding the overwhelming and horrific conditions of the battlefield, was not amputation.

But in trying to save a limb, infections were unavoidable.

Doc Burnett could only speak for himself, but by the war's end, his standard procedure was to cut away dead tissue and inject the wound margins with bromine — while the patient was under anesthesia, if possible. He'd then pack the wound with a bromine-soaked dressing and isolate his patients in a separate tent with their own bandage supply. Doc's assistants dressed the wounds, and he insisted that they wash their hands in chlorinated soda between patients.

He'd learned a great deal in those bloody days, but he hadn't had the luxury of applying any of that knowledge here.

"Then cut her. Do what you have to do."

"I can't."

The gunslinger's eyes narrowed, and Doc knew the man was about to explode again. "What do you mean, you can't?"

"I can't because, as I *told* you, the specific surgical tools I need are back in Elkhorn. I can't because she is in severe pain, and the strain of an operation without chloroform and morphine will *kill* her."

He stared at the young man, letting the silence hang for an extra moment.

"Do you want her to die?" Doc finally asked.

Lucas turned abruptly and headed for the door.

Doc watched him stride out into the afternoon sunlight and wondered if the road agent was going out there to tell one of the others to dig two graves.

No, digging graves was too much to hope for. No doubt they would come back in, guns blazing and shoot them both. Then Lucas's partners would drag the dead bodies of an innocent stagecoach passenger and an ornery Elkhorn medical professional out to some ditch or ravine where the scavenging wildlife of the area could have their way with them.

146

Doc wasn't about to delude himself. That was what had been done for that miner when he was no longer of any use to them.

The pile of parcels and letters spilling out of the opened Wells Fargo strongboxes drew his attention.

Damn, he chided himself. He should have written to his daughter while he'd been stuck here. When these outlaws were done with this place, they'd no doubt take anything valuable and ride away. But Doc guessed those letters would stay where they'd fallen. And who could say but that in a month, or six months, or a year, some drifter might possibly pass through and find the letters. Perhaps he would take it on himself to carry them back to civilization.

There was so much he'd like to say to Sheila. He wished he could explain why he'd gone away and why he'd stayed away. He would tell her that, despite the long years they'd been apart, he loved her. To die out here without at least trying to leave some last words for his daughter would be a tragedy.

The woman shivered, moaning low. Her pain had to be horrendous now, but it would be excruciating once the medicine ran out. He'd continue to stretch it as far as he could, but during the day tomorrow, it would be gone.

Doc considered cleaning the wound first before covering it again. He stood up and crossed the room to the stove. The fire was out, but he picked up the pot of water he'd had Lucas fetch earlier. His bandage supply was limited, so he'd been boiling the used cloths each time he changed them.

When he returned to the bed, her eyes were open. Though they were feverish, she was more alert than he'd seen her. Her face was flushed and blotchy. In her condition, he expected that she would drift in and out of sleep, though when she was awake, the pain had to be agonizing.

Doc immediately glanced at the door to make sure Lucas wasn't coming. There was no sign of the outlaw. He sat down beside her.

"Am I dying?" Her voice was hoarse and weak, as if she were trying to call up from the bottom of a deep well.

"You heard what I told him, didn't you?"

Her chin moved slightly up and down. "How much time do I have?" she whispered.

"I exaggerated somewhat." Doc glanced at the door again to make sure they were alone before speaking. In his experience, it was better if the patient didn't hear the worst. "It is true that the wound is beginning to look suspicious. What I said about having to operate again is the truth. You'll not be getting better if I don't reopen the wound."

"Then do it."

"You are a brave woman. You have already suffered a great deal at the hands of these ruffians."

Her face was surprisingly calm as she looked steadily into his eyes. "Do what you must, Doctor. I trust you."

He shook his head. "But I was telling the one who watched us the truth when I said I can't operate without the correct medical instruments and anesthetics."

"I heard you ask him for it."

"But I don't know if they're paying any attention to what I say." He laid his hand on her forehead. She was even hotter. "Can I get you anything?"

"Thirsty. I'm very thirsty."

Somehow he had to keep her strong enough to stay alive. But his options were limited. He had no broth. Nothing but some dry biscuits and water and coffee.

During the past days, he'd been soaking the hard biscuits in cold coffee to soften them. He gave her a bit at a time whenever she came around. Since she was awake, he wanted to give her something stronger to

149

help stretch the effect of the laudanum.

He crossed the room again and picked up the bottle of brandy Lucas had been drinking from earlier.

"Tell these fellas exactly what you need out of your house."

The young outlaw's voice startled him. Doc whirled and found Lucas at the door, flanked by two others. They were the same gunslingers who'd been waiting for him and the miner outside of town. The younger man was the one who'd shot and killed Smith with no more feeling than if he'd knocked a bottle off a fence post.

Doc stole a glance at his patient. Her eyes were closed.

Smart woman, he thought. She knew she was safer pretending to be unconscious.

The older road agent spoke up. He was shorter and thinner than the other and had a face like a hawk. "What do you need? And where would we find it?"

Doc calculated how long it would take them to return to Elkhorn. They'd be mainly traveling in the dark and would more than likely arrive at his house before dawn. But even if they got there later, it was unlikely they'd find his housekeeper there. Without having to prepare meals for him, Mrs. Lewis didn't come around when he was away.

He took a notepad and the stub of a pencil from his coat pocket and wrote down his list.

"Here are the things that I need," he said, tearing off the page.

Lucas took it and handed it to the older man. "Can you read that, Wendell?"

The hawk-faced gunman looked at it and nodded.

"Take my bag." Doc picked up his leather valise and put the empty bottles back in. With his back to them, he pushed his surgical instruments farther under the cot with his foot. "Don't bring the large bottles in my office. I don't want them broken in transit. Only fill these bottles."

Wendell took the medical bag from him.

"Where's your house?"

"You know already." Doc had no doubt these two had been watching Smith from a distance when he came to Doc's door. The man's nervousness spoke of it.

"Tell us again."

"First lane off Main Street as you go into town. The only house with a porch out front."

As the two men turned and went out the door, Lucas went after them.

Doc peered out the front door and

watched the young outlaw speaking fiercely to each man. When he was finished, they nodded and walked away.

Turning back to his patient, he saw the women's eyes were once again open.

"Well, that kid Lucas is, no doubt, in charge of this outfit," he told her. "Let's get you better. I think, between the two of us, we can handle him."

CHAPTER FOURTEEN

Caleb moved toward the sound of shooting until he reached a bend in the trail formed by an outcropping of solid rock. From here, he still couldn't see the gun battle, but the sound of rifle fire was loud and close. Any farther and he'd be smack in the middle of things.

That wasn't what he had in mind.

He looked around, considering his options. Since midday, the trail had been winding in and out along the rugged hillside. Its path had been dictated by the contours of the land as well as by shale and brush and rocks jutting up from grassy areas. These boulders varied in size, some of them as big as a barn. To his right, the land rose sharply into a forest of firs and brush, cutting off his ability to see more than a few paces. To his left, the slope beneath the trail dropped away quickly, so steep that he looked down on the tops of full-grown trees.

Unless he wanted to backtrack for miles and find another way through the pass, Caleb realized, he wasn't going to get around this confrontation easily.

"Best find out what this is all about," he muttered to himself. To do that, the only way would be to get to a place above the shooting where he could see what was going on.

Turning away from the gunfire, he moved back the way he came until he found a spot where he could leave the trail. Scaling a steep embankment, he began his climb through groves of evergreen and worked his way through patches of thick brush and rock. His boots often slipped on patches of gravel or fir needles. The going was made more difficult because he was carrying his Winchester and had only one hand free.

From the position of the sun behind him, when he could see it, he figured he still had an hour of daylight, maybe two, but he didn't reckon going back down this way would be easy or even possible in the dark. He couldn't waste much time up here.

A few minutes later, he reached a steep, narrow band of meadow grass. A little higher and off to his left, a boulder that looked like an old man's face jutted out from the side of the hill. He was getting closer to the shooting. He decided that the old-man boulder would give him the best vantage point, and he started for it.

As he made his way, he found himself almost immediately at the base of a jagged bluff. It looked like a thirty-foot-high stack of flat rocks piled on top of each other by some giant hand. Around him, that same giant had buried dozens of similar rocks half in the ground.

Caleb decided to climb the bluff. From the top, he could get to the old-man boulder quicker.

He reached for the lowest ledge and then yanked his hand away. As he fell backward a step, a dried snake skin dropped to the ground in front of his boots.

Rattlesnake skin. The monster that shed that skin had to be six feet long.

Caleb cursed himself. Any greenhorn could tell you that only a fool would blindly stick his hand up where it could be bitten. Colorado was full of rattlers, but he rarely saw the damn things this high in the mountains.

Deciding against the climb, he worked his way along the face of the bluff until he found a break where he could continue his upward scramble.

Whoever was facing off, they were continuing to blast away at one another with rifles and pistols. Gunshots echoed back from across the wide chasm of the pass. From the sound of things, they wanted to finish it before sundown.

When he thought he'd climbed high enough, Caleb moved along the steep slope. Finally, forcing his way through brush, he found himself standing on a narrow ledge. The valley opened up in front of him.

Across the way and far below him, the forests and the river were already in deep shadow, and the golden sun was dipping quickly toward the mountain ridges. The boulder that looked like an old man was just below him. He dropped down onto it, then crouched and edged out to the end. Lying on his belly, Caleb took stock of the battle.

Five gunmen were strategically positioned along the slope face, hidden between rocks and trees. They were eighty yards or so above the trail, and anyone coming along would ride directly into their sights.

From where he was, Caleb could see only two of them clearly. From this distance, there was nothing to distinguish them from most other cowpunchers, drifters, or miners. One, wearing a wide-brimmed sombrero, was shooting an old Sharps carbine. The other, sporting a battered stovepipe hat and a green coat, was raining down bullets with a Winchester. They were firing down the steep hill and didn't seem to be too concerned about running short on ammunition.

Though he couldn't see the other three, he knew where they were from the crack of their rifles and the puffs of gun smoke each time they fired down on the men pinned down below. These fellows had deliberately positioned themselves to ambush someone coming along that trail.

There appeared to be a path, of sorts, running on an angle up from where the shooters were to a wooded ridge. Caleb decided they more than likely had left their horses there, in case things didn't work out the way they planned.

Somebody in that bunch was thinking.

Caleb turned his attention to the carnage down the hill.

The carcass of a small sorrel stretched across the trail, its eyes open, a black circle of blood on its shoulder marring the handsome color of its coat. Not far from the dead horse, a man lay sprawled in the grass, motionless, half-hidden by a protruding rock.

Three others had somehow found cover, two behind rocks and a third behind the rotted trunk of a fallen fir tree. Because of the angle the tree had fallen, Caleb decided it didn't afford the best protection. In their scramble for safety, they apparently had no chance of grabbing their rifles out of their scabbards.

Their horses were nowhere in sight. They hadn't come back down the trail toward him when he came upon the shooting, so he figured they must have run off ahead or gone down that steep slope. If the slope was where they went, he didn't hold out much hope for them surviving. But then again, from the looks of things, their riders probably wouldn't be needing them. Not in this life, anyway.

Not that the men weren't putting up a good fight. As he watched, somebody's head or hand would pop up, and he'd empty a six-shooter in the general direction of the bushwhackers. They didn't have much chance of hitting any of them, what with the distance and the fear of catching a rifle slug in the eye. But they were trying to keep the boys up the hill from moving around too freely. And Caleb guessed they were praying that the sun would drop as soon as possible.

He considered staying out of it and letting the contenders play out the hand. He never liked getting in the middle of a brawl — whether it was a card game or a street fight — without knowing the bone of contention that started the fight. And even then, he'd made it a personal policy not to interfere.

One time, when he was wearing the tin star up in Greeley, he found a pair of newlyweds duking it out in the front parlor of the rooming house he was living in. When he tried to separate them, the two turned on him. No sooner had he subdued the husband than he had the new wife on his back. He thought he'd have to shoot both of them before they calmed down.

These two gangs of fellas didn't appear to be newlyweds, though, and that made Caleb even less motivated to pick a side.

The bushwhackers above were keeping them pinned down, but it was only a matter of time before they realized the shooters on the far left and far right could move, get a better angle, and finish it.

Then, just as Caleb was starting to feel bad for those boys down by the trail, one of them raised a white handkerchief and started waving it. The firing died down, and he stood, shouting that he didn't know what they wanted, but he and his friends meant them no harm. A second man stood as well, holding his revolver out to the side.

The third man, who'd been hiding behind the fallen log, started to stand too. Caleb recognized him.

The truce-seeker was still talking when Stovepipe Hat levered a cartridge into that Winchester and — easy as you please — put a bullet square into his face. The second man stood frozen, unable to move. He didn't stand there for long. Before that white kerchief floated halfway to the ground, the Winchester again spit fire, sending him spinning out of sight.

The blackguard then swung his rifle around and took leisurely aim at the third man. He figured he'd just drawn an inside straight.

But that was one card too many for Caleb, and his bullet was on its way before the dog could pull the trigger. The shot was rushed, but he didn't miss. The stovepipe hat tipped up slightly on the man's head, and a spray of pink mist exploded onto the rock in front of him.

The man in the sombrero spun around, looking for the new player in the game. Caleb put one right in the center of his chest. The Sharps in the man's hand tipped forward and dropped as the shooter slumped to the ground.

As the echoes died away, Caleb turned his eye toward the remaining three shooters.

Suddenly, a bullet ricocheted off the boulder so close to him that a stone chip took a chunk out of his face. The shot had come from above and behind him. Whoever it was, Caleb wasn't about to give him a second chance.

When he crawled out onto this rock, he hadn't decided whether to get involved or whose side he was on.

Rolling for cover, he realized his decision had been made.

As the shots died away, Caleb turned his
toward the remaining three shooters.
Suddenly, a bullet ricocheted off the
boulder so close to him that a stone chip
tore a chunk out of his face. The shot had
come so close. Caleb wasn't about to give him a
second chance.

CHAPTER FIFTEEN

Caleb wiped the blood from his face with
the back of his hand and pressed himself as
flat as he could manage into a shallow
depression in the rock face. Bullets from
the gunman above him were chipping away
at the stone a foot in front of his boots.
Where the slugs struck just over his head,
dust and gravel rained down.

He cussed at himself as he loaded cartridges into his Winchester. When he'd realized that one of these boys had a brain, he
should have considered that they'd leave
someone up with their horses. That fella was
also watching their flank. Caleb was fortunate that the knothead hadn't been on
target with his first shot.

Peering over the edge of the boulder at
the ridge below, he knew he couldn't stay
where he was. Three guns remained down
there, but they wouldn't wait for sunset to
move. It wouldn't take much for one or two

of them to get to a place where they had a clean shot at him. And with this blackguard above keeping him pinned down, Caleb wouldn't have much chance.

He had to move now.

Turning slightly, he fired two shots up the bluff and two quick ones in the general direction of the gunmen below. Hoping that was enough to hold them off for a second or two, he scrambled back the way he'd come.

Bullets pinged and thudded into the ground around him, but he made it into the cover of the brush and kept going. The gunman above him was moving too, following along and taking potshots as he went.

Caleb had very little cover as he cut across the steep hillside, but he used what he could. The fir trees below him and the dark shadow they threw looked tempting, but going straight down to them would expose his back. Bullets continued to cut through brush and saplings, and he didn't want to push his luck.

Besides, he had an idea.

Sometimes, when they had the chess board set up in the parlor of Doc's house, he'd find himself with his own king on the run. Damned if old Burnett wasn't relentless in chasing him when that happened.

Sometimes — not always, but sometimes — he would gull that medical man into moving too quick, committing himself where he shouldn't, and then Caleb would strike, leaving Doc scowling and cursing at his own impetuousness.

Caleb knew his idea wasn't a great one, but this was a deadly game they were playing, and his moves were a mite limited at the moment.

Moving on an angle down from his pursuer, Caleb spotted the thirty-foot-high stack of rock slabs and raced to get to it. Then, halfway across open meadow, his boots dug into a soft spot, and he tumbled what felt like a mile down the hill, coming to a stop when his ribs made themselves at home against a boulder sharp enough to cut rope.

Trying to force air into his lungs was about as easy as stuffing a bobcat in a sack. It didn't help that he had bullets thudding into the ground and raising sprays of dirt all around him.

Grabbing his hat, he limped and ran as well as he could until he reached the score of rocks that lay half buried in the grassy slope below the jagged cliff face. As he recalled, most of them were bigger than a man.

164

The top of the bluff shielded him from the shooter, but it wouldn't be for long. In a few moments, that bastard would be standing on top of the cliff. He'd have a commanding view of the slope. That's what Caleb was counting on.

Quickly propping his hat and rifle up near the top of one of the jutting rocks, he raced to another jagged boulder twenty yards beyond it and took cover. With his back to the boulder, Caleb drew one of his Colts and waited.

Less than a minute later, he heard gravel and sand come tumbling down the face of the cliff.

"Come for my king, fella," he murmured.

In the silence that followed, Caleb could feel the shooter scanning the scene below him. He played it out in his mind. If he'd positioned his hat and rifle in the right spot, the pursuer would soon see them. Focus only on them. Put them alone in his sights. Positioned at the top of the slabs, the gunman would figure he'd have a clear shot at him if he tried to make it to the firs.

All Caleb wanted was for him to feel that he was in control of this chess board. Confident that the chase was over. Sure that he was closing in for the kill. And then, move just one space too far.

He heard the scrape of a boot far above him. Caleb slowly turned and raised himself until he could peer over the rock and then eased back down. The shooter was set at the top of the bluff, positioned close to the edge. He was on one knee, his rifle fixed on the hat and gun.

Caleb judged he was about forty yards from his target. He'd only have maybe one shot. He took a breath, ready to make his move.

Funny thing about life, though. It ain't chess. Caleb knew that well enough. Chess was a board game that pitted two opponents against each other. The rules were set. It was a contest of intelligence and strategy. There was no element of luck involved.

In the game of life, fate was bound to throw the unknowable at you. Often when you least expected it. Often when you could least afford it.

The movement at the base of the rock eight feet from him caught his eye just as he heard the rasp of serpentine skin on the grass and gravel.

CHAPTER SIXTEEN

The snake winding quickly toward him was as thick as Caleb's arm, and it had to be seven feet long. The head of the monster was as big as a fist, and the forked tongue flicking at him was brown and nasty.

However big it was, the critter had to be a tough old cuss to be living this high in the mountains. Two dark lines ran on a diagonal on each side of its face, from its eyes to its jaw. If the dark, diamond-shaped patterns along its back weren't a dead giveaway, the rattles at the far end of him told Caleb exactly what was coming.

He was definitely on the horns of a dilemma. One killer was poised on a rock, ready to shoot his eye out, and another one was gliding toward him, smiling like Caleb was some oversize prairie dog.

Scooping some gravel from the ground beside him, he flung it at the rattler. That was only good enough to encourage the snake to stop and curl up within striking distance of his foot. The triangular head of the beast rose up, swaying from side to side, and those rattles struck up the first chords of a tune Caleb didn't find himself partial to hearing.

If for no other reason, the closeness of the beady-eyed killer won out for his attention.

The Colt barked once, but he didn't have any time to see how effective his aim had been. He and that rattler were close enough to shake hands, but he had other fish to fry. Springing to his feet, he spun and fired twice at the kneeling figure at the top of the bluff.

Beneath a long, drooping moustache, the gunman's mouth opened in a surprised O. The rifle dropped from his hand as he clutched at the two patches of dark red spreading out on his chest and his belly. He kept staring at Caleb as he tried to rise, and he was wearing a look that was both per-plexed and sorrowful. A moment later, the gunman fell to his knees, tipped forward, and tumbled headlong off the bluff, hitting a slab ledge halfway down before landing in the grass at the base of the cliff.

Caleb didn't reckon he felt that ledge at all.

He turned and looked at the rattler. The

carcass was missing a head, and Caleb had no interest in looking for it. He picked up the snake by the rattles, though, and held it at arm's length. The thing was longer than Caleb's own six-plus feet of height, and the weight of it had to be fifteen pounds. As he laid it down, he felt an unexpected pang of disappointment at having to kill it. The creature had to have been living here for quite some time.

As he turned and looked at the gunman's body, however, Caleb felt none of that remorse. He never liked killing a man, but this fella had come after him with just one thought in mind, and that was to kill him. If he'd stayed by the horses — if that's what he was doing — he'd still be breathing.

The sound of rifle shots refocused Caleb's attention. Grabbing his Winchester and jamming his hat on, he started back toward the confrontation.

Instead of climbing higher, as he'd done the last time, he now followed the line of firs until they ended and he was looking across at the open slope. He was still above the trail, but from here he could see the positions of the remaining ambushers.

These three were obviously not the brains of this operation. Instead of spreading out and finishing off the last man down below, they'd clumped together behind some rocks and brush.

The return fire from the fella by the trail was intermittent. It was just enough to let them know he was there and still had some fight in him.

Caleb levered a cartridge into the chamber, ready to lend a hand.

The man closest to him must have been reading Caleb's mind. Leaving the other two, he moved stealthily to his left, looking for a clear shot. When he found the place, he grinned and nodded back at the other two.

It was a good decision, but his timing was wrong. Dead wrong. When he raised his head to take his shot, Caleb put a bullet in his brain.

That was all it took. The other two were off and running like a pair of jack rabbits with a hungry coyote on their tail. As they scampered up that trail toward their horses, he might have taken out one or both of them, but he had a pretty good idea he wouldn't be seeing either of them too soon.

The survivor down below stood and let out a whoop they probably heard back in Elkhorn.

As Caleb climbed down the slope, the man met him with a grateful look on his face. Recognition and surprise registered as well in the next instant.

"Ain't you Marlowe?" he asked as Caleb drew closer. "Fella, I ain't never been so happy to see a gunslinger as I am now, seeing you. Thought I was a dead man."

Caleb had remembered him the moment he stood up looking for a truce and nearly got cut down for taking the trouble. He recalled Doc Burnett introducing them at the bar in the Belle Saloon. Doc told him later that the man worked a silver claim near Elkhorn. He was yet another soldier who'd shed his blood and watched brothers die during the war between the North and South. Like so many others, he'd come west looking to leave the past behind.

Caleb wondered what brought him so far from town now.

"Do you recall? I'm Zeke . . ."

The miner stopped short, remembering something obviously important. Turning on his heel, he hurried back to where he'd taken cover.

As Caleb followed him, he heard a man groan in pain.

CHAPTER SEVENTEEN

"Everett owns the claim next to mine," Zeke said to Caleb as he crouched beside his friend and helped him sit up.

Zeke was the two-legged version of a wild boar, if ever Caleb saw one. Short and solid, he was as wide as he was tall. Whiskers and eyebrows nearly obscured every bit of his round, scowling face. He wore a gray wool coat over a gray wool jacket and gray wool waistcoat. Only his scuffed, dirty boots and wide-brimmed hat altered the scheme. They were black. Or, at least, they were at one time.

"How bad you hit, old man?" Zeke asked.

His friend Everett was sitting between two boulders, trying to pull himself together. Caleb had noticed he was taller than the others when they stood and tried to make peace with their ambushers. Even sitting, he appeared to be all arms and legs, and his recently shaved face was long and thin. He didn't seem to be very old, maybe thirty, but he was nearly bald on top of his head, and stringy, brown side hair hung almost to his shoulders.

The bullet had struck him near the shoulder, sending him spinning away. The right arm hung inert at his side. But the man was feeling around on his head, just behind the ear. He groaned slightly each time he touched a tender spot.

"I'll live, I s'pose."

Caleb looked around him, assessing the damage. Though it could have turned out worse for these two men, the bushwhackers had exacted a heavy toll for coming along that trail.

The would-be truce maker, who'd thought a white flag might make a difference, was lying on his back, his head pointed down the hill. He was hatless now and had blond hair that was almost white. His blue eyes were open, staring sightlessly into the last golden rays of the sun. The other man — shot dead before Caleb arrived — lay sprawled out by the trail.

The lifeless sorrel blocked the trail, and there was no sign of any other horses.

Caleb tallied it up. Two dead down here. Another three up on the slope. One more, counting the fella over by the bluff. One horse. And one rattler.

One bloody evening.

He helped Zeke sit his friend up against a rock.

Everett, the wounded miner, was watching Caleb's face intently. "We're much obliged to you, Mr. Marlowe."

"That's all right. Them fellas had the drop on you. I didn't much like the odds."

"I was sure we was goners."

Zeke positioned himself on one knee beside his friend. "Let's take a look at that shoulder."

Caleb and Zeke eased Everett out of his brown coat. The sleeve had been cut by a bullet high up on the shoulder.

"I'm fine, boys," he said. "It was the fall against that boulder there that did the most damage."

He showed them a welt the size of an egg behind his ear.

The damage from the bullet did not appear too serious. The slug had carved a groove about half an inch deep in the muscle two inches below the shoulder joint. Pulling a bandana out of his pocket, Everett slid it under his shirt until it covered the wound.

"There, you see," he told them. "Good as new."

He lifted the arm and flexed his hand, wincing as he did so. It was obvious that his use of the limb would be limited for some time.

"You were dang lucky them varmints didn't take your arm clear off," Zeke asserted. "Or worse."

The wounded man nodded, feeling around the nob on his skull and frowning fiercely. "Could've ended up like them poor souls."

Zeke went over and picked up the white handkerchief from the ground. He laid it over the face of the blond-haired man who'd dropped it.

"This young feller is . . . or was Olaf Olafson," he said, sadness in his voice. "Told me he come out here from Wisconsin cuz there was ten other fellas named Olaf Olafson in his one little town. Said he walked until he got to some place where there weren't no other Olaf Olafsons. That was Elkhorn. Said he would have walked all the way to China if he had to. Figured there weren't no fellers with that name there."

"Was he a miner?" Caleb asked.

"Nope. Worked as a carpenter in town. Olaf didn't want nothing to do with going under the ground. Said he'd be spending enough time there soon enough. Don't think he figured it'd be this soon. Don't think he was even twenty years old."

He rubbed quickly at his eye and shook his head as he stalked to the other dead man. These were Zeke's friends and partners. Out of respect for his loss, Caleb stayed close to him.

"This here was Smollett. Tobias Smollett. Claimed his great-grandpap was some famous Scotch author. The limey sumbitch spent more time drinking and gambling in the Belle than he ever did digging silver. He was broke as a baby this month, and I talked him into coming out with us. Dang it!"

Caleb said nothing. Losing a friend was a difficult thing. Feeling responsible for it was worse.

"Smollett always claimed he was the luckiest man this side of Frisco. I never seen it. He couldn't win at cards, and I don't know that his mine was worth spit either."

Zeke stood grimly silent for a moment and then slapped his battered hat hard against his thigh.

"The sumbitch never knew what hit him. Lay there on the trail after we took cover, a-moaning and a-moaning. But we couldn't do nothing. After a while, he just gave up the ghost."

They stood for a while as the shadows grew deeper. Finally, Zeke walked over to the sorrel.

"This little lady was mine. Them bastards shot her out from under me." He crouched down and stroked her neck. "She was a fine, fine horse, Marlowe."

Caleb understood, as well as anyone, the connection a man developed with his horse. Over the years, he'd ridden a number of fine mounts, but the buckskin gelding he'd left tethered in the grove a short way back on the trail was one of the best. And he needed to get her before the darkness settled.

Zeke moved around the animal to unbuckle the saddle and the bridle. The miner's old Yellow Boy was still in its scabbard. Caleb had figured right; when the ambush started, he'd obviously never even had the chance to grab for the rifle.

"What are you all doing out here?" Caleb asked as he helped him.

"Working for Judge Patterson. Every few weeks, he has a bunch of us fellas out looking for a band of outlaws that've been hitting the Wells Fargo coaches. Started a couple of months ago, once the winter eased up. Nice, steady wages." He waved a hand in the direction of his two dead partners. "Till today, it was a nice break from scratching away in that mine."

Caleb recalled from his meeting with Patterson that he had his own men out searching for the outlaws.

He gestured up the slope from the trail. "Do you think them fellas were the ones you've been hunting?"

"Doubt it." Everett piped up from where he was sitting. "The gang we're looking for don't waste their time on low-down villainy like this. They don't rob no homesteader coming through, nor no carters hauling goods, nor anyone else. If there ain't no Wells Fargo strongbox involved, they ain't interested."

Caleb considered that information. He looked up the slope where the attack had come from. "Maybe you fellas just got too close to them."

Zeke shook his head. "I ain't heard of even one ambush like this one. And like I said, we been dogging them off and on for a couple months now."

Everett was trying to get to his feet, but his long legs were wobbling some. They went over to him.

"Also, when you run them mangy hounds off," Zeke continued, "I believe I heard them horses heading south." He pointed in the direction of the Denver road. "*Our* gang of road agents wouldn't have no call to be

178

going that way."

"Why?"

"Far as folk can tell, they only come down from that wild country up beyond this Devil's Claw pass when they're bent on robbing Wells Fargo. And there ain't no stagecoach coming through for the next few days." Zeke paused and stuffed a chaw of tobacco in his cheek. "What brings *you* to these parts?"

Caleb had tucked the tin star into his pocket last night before turning in, and he saw no reason to share with them that Patterson hired him as deputy to do the same thing they were doing. At least not yet.

"Doc Burnett's gone missing. I'm searching for him."

"You don't say. When?"

"Early Wednesday morning. Today being Saturday, he'd have been back if there was no trouble."

"Wednesday?" Zeke pondered that. "The gang hit the stage on Tuesday evening. They killed the driver and the guard. But it looked like a passenger got shot too, and they took him. Maybe there's a connection."

"That's what I reckon." Caleb nodded. "Did you all go out to the claim belonging to a fella named Smith a couple of days ago?

He's got a cabin not far from the Denver road."

"Nope. Don't know no miner named Smith out this way."

Everett concurred. "That weren't us. Why do you ask?"

"The judge told me he sent some men out there. Smith was the one that fetched Doc. Nobody's seen neither one since."

Zeke lifted his broad, burly shoulders. "Well, that's the way the judge works. When he sets his mind to getting something, he has men going out every which way, all doing the same thing. In the last month, we've been falling all over each other trying to find this outfit. But he wants them found, and he's as tough and persistent as a starving dog hunting a buried bone. He ain't an easy man, the judge, and he don't accept no failure."

"But when he has a job that needs doing," Everett added, "the money's awful tempting."

Meeting Patterson, Caleb had read him exactly the same way. A man didn't reach a position of power like that unless they were tenacious *and* ruthless. And the judge was very persuasive when it came to getting someone to work for him.

"He's paying you too," Zeke asked. "Ain't he?"

"What he's paying ain't as important to me as a private favor he's promised to do," Caleb said honestly. "He has connections."

"There's nobody in the state that can't pull strings better, if that's what you need."

"And he's good for his promises," Everett added.

Caleb had to take their word for it. For now. He gestured toward the wounded man's arm. "When you fellas get back to town, who'll see to that with Doc gone?"

Everett stretched his arm again. "That bullet just grazed me. But I'll get one of the girls at the Belle to give me some loving attention."

It was nearly dark, and Caleb knew they had tasks to accomplish, but Zeke had that talkativeness that sometimes comes with having just escaped death by a frog hair.

"Marlowe, you aiming to go out beyond the Devil's Claw on your own?"

"That I am."

"Well, if you want, you could come back to town with us or even wait around here for a spell. Everett and I can gather more men and supplies and meet you back here."

"Much obliged for the offer." Caleb gestured north, through the pass. "But maybe we can meet up on the other side."

"Been out in that country afore?"

"Some."

"Then you know there's divides and valleys and gorges that lead nowheres. There's still a few working miners' camps and cabins hidden away behind hills and in gulches where you won't never see them. And there's outlaws out there that have nothing to do with the Wells Fargo gang. But whether you're looking for them or not, they'll still kill you on sight."

"I know, Zeke."

"And you still want to venture on alone?"

Caleb wasn't about to share all he'd done in his life, where he'd gone with Jake and on his own afterward. He had no doubt he could tell Zeke stories that would rob him of sleep for many a night. Besides, it was better to make a man feel his worth rather than cut him down, especially when he was already feeling whipped.

"This is what we'll do," Caleb replied. "I'll get a head start and take my time. Just scout around some. More than likely, I won't hazard out too far beyond the pass. When you come back with help, we'll join up."

Zeke nodded and turned a sad eye on the dead men. "I'd surely like to get these fellas back to town. Wouldn't feel right leaving them out here."

Caleb agreed. "You're going to need some horses to do that. Except for that sorrel, where are yours?"

Everett pointed up the trail. "They lit out quick, soon as we were off of them. They might be halfway to Canady by now."

"Zeke, with the little light we got left," Caleb suggested, "why don't you take your rifle and try and find them? While you do that, I'll go up to that ridge and see if they left anything behind. My guess is there are four more horses up there."

As the miner turned and started along the trail, Caleb left his rifle with Everett and climbed the slope. When he reached the three men he'd shot, he gathered their weapons and gun belts and anything of value they had on them.

It wasn't much, but there would be enough to pay for burying the two men in Zeke's posse. These fellas up here would be lucky if Zeke and Everett conceded to piling some rocks on their miserable carcasses.

Following the path where the other two had skedaddled, Caleb soon reached another trail. Sure enough, those sorry blackguards had left four half-decent horses to the mercy of the wolves. Stringing them together, he led the mounts south until he reached the top of the bluff where he'd outmaneuvered both rattler and rogue.

As he climbed down from the lead horse, however, the hackles on his neck prickled and stood on end. Drawing a revolver, he scanned the surroundings. Dusk was quickly giving way to night. To the left of the trail, giant slabs of rock like the ones below formed jagged ledges and escarpments and rose steeply up the mountainside until they were lost in the gloom. Not thirty paces from him, an abandoned mine yawned in the hillside.

And his instincts told him there was someone in there.

Caleb moved quietly to one side of the opening, listening. There was indeed someone in there. Man and horse, he judged.

If this was one or both of those bushwhackers, they'd made another mistake by not hightailing it out there. He wasn't going to give them any more chances to run, though.

He drew his other Colt and cocked the hammer.

"Whoever you are in there, come out now. And your hands better be high and empty."

Silence answered him.

"Last chance. I ain't telling you again."

"I'm coming out," an old voice called out.

"I'm coming. It's just me . . . Preacher."

"Then you come ahead," Caleb snapped. "But if you got so much as a prayer book in your hand, Preacher, a legion of angels won't be no help to you."

"I'm coming. It's just me . . ." Preacher.

"Then you come ahead," Caleb snapped. "But if you got so much as a prayer book in your hand, Preacher, a legion of angels won't be no help to you."

CHAPTER EIGHTEEN

The man that emerged was a scrawny, hard-bitten creature, dressed all in black, from stovepipe hat to dusty boots. His clothes were ragged and so old, Caleb figured this preacher had to be an honest man. Or the worst sermonizer west of Jerusalem.

He was leading a broken-down mule that must have been old when Noah passed over him before the Flood. That beast was little more than a bag of bones and, coming out of the mine, the mule wore an expression of weary resignation as he eyed Caleb. But as soon as he saw the string of horses, the animal's long ears pricked up, and he shot a look at them that was positively venomous.

The preacher was unarmed except for a five-shot Colt Baby Dragoon in a holster strapped to the mule. He had a long, drawn face as wrinkled and brown as an old, dried walnut. A gray moustache drooped around a frowning mouth, and thin whiskers hung like a goat's beard beneath his chin. His brown eyes were clear and alert. Like his mule, though, he wore a tired and stoic expression, and Caleb guessed the man had looked down the barrel of a gun more than a few times before. Even in the darkness, he looked to be the ugliest fella Caleb had ever run across.

"Mind if I lower my hands?" Preacher asked. "These old bones can't take being raised for too long."

Caleb nodded. "Just open that coat of yours. I don't want to see you pull any weapons out of there."

Preacher did as he was told. "I do carry a knife in my boot, and my old pistol up there." He pointed to the holstered Colt on the mule. "But that's all. I have a higher power that protects me."

"That may be so, Preacher. But I reckon the same higher power also looks after the hungry grizzlies I've seen up in these mountains."

The minister sighed and looked at his mule. "This ornery old cuss and I have been traveling through these hills for nigh on ten years, and I reckon we're both too old and too tough even for a grizzly to chew on."

"Ten years, you say?" Caleb holstered his twin Colts. "So you know the country out beyond the pass?"

"I do, indeed, stranger. I've been carrying the Good Word to the heathen, the devout, and the fallen throughout this entire wilderness. Though I can attest to the fact that there are more of the fallen out here than anything else. So, from camp to camp, I roam and will continue to do so until I go to my eternal reward."

"Well, if you'd been any slower in answering me just now, you'd have claimed that reward this very night."

"Maybe so, but not one sparrow falls without it being His will, so the Book says."

"So I hear," Caleb replied, feeling an old anger sparking within him. "But I can tell you a flock of sparrows went down this day, so maybe it ain't worth pressing the issue."

"I heard the shooting."

"And decided to stay clear of it?"

"Yep." The old man looked at Caleb, sizing him up. "I don't think you intend to shoot me, though."

"We'll see. But for right now, I want you to come with me."

"What for?"

"I think you're a fella I'd like to talk to," Caleb said. "And not about any sparrows."

He walked to the lead horse and took hold of the bridle. The preacher followed along, muttering the whole way, and Caleb couldn't tell whether he was praying or talking to his mule. Not far along, the path descended through a gulley and came out on the trail, close to where Pirate was tethered.

By the time they reached the place where the fight had taken place, Zeke had returned with their three horses and was laying blankets over the bodies of his dead friends. Everett had started a fire at the widest point of the trail he could find.

Seeing the small herd of horses Caleb was leading was surprising enough, but the sight of the traveling minister and his mule was almost more than Zeke could comprehend. At first wary that the man might have been part of the gang of bushwhackers, the fierce little miner needed a few moments for his suspicions to be allayed. Luckily, Everett had heard of the itinerant preacher who made these mountains his church and the folk living up here his congregation.

Everett and the preacher started beans and biscuits for the four of them. The moon was just on the rise, so Caleb and Zeke led the horses up the trail a ways to a spring-fed creek where they let them drink and graze on the long grass, silver in the moonlight.

"How did you move that sorrel of yours, Zeke?" Caleb asked while they sat on a fallen log and waited.

"Everett took hold of one hoof and I took the other, and we rolled her. Only took the once, and she went sliding down that slope into the darkness below. My heart broke a little, watching her go, let me tell you."

They sat watching the horses for a few moments until Caleb broke the silence.

"Tomorrow, we'll put those friends of yours up on these horses, and you and Everett can take them back to Elkhorn." He gave Zeke the money he'd found on the ambushers. "This should take care of the undertaker."

Zeke nodded and said nothing more for a while. Eventually, they talked about the mines and Doc and the arrival of his daughter, which the miner knew nothing about.

Caleb regretted not stopping and talking to Sheila after speaking to Judge Patterson. She didn't need to be told her father had been taken by outlaws. Still, it might have given her a little peace of mind to know Caleb was also out there searching for him.

When they could smell beans and coffee in the air, they brought the horses back to the camp and readied them for the night.

As they ate, Preacher proved to be a garrulous fella. He and Everett could both talk the ears off a tin jackass, and once the minister took the bit in his teeth, he was off and running. After he'd gone on for a while, Caleb decided it was time to steer him in the direction he wanted the man to go. It didn't take much to do it.

"Ten years you said you've been preaching to the folk up in these hills," Caleb said.

"That I have, pilgrim. In summer and in winter, in sickness and in health . . ." He paused and chuckled. "Sounds a bit like a marriage, don't you think? And in a way, I suppose it is a marriage of sorts. Like a husband to his wife, I made a commitment to my folk out here and —"

"And there's a good number of miners still working claims up here?"

"Not as many as there once was. A lot of the old mines are abandoned and the camps deserted." Preacher helped himself to more coffee. "But there's still a few hardy souls out there, sure that they'll strike it rich as Croesus one day."

Caleb realized that Zeke and Everett saw what he was trying to get at. As they listened, they just sat back, nursed their cups, and stared into the fire.

"Must be dangerous out here, though, traveling alone as you do."

191

Preacher raised his bony shoulders. "From what I recollect, a man can get into a peck of trouble in the towns too. I know that was true for me, before I found my calling. Out here, there's no laws to get a man's back up. Except, of course, the laws in the Book I take to them. But when a man is digging for his fortune and minding his own business, those ten laws are not so tough to keep."

Caleb frowned. "You know your flock, Preacher. But five fellas laid in wait here today. And I think them laws of yours say something about not killing."

"As I said, friend, there are quite a few of the fallen out here as well."

"Then you know that, with all the deserted camps and the rugged lay of the land, more than a few outlaw gangs have taken to hiding out up here."

Preacher fixed his gaze on Caleb's face. "You a bounty hunter, pilgrim?"

He shook his head. "I ain't. But I am looking for some road agents that have been helping themselves to every Wells Fargo stage they can lay their hands on."

The minister said nothing for a moment.

"I believe one of them laws in your Book refers to stealing," Caleb added, prompting him.

Preacher nodded. "I know who you mean. You're talking about some fellows who waylay *only* Wells Fargo stagecoaches."

"Those would be the fellas."

"Well, as it happens, in my travels I've gotten to know those men somewhat. I've been to their camp a half dozen times. I've sat with them at their fire, just like this. I've broken bread with them. Even prayed with a couple of them. And I know a few other things about them. I'll tell you one thing, these are good men."

"Good men?" Caleb felt his temperature rising. "Do you also know that this gang killed the driver and the guard in a robbery a few days ago. And they may have a passenger they wounded, as well. But we can't be sure, cuz he's missing."

"No, friend," Preacher retorted adamantly. "These are not killers. They don't go out hurting others. I know them."

"You may think you do," Caleb snapped. "But they also have a friend of mine, a doctor. And the chances are they killed a miner who helped them take Doc."

He paused as that information sank in.

"So I would be much obliged if you could tell us exactly where these fellas are holed up."

A troubled frown creased the minister's

face. "This must be someone else. Someone who is trying to drag down their name. It's not them, I tell you."

"And I'm telling you, it is."

Preacher glanced at Zeke and Everett, but their hard faces offered no help.

"I want to know where this gang is holed up," Caleb demanded.

The minister tossed the remainder of his coffee into the fire and chewed on those words for a bit. Putting his cup on the ground, he pulled at his goat beard, took off his hat, batted some dirt from it, and jammed it back on his balding pate.

"That is the one thing that I can't tell you."

"Why?"

"Two reasons, mainly," he replied.

Caleb's patience was worn about as thin as a demon's promise. "I'm waiting."

"First, once you travel out through the pass here, the land is wild and uncharted. I don't think I could give you good directions to find them."

"Ten years, Preacher. I reckon you can."

The minister hesitated, looking away evasively. But when he spoke again, he held Caleb's gaze.

"Second, I'm a man of God. These fellows — and a few other outfits that have taken up residence out beyond the Devil's Claw — they trust me. If I betray that trust, my mission out there is finished. So you can beat me or kill me, pilgrim, but I'll *never* give that up."

colon my residence o−? beyond the D−
Chaw−dhaw nuss realld betray the crin−
my master my master is finished So you can
best me or Kill me, plignit, but I'll s−ver
preothal my−

CHAPTER NINETEEN

Sheila opened her eyes with a start, listening intently for the sound that had awakened her. The distant creak of a floorboard.

She waited, gripping the arms of the reading chair, holding her breath, waiting to see if it repeated itself. There was nothing.

It was only a dream.

She'd been having a nightmare. In it, outlaws had broken in and were rummaging through the house downstairs. Desperate men, here to rob and murder. And worse.

Suspended on that frightening edge of the dreamworld, Sheila was too paralyzed to move, afraid even to breathe. She strained to hear the sound again. The silence was broken only by the scratch of a branch against the window.

The oil lamp at her elbow flickered, and monstrous shadows loomed on the wall. She couldn't look away from the wavering, threatening figures. She couldn't even blink for fear that they could actually *be* some horrible intruder who had invaded this house, this room.

From the windows, the moon spilled its cold, blue light, illuminating carpet and bed. The figures were just shadows. She stole a glance at the corner next to her chair. Her father's shotgun sat at the ready where she'd left it. Even though this was not New York City, she was still a woman alone in an unfamiliar place.

Heartened by the sight of the weapon, Sheila plucked up her courage. She reached for the watch she wore pinned to her shirt and realized it was covered by the woolen charcoal-colored waistcoat she'd borrowed from her father's wardrobe. Her excuse was that the evening temperature cooled last night. But the truth was that she wanted a part of him near her, a sense of him with her, as she waited and fretted over his delayed return.

Worries about his well-being had been dogging her ever since she arrived on Wednesday. What if he'd been thrown from a horse and hurt in the fall? He could be lying out there, injured and alone in the wilderness, fighting off wolves. Or brigands. Or natives.

He could be sick, battling fever. On the endless train ride from New York to Denver, she'd read in the newspapers that the President's Quarantine Act had not stemmed the yellow fever epidemic that was sweeping outward like a wave beyond New Orleans. What if the contagion had already spread this far? What if her father had gone to some nearby mining camp where the fever had struck everyone down? What if he contracted it and had no one to care for him?

And in the back of her mind, another thought had nagged at her. A thought that annoyed her for its selfishness, but she couldn't shake it. If the worst had happened, if her father was dead or had simply gone off, what would become of her?

It had been a very long time since she'd seen him, but he was still her father. Distance and years had divided them, but she loved him. And she hoped he would want her to be part of his life now that she was grown and mature and independent. She desperately wished that he wouldn't send her back to New York.

Sheila looked around the room, orienting herself. As she did, the hot panic in which she'd awakened, along with her pounding heartbeat, gradually subsided. Her hands rested on a book that lay open on her lap, and she pushed it to the side.

Since arriving here, she'd learned a few things. It *had* been a terrible idea to go to Marlowe's ranch after dark, alone and unarmed. Even now, she cringed at the thought of how poorly he must think of her. She'd showed bad judgment and a lack of understanding of the danger she'd put herself in.

New York City had its hazards, of course. And it wasn't always safe for a woman to move around the different neighborhoods by herself. Even for men, some areas were positively unsafe. Perhaps her impetuous behavior had been the result of her sudden freedom. Her grandparents had seen to it that she always had a chaperone or a man-servant on hand to follow her and watch over her. In the city, she was never alone. Never exposed to danger.

Elkhorn was not New York, but in this town, she had already experienced the difficulty of walking the few blocks to the general store and the butcher shop and the hardware store to speak with Mrs. Lewis. Harassment at every turn. Drunkards slouched against walls and sat on steps to the street. Dust-covered cowboys called out comments as they drifted by on their horses.

Miners and ne'er-do-wells stumbled from the saloons, unable to focus eyes bloodshot from liquor and lack of sleep. Even the large, slovenly man wearing the sheriff's badge had paused to leer at her as she walked past.

The bright spot in her day had been when Mrs. Lewis stopped by to visit this afternoon. The kindly woman had brought her supper and offered to stay the night. Sheila had refused. With a gun at her side and a good book on her lap, she was fine.

She peered at the tiny hands of the watch. It was almost four in the morning.

Four in the morning. Since Sheila arrived here, she'd found herself completely unconcerned with routine. Her days and nights were so different from the world she left behind. No one dictated when she slept or if she slept. Her days were spent as she pleased, and the hours had largely been filled with poking around her father's house.

At first, she'd excused it with the thought that she was looking for some clue as to where he'd gone. She soon realized, however, that she was searching for something else. She was looking for hints as to *who* her father was in the hope of finding answers to a thousand questions she had about why he'd abandoned her.

Answers like that, unfortunately, didn't sit in medicine cabinets.

Sheila stretched. She thought perhaps there was yet enough night left that she should get up and put on her nightgown.

And then she heard it. There was no mistake this time. It was no dream. No nightmare. The sound of someone walking. Moving about downstairs.

She listened and waited, trying to convince herself that he *had* returned, after all. She prayed that these were the sounds of her father's boots. She tried to imagine him coming in after his difficult journey. Exhausted after a long ride through the dark of night.

If her father was in fact the person downstairs, he would have no way of knowing that she'd arrived in Elkhorn and that she was upstairs. The owner of the livery knew. Caleb Marlowe knew. But her father might not have seen either of them at this time of night.

"Where is the dang cabinet?" A man's voice reached her.

Sheila's hopes took flight like a bird with a shattered wing, immediately plummeting downward with ever-increasing speed. Optimism turned to caution. And then to fear. It wasn't him. Someone else, knowing the town doctor was missing, had broken in to steal his valuable surgical equipment and medicines.

What would he do if he found her here?

The sound of someone else reached her from the kitchen. There was more than one person downstairs.

Cold fear prickled in her scalp and washed down her neck, spreading through her like icy spring floodwaters. Iron claws clutched her throat, squeezing it in a grip so tight, she could taste the burning bile.

She had to do something. She couldn't stand and wait and surrender like some damsel in a dime novel.

Sheila reached for the shotgun. It was loaded, both barrels. It was similar to a longer gun she'd fired many times, target-shooting at the home of a friend on the banks of the Hudson. But could she shoot a *man*?

She heard the sound of footsteps again, right below her. The floorboards were creaking under someone's weight, and then a door squeaked. Whoever it was, he'd gone into her father's consulting room.

Sheila looked wildly at the door, at the window. She had to get out.

When she was up and halfway across the room, she stopped dead. A man was coming up the stairs.

A gruff voice called up sharply from the foot of the stairway. "Where the hell you think you're going?"

"I heard something." The answer came from the upstairs hallway.

Panic tore at her. Her brain was on fire. She could barely think. Barely breathe.

Sheila forced her leaden legs to move. She backed toward the window. She had to jump. It was only the second story. But before she could push the window open, her door swung inward.

"Damn my eyes. What do we have here?"

"Stay where you are." Sheila pressed her back against the wall and pointed the shotgun, ready to shoot.

The man was tall and burly, and his wide body filled the doorway. From the sound of his voice, he was not much older than she was, if that. He wore a dark-brown coat, a black waistcoat, and a bandana. Tan pants were tucked into boots. The wide brim of his brown hat cast a shadow across a round, boyish face. He wore a smirk, however, that was as menacing as his voice.

"Ain't this a nice surprise."

Sheila's heart hammered in her chest. Her palms sweated. She didn't think she'd ever been as frightened as she was at this moment. Suddenly, the future her grandfather had planned for her in New York felt very appealing.

"What do you want?" she asked.

"Want? You'll find out soon enough, sweet pea."

She raised the weapon an inch, pointing it at the man's chest. "You take even one step into this room, and I'll blast you back into that hallway."

"Will you now?" he sneered. "Well, maybe I'll just test your spunk and . . . ."

A hand appeared from outside the door, clutching his collar and yanking the intruder back into the hallway.

"Dodger, I am sick and tired of you being such an ass."

"Are you?" The response was low and cool and laden with threat.

"You *will* do as you're told. Hear me?" The other man's voice was sharp and commanding and clearly unimpressed by his companion. "You will follow orders and stop trying to act like such a young tough every dang minute."

Sheila took a step to the side to see what she could of the other man. The one who had hauled the menacing intruder back into the hall was older, shorter in stature, but hardly lacked in confidence. He wielded

204

authority like a seasoned general.

They stood with locked horns in the dim light of the hallway. Tension sizzled in the air, and Sheila's hand was shaking as she kept the shotgun up and pointed at them.

"Do you have a problem with what I'm telling you?" the older one hissed into the face of the other. His hand sat on the handle of the pistol in his belt.

The big man took his time answering.

"Not at all, *Wendell.*" The emphasis on the man's name carried an unmistakable hint of taunting. "You're in charge."

Sheila let out the breath she'd been holding, realizing she'd already taken sides.

"And you just remember," the man called Wendell continued. "We ain't even guests in the doctor's house. We're on an *errand* for him."

Her attention flew to the older man's face.

"I hear you," Dodger replied gruffly. "But don't you never touch me again."

Wendell took a long moment. "Then don't make me. Now go down there and fetch what Doc Burnett wanted."

She waited until Dodger had trudged down the stairs before moving an inch.

Wendell tipped his stovepipe hat to her. He too was wearing a dark coat. His vest was wool, dark green, and missing two but-

205

tons. The corner of a bandana hung out of one pocket. He had the sharp features of a bird of prey, but his dark eyes were not threatening when he looked at her. He had the weathered face of a man who'd seen hard times, and he made her think of the old, seasoned war veterans she'd seen in New York.

Sheila was hardly willing to trust either of them, though, and held the rifle steady.

"I am sorry, ma'am, for busting in here and surprising you. We didn't mean to cause no trouble. But Doc didn't say nothing about nobody staying in his house. If we knew, we'd have knocked first afore coming in."

"How do you know my father?"

"Father?" He removed his hat and ran a hand through thinning hair. "Well, now. That's another surprise. Doc definitely made no mention of no family."

"I arrived in Elkhorn this week. We missed each other by a few hours."

Sheila realized she was revealing too much. She shouldn't be offering information. She should be asking questions.

"I still want to know how you know my father," she demanded. "And I want to know where he is."

He gestured to the gun she still had pointing at him. "Would you mind tilting that a few inches that a way, miss? I don't want you hurting yourself. Or me, for that matter."

"Answer me first."

He nodded. "Fair enough. The doctor's been staying out at my claim since the middle of the week, tending to my wife."

"Where is your claim?"

"In the hills about ten miles or so yonder. I have a cabin and a mine that shows real promise. Indeed, it does."

"What's wrong with your wife?"

"Attacked by a rogue wolf, the poor thing. The critter got her here . . . and here." He pointed to his neck and to his chest. "Tore her up bad, but Doc thinks he can save her."

The man's expression was sincere, and he dipped his chin and shook his head as he stared at the tips of his boots.

"That's horrible. I'm so sorry."

"We're hopeful, miss. Very hopeful."

Sheila heard the sound of Dodger stomping around downstairs. "Who is that vile man you have with you? He intentionally frightened me."

"I'm sure, miss. And I do apologize for Dodger's manners. He has none. Raised bad, I reckon. Safe to say he don't understand polite society. He works for me in the mine."

Everything she was being told was plausible and tugged at the strings of her sympathy. But it was all very convenient, and every word could be a lie too.

"Why should I trust you, Mr. Wendell?"

"I'm just a miner with a hurt woman at home, miss. If I meant to make trouble for you or anyone else, why would I be coming here to Doc's house looking for medical supplies that he sent me for? What good would they be to a feller like me?"

"What supplies exactly?"

"He sent me with his medical bag. Got it down there." He motioned toward the stairs with his hat. "We're to fill up some medicine bottles and fetch a surgery box."

Sheila had already gone through the room her father used for surgery and consulting. A large cabinet contained bottles of ointments and medicines and supplies. She'd also seen where he kept his box of surgical instruments.

Wendell pulled a piece of paper from his pocket.

"I have a list of what Doc wants right here, made out in his own hand." He held it so that she could see the writing. "And I don't mean to push you none, but he said to be quick about fetching these things, cuz my wife could die."

Even at a glance, Sheila recognized her father's handwriting from his letters. She had little reason to doubt the man any longer.

The most important news to her, however, was that her father was alive. She lowered the weapon and decocked the hammers.

"Have you found the items that my father needs?"

"We just found his medical room when Dodger got distracted and came barging in here." He directed a hopeful glance at her. "You being the doctor's daughter, we could surely use your help, miss."

Not wanting to leave the shotgun up here, she carried it with her. Wendell stood aside and allowed her to go in front of him downstairs.

In the large room her father used as a surgery and for consultations, she once again felt her stomach clench as Dodger turned and eyed her. He looked at Wendell and then back at her. The disrespectful smirk had returned to his face.

Her father's medical bag sat open on a worktable. It was the same one he'd carried since she was only a child. The gold lettering of his embossed initials had long faded, but she could still read them clearly.

"Doc said to fill up them bottles inside his bag," Wendell told her, handing her the list. "Would you mind doing the honors, miss? My eyesight ain't so good, and I don't trust this one to do it right." He jerked a thumb at Dodger.

She couldn't hold on to the shotgun and do what he asked. Reluctantly, she went over and placed the weapon in the rack where she'd gotten it earlier.

Keeping the worktable between her and Dodger, she took out the empty bottles and examined them. They were all clearly marked in her father's hand.

The much larger jars were lined up in the cabinet like soldiers on parade. The two men stood aside and watched while Sheila went back and forth, refilling the smaller jars per the list.

"What else did my father ask for?"

"A box of surgical tools."

Sheila went to another cabinet, took out a wooden case, and brought it back to the table. The case contained a number of instruments, an array of curved needles and cat gut used for stitching wounds. "Everything should be in here."

She closed the case and the medical bag.

"Before you leave, Mr. Wendell, I'd like

you to give me more information as to where your cabin is exactly and when I should expect my father back. I've been quite worried about him, as have a number of other people in town."

"Sure enough, miss," Wendell replied with a thoughtful nod. "But . . . rather than try to fill your head with directions that wouldn't make no sense whatsoever, I reckon it might be a very good thing if you were to come with us. You can see how your father is doing yourself, and provide him with company for his ride back."

"Come with you?" she asked, surprised by the offer.

She shot a glance at Dodger. He appeared to be in complete agreement, and her stomach sank at the way he was running his eyes over her.

"I don't think that will be necessary. Thank you for the offer, but I'll wait for my father here."

Wendell had moved closer to her, and his dark eyes had lost their friendly look. "That weren't an offer, miss. You're coming along."

In one quick movement, he took hold of her arm and clapped a hand over her mouth.

Sheila fought her assailants, but they were too strong for her. A moment later, she stood with her hands tied tightly in front of her.

"I'm a-gonna take my hand off your mouth now, miss. But if you make so much as one peep, we'll be forced to shut you up, and you won't like that none. You understand me?"

She looked into his eyes and nodded.

Wendell took his hand away, still holding her arm in a viselike grip.

"Go to the livery stable," he ordered Dodger, "and bring back a horse for her. No trouble and no noise, you hear? I don't want no one knowing we're taking her. And don't show your face. Got it?"

"Got it." With one more look at her, Dodger went out. She heard the front door of the house close behind him.

"Why?" Sheila asked. "Why are you doing this?"

"I get a feeling your father needs a little prodding. And you might be just the poke he needs to get the job done."

CHAPTER TWENTY

Caleb opened his eyes and breathed in the cool, clean mountain air, marked only by the scent of a dead cooking fire, healthy horses, and his three snoring companions.

He looked up into the deep, endless blue-black canvas, still studded with stars so bright, they looked alive. But as he tilted his eyes to the east, he saw the faint lightening of the blue and knew dawn would soon be breaking. He sat up and pushed off the bearskin covering. Even now, his eyes could distinguish the ridges and the craggy boulders and the lines of treetops plunging down on a sharp angle to the river far below. Above their camp, a pair of deer moved cautiously along the slope and disappeared into the firs.

Caleb rose, picked up the coffeepot, and padded off along the trail. Leaving the camp behind, he entered the darker gloom of a wooded grove. The air immediately became cooler, and the earthy forest smell filled his lungs. Here, with the evergreen canopy above and a carpet of needles beneath his feet, it was silent as a church on a Wednesday, and he had no desire to disturb the peace.

In a few moments, the burbling sound of the creek falling with whispers and murmurs over the rocks reached his ears. The light ahead brightened a little, and he soon came to the grassy banks where the trail crossed the shallows. It was the place where he and Zeke had watered the horses last night.

Dropping his hat on a flat rock beside a wide pool, he went down on one knee and rinsed out last night's coffee before scooping up cold water in both hands. After drinking deeply, he washed his face and neck and dipped his head in the water.

As he wiped his face, a glance at the soft earth by his knee caused him to pause.

Two fresh prints, side by side, caught his eye. Four toes and a palm pad, each print as big as a man's fist. Cougar.

He ran his eyes around the edge of the open area. The cat had been here not long before him, no doubt stopping for a drink after a long night of hunting.

And Caleb had left his gun belt back at the camp.

Traveling in these hills at any time of day could be hazardous. Travel at night was another thing entirely. Black bears, grizzlies, wolves, and coyotes stalked their prey along these trails. But they were not the most dangerous. Aside from the two-legged predator, cougar or puma or mountain lion — whatever the locals chose to call it — the big cat was the cruelest.

Caleb hadn't been concerned about mountain lions yesterday as he climbed the slope. The crackle of gunfire would have been enough to drive them off. But the rock slab overhangs and shallow caves and ledges, like the bluff where he'd encountered the rattler, provided perfect lairs for the big cats. There, they would lie comfortably, still as death, eyes shining, and watch their evening meal grazing below them in the grassy hillside.

Caleb had encountered dozens in his travels and seen signs of a hundred more. In lands farther to the south and west — places like the red rock hills of Mormon country and the woody river valleys of New Mexico — a man couldn't spit without hitting one. He'd seen many over the years. And killed a few.

The cougar was a strange animal, though. As predators go, they were easily the most unpredictable. Caleb had run across some that would be scared off with a mere wave of his hand. Others — maybe the hungrier ones — would stalk you craftily for an hour, showing up only now and again, their green-gold eyes glowing. Those were usually the ones that wouldn't take a friendly warning. And when they were ready, they could bring the fight to you with such speed and ferocity that a man couldn't help but pay attention. When that happened, a cool head, a sure hand, and a dead aim were the only things that could deter the big cat's dinner plans.

On one of his early travels with Jake out in western Wyoming, they ran across a man who herded Appaloosas. Caleb recalled sitting around a campfire, listening to the man complain that mountain lions cost him thousands of dollars every year. No one ever hunted them, he said. They couldn't be hunted. And wherever there were deer and horses, the cougars lived fat. He had a score of stories, and Caleb remembered every one.

He thought of the deer he'd seen above the camp, moving silently into the trees.

Caleb stood and gathered his things. He had work to do before he sent Zeke and Everett back to town. They had bodies that needed to be strapped across the backs of their horses and dead blackguards that needed tending to as well. That is, if wolves hadn't already dragged them off in the night.

As he started back along the trail, he stopped short.

The braying of the mule and the shouting of Preacher were enough to wake the dead.

Caleb ran hard toward the sound. He rounded a bend and saw them in the distance.

It was just as he'd feared. The minister was shouting like a madman over the terrified sounds of the mule. His arms were up, and he was waving a branch of evergreen at something Caleb couldn't see. That branch wouldn't have done a lick of damage to a newborn lamb.

He knew what Preacher was trying to do, though.

Caleb was covering ground quickly, but he was still several hundred paces from them. He ran full speed, leaping to avoid protruding rocks and roots. The trail dipped into a wash, and he lost sight of them for a moment. The hoarse shouts of the minister and the continuous braying urged him on. As Caleb raced up the incline and caught sight of them again, he figured he was still more than a hundred paces away.

Suddenly, tawny fur flashed across the ground. A cougar that looked to be the size of a pony leaped onto the hindquarters of the mule. He barely got his claws into the mule's haunches, however, when the old beast let go with a ferocious kick using both back hooves, sending the big cat tumbling and rolling across the forest floor.

Caleb's lungs were burning. Still carrying the coffeepot, he was a good seventy paces away, but he yelled with as much breath as he could muster.

The lion crept into view, his broad face, tawny and white, held low to the ground. Even as Caleb pounded along the trail, he could see the bared teeth and golden eyes gleaming in the murky dawn light. The big cat was moving closer to the preacher. It had clearly decided that the old man — fearless as he appeared with his flimsy weapon of fir — was easier prey than the sharp-hoofed mule.

"Heya! Heya!" Caleb shouted, but the confrontation ahead was focused and deadly.

He was still fifty paces away when the trail turned slightly, and he lost sight of them for an instant.

By the time he saw them again, he was thirty paces away.

This cougar was the largest he'd ever seen. The powerful back legs were quivering, ready to launch him once again. The ears were back, nearly flattened against the head, and the mouth opened with screech that showed long teeth, sharpened on the bones and gristle of a thousand animals.

Twenty paces from them, he shouted again, using the sharp sounds of the seasoned cattle puncher, trying everything he could to divert the fearsome hunter.

But the mountain lion was not to be distracted. He took two smooth steps forward and lunged at the preacher, who threw up his arms as the cat bowled him to the ground. The powerful front claws ripped and grabbed hold, trying to catch the man's face between those cruel jaws.

Caleb flung the coffeepot at the beast's head. He saw the lion's eyes and ear flick toward him, but the animal was intent on finishing the battle with the struggling preacher.

Without slowing his pace at all, Caleb launched himself into the fray. The cat, seeing a more formidable opponent so close, released his prey and spun toward him at the exact moment Caleb found a handhold in the thick, tawny fur. Using his momentum, he leaped over them both, hauling the beast with him.

The lion, dragged off-balance for a moment, was not about to give up the fight. Spinning and slashing at the new foe with lightning-fast swipes of its deadly front claws, it scrambled to regain its footing. It took the predator only a split second to get its rear paws on the ground.

Caleb released the big cat and sprang backward, hoping the combined force of two humans would be enough to scare the hunter off. But the animal was aroused, and blind rage was driving it now.

The lion came with almost unimaginable quickness, leaping with its front legs fully extended. Outstretched claws as sharp as razors reached for Caleb's neck and throat. He looked into the gaping mouth and fangs, at the jaws ready to crush his head.

Over two hundred pounds of raw muscle and fury hit him, gripping him and driving him back. As the beast surged forward, Caleb threw his hands up, his two fists grasping the fur high on the cat's chest. The hunter's front claws had his shoulders, and he could smell the cougar's foul breath, hot on his face.

Turning and falling backward, Caleb used the animal's weight and motion to yank the lion toward him, intending to throw it to the ground. But the trail behind him had disappeared.

The two of them tumbled over and over, down the steep slope. Even as they fell, Caleb knew that the cat's four paws would be quicker at finding a foothold, so he hung on as they plunged and rolled.

When they hit a small sapling and stopped, Caleb found himself momentarily on top. He was not about to surrender his advantage. With the big cat's body still writhing beneath him, he managed to pin the clawing back legs with his own.

Jerking a hand free, he reached for his boot and drew the hunting knife that had served both him and Jacob Bell so faithfully.

Caleb struck hard, driving the blade deep into the cougar's chest.

CHAPTER TWENTY-ONE

Sheila was not taking their threats lightly. These were hard, tough men.

The three of them had been riding for some time — Wendell in front, then her, then the despicable Dodger behind her. The sky in the east was brightening, but there were times in the last few hours when she wondered if she'd live to see another dawn.

After they took her prisoner, she and Wendell had waited and waited for Dodger's return. It seemed like forever for him to come back with a horse from the livery stable, and the older man had stood fuming by a front window the entire time. And with every passing minute, his hawkish face grew darker and angrier.

The duster she'd worn out to Marlowe's ranch was hanging on a peg by the front door. While they waited, she asked if Wendell would mind if she wore it — the night air being so cold. She'd hoped he'd unbind her hands, but he didn't. The villain only yanked it from the peg, threw it around her shoulders, and buttoned it roughly at her neck. He was not going to untie her.

When the vile younger man finally showed up with a horse for her, Wendell practically dragged her out to it. He hoisted her up into the saddle and snapped orders at Dodger to fetch the surgical instruments and supplies. The tension between them was obvious, though, and Sheila didn't want to get in the middle of any trouble.

Wendell had not minced words. If she made so much as a sound as the three of them rode out of Elkhorn, he'd shoot her dead. If she tried to make a break for it, he'd shoot her dead. After all, he said, the things they really needed were in that valise and that case. If he had to shoot her, he told her, Doc would never be the wiser.

She'd decided she had no choice for the moment but to go along willingly. The threats were real.

When they headed east out of town, no lamplight showed in any window. No one was out and about on the sidewalks, except in front of the saloons farther down Main Street. But she had no illusions concerning the raucous, drunken men reeling about in the distance. Even if she'd screamed at the top of her lungs, not one of them would have turned a bleary eye in the direction of the sound. Not one of them would have come and rescued her from these two villainous rogues.

They rode in silence, the bright light of the setting moon casting shadows on the road in front of them. An hour or so outside of town, Wendell led them off the Denver road onto what seemed to be a little-used trail.

Sheila chided herself bitterly for putting herself in this position. She'd been a fool believing Wendell's story about his injured wife. What made her believe him? How could she have simply put the shotgun down?

If Wendell had revealed his true colors at that moment, though, could she have shot him?

She knew, even now, that firing that gun would have been problematic.

But the other one? In spite of her feelings about killing another human being, she had a strong sense that she *could* have pulled the trigger and blasted Dodger. He'd terrified her. But Wendell had intervened, putting himself in front of her. And the way he'd presented himself was far less threatening than his partner.

Out on his ranch, Marlowe told her he'd killed those rustlers in defense of himself and his property. It had been much the same situation for her. But if her conscience had stricken her after the first death and she hadn't been able to fire that gun again, what would have happened to her? She shuddered at the thought of what Dodger would have done to her if he had her alone.

Now, with the sun beginning to edge up over a forested mountain ridge, with the relative law and order of the town far behind her, Sheila knew she was in greater danger than she'd ever faced in her life.

"Get going, you prissy bitch," Dodger called out sharply from behind her.

It was not easy for Sheila to control the horse on this trail. Her hands were still bound in front of her, and the saddle was anything but comfortable. She urged the horse on with a light kick of her heels, but the change was negligible.

It was astounding how drastically her life had changed in a matter of one month. Back in New York, she'd found herself in a dreadful predicament. Her grandfather, J. T. Spencer, had suggested she should accept the offer of marriage from his financial partner.

Suggested was too kind a word. Her grandfather had given her an ultimatum.

She would marry Rudd Hughes. Period. There was no alternative in the matter.

The idea of such a union was ridiculous. True, at twenty-five years of age, she was getting a little old for marriage, but she had no desire to marry the man. Mr. Hughes was a widower in his fifties. He had daughters older than Sheila. Even if he didn't look like a troll in fine clothing, the age difference made the match absurd.

Then, there was the obvious fact that she didn't have any affection for the man. She'd seen him, spent time with him socially, and was a friend of one of his daughters. She'd witnessed firsthand how poorly he treated his own family. No, it wouldn't do.

Sheila could never consider such a marriage that was so obviously intended to unite their financial holdings under one roof. But to stay in New York meant defying her grandfather, and he was a man accustomed to having his own way.

J. T. Spencer had grown up in a fairly well-to-do old New York family, but his real fortune came during the Civil War. Sheila had only recently learned the details of it. Through political connections in Washington, he'd managed to have his bank syndicated at the outset of hostilities. The federal government needed money to fund the war.

Acting as an agent of the Treasury Department, he had used his bank in the effort to sell war bonds to the general public. In the process, he'd accumulated substantial wealth for himself.

After the war, he partnered with Mr. Hughes, a man keen on investing in railroads, mining companies, and heavy industry. The two of them had been making a fortune together ever since.

Sheila never realized it until a few months ago, but as the sole heir to the Spencer family wealth, she had been educated and raised specifically to secure her grandfather's financial holdings for future generations.

Presented with his demand that she marry his partner, she'd found there was no way to reject the proposal. Not if she wanted to remain with her grandparents in New York.

She had few places to turn for help. Her mother had died young, and her father had left her to be brought up in the house of her mother's parents. She'd made her decision practically overnight. She left New York, the only life she'd ever known, and boarded a train west. In Denver — a bustling, riotous city — she climbed into a stagecoach bound for Elkhorn and her father.

And here she was, in the wilds of the

frontier, kidnapped by dangerous outlaws. But no matter what happened, she hadn't one single regret about walking away from the future her grandfather had arranged for her.

A sharp cry startled her. Looking up, she saw two ravens harassing a hawk just above them. She took a deep breath, pushing the thought of her past behind her. The birds disappeared into the trees.

Here, on this mountain trail, there was a comfortable coolness in the air. Except for the dull, clopping thuds of their horses' hooves, the squeak of leather, and the occasional jibe from Dodger, it was peaceful and quiet. They passed beneath bulging stone ledges and soaring bluffs, through evergreen forests and groves of trees just opening their leaves, through open meadows of silver grass. It was all so different from the smoke and the smells and the constant noise of the city she'd left behind.

Sheila had lost any hope of finding her way back to Elkhorn, if she were ever able to break away from her captors. She only knew, from the direction of the bright sun, rising above distant peaks, that they were continuing to ride to the north and east.

The sight of her father's medical leather bag and his surgical case, hanging securely from Wendell's horse ahead of her, did provide some comfort to Sheila. He had to be alive, or these two wouldn't bother to bring his things back with them.

She no longer imagined that it was for Wendell's wife, however. She could only think it was one of their outlaw friends who'd been injured. Whatever role they intended that she play in their nasty game, though, remained a mystery.

Ever since leaving the main road, they'd been riding single file. Lately, however, Wendell had been getting increasingly annoyed when Dodger would fall behind, often out of sight. As far as Sheila was concerned, those were the preferred moments. She would not have lost a wink of sleep if the vile creature had fallen into a ravine or been eaten by wolves.

At the bottom of a grassy knoll, Wendell reined in to wait for his partner to catch up. She heard him cursing under his breath as he looked back along the trail. A moment later, Dodger appeared and rode up to them.

"They know I've gone missing," she said to Wendell before they could start off again. "They'll come after me."

"Who knows you've gone missing?" he scoffed. "Your own pa didn't have no idea you was there."

"Since I arrived, my father's housekeeper comes every day to check on me. She'll know right away. You can have little doubt she'll notify the sheriff."

Wendell didn't seem bothered at all by the threat, but Dodger wheeled his horse and rode back toward the top of the hill, ignoring the call for him to stop.

"Look what you done," Wendell snapped. "Now he'll be dragging behind twice as bad as afore."

She shrugged and directed an accusing look at the man. "Everything you told me back in Elkhorn was a lie, wasn't it?"

"You're as green as can be, missy." He kept his eye on the trail behind them. "Don't know what it's like where you come from. But you'll learn soon enough that, out here, you can't trust everything you hear."

"So you intend to let me live? I'll actually have a chance to learn the ways of the West?"

The hawk eyes flicked toward her and then back in the direction Dodger had disappeared. "Don't you fret about that. If Doc does what he's s'posed to do, the two of you will be heading back to Elkhorn in no time."

"Is this another lie?"

"There you go." The hint of a grin tugged at his face. "You're already learning. But this here *is* the truth."

The last time he'd lied to her, she was pointing a shotgun at his chest. Now, she was his prisoner. Sheila wanted to think the man had no reason to lie.

"I'd like to trust you, Mr. Wendell. But that friend of yours . . ." She tipped her chin in the direction of Dodger. "I don't care for him at all."

"Yeah. I get it." He shrugged. "And it's just Wendell. Not *Mr.* Wendell."

The sound of Dodger's horse approaching drew her attention.

"Ain't nobody coming," the younger man said when he rode up to them.

"Of course, no one is coming, you dang fool. Now let's git." Wendell turned his mount and started off again.

The trail was wide enough here for two to ride abreast, and Dodger kicked his horse and rode up alongside Wendell.

"Who you calling a fool, old man?"

Sheila was right behind them, and she could hear every word passing between them.

"A fool is as a fool does. Ain't that the old saying?"

"What do you mean?"

She could hear the note of danger in Dodger's words, but Wendell was ignoring it.

"You answer me this," he said sharply. "Back in Elkhorn there, why'd it take you so godawful long to bring back a horse for her?"

Dodger took a moment before he answered. When he did, the threat in his tone was gone. "Didn't you say, don't make no trouble?"

"Was there trouble?"

"If you're asking if I shot somebody, I didn't." Dodger raised his voice a little, and Sheila sensed he was speaking for her to hear as well. "And I didn't do no stabbing or throat cutting or head bashing, neither."

"Well, that's a nice change."

Sarcasm dripped from Wendell's words, but Sheila shuddered. She had a strong feeling he meant it. She was now more fearful of Dodger than ever.

"You got a problem with how I do my job?" His voice was again low and threatening.

Wendell was clearly unimpressed. "Your job is to follow orders. It ain't to go off half-cocked and acting like a dang hothead. It ain't your job to spill blood any time you imagine someone is looking cross-eyed at you."

Dodger stared straight ahead, and she didn't know how he was taking this.

"What is it about your gang?" he said finally, scoffing. "You have a good thing going here. You rack up loot real steady, hitting them stagecoaches. But you ain't the cutthroats and thieves that folks think you are. All you do is take the cut you're given without a whimper and take orders from —"

"That's enough." Wendell reined in his horse sharply. His hand was on the pistol at his hip. "You keep on talking. Keep on disrespecting the boss. Cuz one more word and I'll shoot you dead, right now. You got it?"

Sheila hadn't seen Wendell this angry before.

Dodger's manner changed immediately. The threat was gone from his voice, replaced by a fake, almost joking tone. "Hell, I don't mean nothing by it. But a man can ask questions, can't he?"

"Not about that."

When Dodger shrugged and nodded, Wendell nudged his horse, and they all started off again.

"You're hearing me wrong," Dodger continued, not letting it go. "I got respect for the boss. It's just that I'm new to your gang. I ain't never seen a group of gunslingers so good at getting a job done. How can I not respect you all? You been doing this a dog's age without the law catching up to you."

"And the reason for that is cuz we don't cause no trouble where we don't need to," Wendell said, still angry. "In five years, for all the stagecoaches we done robbed, we ain't never killed a driver or a guard. Not till you come along."

"You told me yourself you had a man killed just afore I signed on."

"It ain't your job to avenge nothing, if that's what you're saying."

"I had no choice when we hit that stage," Dodger muttered. "They was shooting at us."

"Not afore you started shooting."

"They saw my face. I ain't having no WANTED flyer out with my face on it."

Wendell stared at the younger man. "And what about the miner?"

"I thought that was the plan all along."

"It *wasn't.*"

"But he saw us."

"Men like that feller are common as rocks out here. They come and go and mind their own business. As we mind ours. The same goes for that old codger who wandered into camp the other night. You had no call to kill him neither."

Cold sweat trickled down Sheila's back. Suddenly, she was afraid they'd never let her go back with her father after hearing everything Dodger had done.

"I'm learning." The killer simply grinned in response to Wendell's reprimand. "When I fetched that horse for her ladyship here, I found a kid sound asleep in a little office they got in that livery there. I could've cut his throat and made sure he wouldn't raise no fuss, but I let him sleep."

Wendell shook his head. "That was mighty big of you. Imagine. Not killing a kid."

The trail narrowed as they entered a grove of firs, and the older man moved ahead. Dodger reined in his horse and stared at Sheila as she passed him. She didn't look at him or give any indication she'd heard even a word. A moment later, she glanced over her shoulder. He was again lagging behind.

"So you're not the boss then," she said to Wendell.

"Nope. And don't wanna be."

"Is the boss more like you or like him?"

"The boss ain't like nobody." Wendell sent her a cross look. "And you're asking way too many questions."

"I only want to know if I'll live to see Elk-horn again," she persisted. "That Dodger is dangerous."

"Don't mind him, miss." He frowned and shook his head. "He ain't nothing but a hired hand. Gunslicks like him are common as rats in a riverboat. He takes one more step out of line, and I'll put a bullet in him, just to put him out of his misery. You're safe with us."

Sheila turned in the saddle and found Dodger had dropped back so far that he was again out of sight. She certainly hoped Wendell was right.

She imagined, though, that in the world of pirates and outlaws, the whip was always wielded by the most ruthless villain of all.

CHAPTER TWENTY-TWO

Most of the blood on Caleb wasn't his own.

"You hurt? We heard the shouting and come running." Zeke sidestepped his way down the steep slope, six-shooter in hand. He stopped and gaped wide-eyed at the dead cougar.

Caleb shook his head and wiped his knife on a moss-covered rock. "How's the preacher?"

"Tore up, some. But he's a tough old bird. That's one big cat there."

Caleb looked down at the bloodied mountain lion, fiercely savage even in death. He didn't want to say it, but he didn't find any satisfaction in killing these majestic animals. In this case, though, it was kill or be killed.

The two of them climbed back to the trail. Everett had tied the agitated mule to a sapling and was tending to the minister, who was sitting with his back against a rock.

The cougar had left his mark on

Preacher's face and neck. The old man hadn't been wearing his coat, and his vest and shirt were blood-soaked and largely torn to shreds. The cat had clawed his arms and chest pretty badly.

"All the years I've roamed these hills, spreading the Good Word, I've never been attacked by one of them."

Caleb crouched beside him. "And you said yesterday that you were too tough for a grizzly to chew on."

"Guess that cougar reckoned he had sharper teeth." He started to chuckle but winced, pressing a bloody hand to his ribs. "Fact is, that monster was after my old mule. I just happened to get in his way."

"From what I saw, you were doing your *damnedest* to get in his way."

"That's true enough." Preacher gazed fondly at his beast of burden, who was keeping an eye on him too. "We've been together for many a year."

"Think you can walk?" Caleb asked.

"I know I can. My knees might be a little wobbly at first, but that cougar didn't get his claws into me down there at all . . . thanks to you."

"Strong enough to walk over to the creek to wash some of this off?"

"The good Lord sent you to save the hide

238

of his lowly servant today. He'll see to it that I have enough strength."

Caleb looked at the other men. "I'm going to walk Preacher over yonder. Why don't you take his mule back with you and start packing up?"

Zeke glanced at his partner and said, "You take the mule back. I got me a mind to go down there and skin that devil. I'll meet you at the camp." He smiled at Caleb and shook his head in admiration. "Nobody gonna believe how big that cat was you killed. Not unless I bring that pelt back with me."

Whatever Zeke was going to do with the cat was his business. Caleb had no interest in it.

Regardless of his belief and determination, the minister was in tough shape. Caleb draped Preacher's bloody arm over his shoulder and helped him walk. The distance they had to go was farther than the man had strength for, but they took their time. Caleb could have easily thrown the wiry little man over his shoulder, but he'd just been mauled within an inch of his life by a ruthless hunter. Caleb didn't want to add insult to the man's injuries.

Though he wouldn't admit it, the effects of the fight with the cougar continued to linger in him as well. Caleb felt like lightning had struck the ground inches from his feet. It was as if something inside of him had shaken loose and was quivering like the plucked wire on a banjo. The waves crackled through his body.

He'd killed cougars before, but this one was the first he'd physically attacked, wrestled to the ground, looked in the face, and killed in a hand-to-hand fight. Well, hand-to-claw.

He'd killed men before, armed only with a knife or his fists. Once, while waiting out a blizzard at a nameless hotel in a nameless smudge of a town in Wyoming, he'd gone across a covered alley into a building that housed the baths. Three men were waiting for him when he came back out into the alley.

He'd been unarmed. They carried knives and staves that they immediately put to use. Two men had gone down quickly. One with a damaged knee he'd be feeling with every step he took for the rest of his miserable life. The other with eyes that stared into starry blackness following the collision between his head and the alley wall. The third man had come at him with a gleaming blade and a rage in his eyes that told Caleb one of them would not survive this fight.

His attacker had been correct, but Caleb felt plucked wire and the lightning bolts racing through his body for an hour afterward.

The rising sun was filtering through the green canopy above them as they made their way to the creek. His brain told him that they were in no danger, but his nerves were still humming. And every shadow and movement drew his eye.

He forced himself to breathe deeply, and by the time they reached the creek, he was himself again. Or that's what he told himself.

He realized he was bleeding from a long gash on his upper arm, and the nick on his cheek that he received yesterday was oozing blood again. Other than that, he'd only be feeling a few bruises. He'd been lucky.

Caleb led Preacher to a rock beside a small pool. As he passed the cougar prints he'd seen this morning, it reminded him how close they'd come to being breakfast for the big cat.

He helped the minister sit, and the old man groaned in pain.

Caleb carefully removed the vest and tattered shirt and inspected the damage done to the wrinkled body. The cougar's claws had ripped through the clothing, and some of the gashes went deep into the flesh.

Preacher had the use of all his limbs, thankfully, but Caleb knew some of those wounds could fester and cause him serious trouble if they weren't looked after.

"We have to clean you up and get you to Elkhorn, Preacher. Hopefully, someone there can stitch you up."

Caleb tore off pieces of the man's ruined shirt and washed off what blood he could. Two deep lacerations ran in parallel lines from his collarbone to the middle of his chest. An inch closer to center and that cougar would had ripped through the jugular. It was a miracle that the minister had survived the attack.

"Do you have another shirt in your saddlebags?" Caleb asked.

"I do."

As Caleb washed the blood off his own clothes, he felt Preacher's eyes on him.

"I owe you my life, Mr. Marlowe," he said, his voice thick with emotion.

"Nothing to it. You and that mule of yours would have finished him without no help from me."

"I'll let that little lie pass. But I reckon I owe you some answers in return."

Caleb understood Preacher's hesitation about pointing him toward the hideout of the Wells Fargo road agents, and he had no hard feelings about last night. As Preacher had reminded him, these people out here, even them outlaws, were his flock.

The wide open lands beyond the Devil's Claw were like so much of the frontier. Life out here lay beyond the reach of sheriffs and courts and their laws. And these folk had only so many choices in how they chose to live their lives. If they chose the outlaw life, the only tie that could hold a gang together was the bond of loyalty and trust. And that went for miner, outlaw, hermit, preacher, and whoever lived on this land. Their business was their own.

Without that trust, men were no different from animals.

At any rate, if Preacher thought that he'd be betraying the trust of these members of his flock by sharing too much about them, then so be it. Caleb could live with that. He'd still find them. All that aside, if the minister wanted to talk, he was willing to listen.

What he wanted most was to bring back Doc Burnett. There was no point in explaining. Doc meant nothing to the preacher. But if Caleb's friend was with them outlaws and he was hurt . . . or dead . . . then the gates of Hell would be swinging wide to welcome a few more residents.

"I won't lie to you," Preacher began. "Knowing you're going after that particular band of road agents, I'm struggling a bit. But there are a few things that sit heavy on my heart. Things that you should know."

"You say what you want to say. I ain't pushing you."

The minister nodded. "I won't tell you how to find their camp. But seeing what I saw last night, you saving the lives of those two fellows, and this morning with this . . . this . . . ." His gaze drifted down the trail before coming back to Caleb's face. "You have a strong relationship with the land. I know you'll find where they're hiding."

It was good to know he had this man's confidence.

"But once you find them, you should know this. They're not the people you think they are."

"You have to speak plainer than that, Reverend."

"They are not murderous dogs, like a few others living out here."

"There are two dead stagecoach men they left behind this week. I'm afraid that contradicts your opinion of them. Aside from that, two other men are missing, and I fear for their lives as well."

"I don't know anything about that robbery. I wasn't there, so I don't know what caused the bloodshed. But for all I know, it might not have been them. It might have been some other gang." The preacher dabbed at the blood still oozing from the wounds on his arms. "I can only speak of the men I have met. They welcomed me to their fire. They shared their story with me. I'm telling you it's not their way to kill in cold blood."

"Go on."

"They do target the Wells Fargo strongboxes. That's all they want. Their grudge is against the company itself. That's who they want to hurt."

"Why?"

"Revenge."

Caleb's face must have reflected his doubts. He'd known plenty of fellas who justified their misdeeds in their own minds with exactly that excuse.

"Do you want to hear the story?"

"It depends who told it to you," Caleb replied. "Was it the leader of this outfit? Cuz I've heard more tales that go from mouth to mouth, getting embellished every time another fella tells it. Did you know Pecos Bill lassoed a twister and dug the Rio Grande?"

"This ain't one of those stories." The

minister glared at him. "I sat around the fire with five members of the gang. The leader doesn't hold with showing himself. He keeps to his cabin when I've been there. But he was that far away." He motioned to the far side of the creek.

That information alone was helpful. If the preacher was right — and there was no reason to think otherwise — there were six men in that outfit.

"When was this?"

"Maybe a month ago. No more than that." He pulled his vest on gingerly.

"How about if we get ourselves back to the camp and get a coat on you. This story can wait."

Preacher shook his head. "No, I'm fine. I want to tell you about them, but I only want to share it with you."

"Okay. I'm listening."

"The leader of this gang wasn't always an outlaw. He was a respectable man."

"That's often the case, Preacher."

"Some fifteen years ago, when the war broke out, he left his wife and children to do his duty. He enlisted in the Illinois Regiment. From the account I heard, he was a good soldier, got promoted, then was seriously wounded at Vicksburg."

Caleb knew about the Siege of Vicksburg.

It was the last major Confederate stronghold on the Mississippi. After it fell, the Union gained control of almost the entire river. Not long after that, Lee was defeated in Gettysburg.

"After they sewed him up, he went back to his unit and fought under Sherman for the remainder of the war. By the end of it, he'd distinguished himself as a fighter and a leader. He was a lieutenant when he was discharged with his regiment in Washington."

Caleb now understood better why no one had caught this gang yet. "How does a man like that become an outlaw? Everyone knows that plenty on the rebel side never stopped fighting, but this fella should have had a future for himself."

"I am getting to it," the preacher said. "After the war, he went west, like a lot of folk. Ended up prospecting for gold in Montana. That's where the bad blood started."

"What happened?"

"Some five years after he got out there, he had an ugly encounter with a couple of Wells Fargo men."

"That's all a little vague, ain't it?"

"There's more. His men told me that these two Wells Fargo agents had worked out a scheme to help themselves. They were stealing miners' gold that was being shipped along the Montana Trail to Utah."

Caleb knew from years back that Montana stagecoaches made for tempting targets. They carried passengers loaded down with gold dust or cash, and the strongboxes were generally a treasure trove of mail containing more cash, land deeds, and stock certificates. When Wells Fargo expanded, buying up other stagecoach companies, they hired all sorts of men to work as agents and provide safe routes. It was no secret that some of them fellas worked both sides of the law.

"He sent a letter to the company bosses in Frisco," Preacher continued. "In it he complained about the thieves and criminals they'd put in charge of the trail. Well, it got back to those fellows in Montana. They sent a gang of men with shotguns to quiet him for good."

"But they couldn't."

"Nope."

"So he's been robbing their stagecoaches ever since," Caleb finished the story for him.

"They told me they've been moving about — Montana, Utah, and even California and Oregon — just to stay ahead of them. That was before coming here."

Caleb wondered if the judge had any idea about the history of these men. He wondered if he'd care.

"Do you know how long they've been at it?"

"One of them said about five years."

"And never been caught."

"That's because they're gentleman robbers."

"Gentlemen robbers," Caleb repeated, almost choking on the word. "What makes you say that?"

"Well, think about it. Here they are, taking in . . . what, thousands of dollars a year. But they swore to me they never once fired a weapon during any robbery."

"I have a hard time believing that."

The preacher shrugged. "That's what they told me, and I believe them."

Caleb shook his head and pushed up to his feet. Two men were dead. Someone else inside that stagecoach was wounded. Maybe there was some truth to this story about how these fellas got started, but he'd also heard that the gang had lost one of their men in a recent robbery. He asked Preacher about that.

"That must have been since I was there."

And maybe, since then, they'd changed their ways.

"I hope this helps you decide how you want to proceed, Mr. Marlowe. I know when fighting starts, a man doesn't always have a chance to ask questions. I just wanted you to go in there knowing what I know."

Caleb nodded and helped the old man to his feet. The minister was still very shaky, but he seemed to do better as they walked.

"But you never met their leader," he asked as they neared their camp.

"Never. He's a mysterious fellow. But a good-hearted one, for all I can see." Preacher paused and looked Caleb straight in the eye. "And I'll tell you this. I got a strong feeling that gang will do anything to protect him."

CHAPTER TWENTY-THREE

The trail had been descending for miles, and for quite some time now, Sheila had been following Wendell along a bluff overlooking the river. Dodger was somewhere behind them. The gushing, roaring torrent was often right beneath them, and Sheila gazed down at the water as it raced along in heaving swells before exploding in bursts of white spray over gleaming boulders and shattered remains of once-great trees.

Over the course of the past few hours, the forest had been changing. The endless expanses of fir had given way to alternating woodlands of spruce and aspen. Sheila was no expert when it came to the flora of Colorado, but she knew one tree from another. The spruces rose straight and rigid to almost delicate silver spear points. And in groves closer to the water's edge, the round leaves of the aspen — which in summer would turn and tremble at the first hint of storm — were now mere buds on the naked, gray-green branches.

The sun was nearly overhead, and she guessed it was sometime around noon when they reached a thickly wooded ravine that opened out onto the river and extended far into the mountainous green hills to the west. The trail dropped once again until they were nearly at the level of the river itself, and the green forest closed around them.

A few minutes later, they reached a stream that appeared to flow out of the very heart of the ravine. Crystal-clear water tumbled over a small waterfall into a shimmering pool. She gazed at the reflected glints of sunlight coming through the trees as Wendell directed his horse toward some shallows where they could traverse the stream.

Sheila's back ached, her legs were cramped, and her bottom was numb from the long hours in the saddle. About an hour ago, as they passed the collapsed entrance to an abandoned mine and the ruin of a tiny shack, Wendell had slowed just enough to hand her some dry biscuits and then his water flask. She ate and drank as he ordered, but now she wished she hadn't.

He showed no sign of stopping, so Sheila urged her horse closer. He turned in his saddle to look at her.

"What do you want?"

"I need to stop."

"Why?"

"I need to . . . to make water."

"Hold it."

"I can't," she whispered. "Please, Wendell. It's urgent."

He looked ahead, clearly annoyed, and his cheeks puffed out as he expelled a deep breath. "We ain't maybe ten miles away from where we're heading. You can wait that long."

She couldn't. "I can't, I tell you. Just a quick stop. Please."

The sound of hooves thundering up behind them caused the older man to roll his eyes and then glower at Sheila.

"What's going on?" Dodger demanded, reining in beside her. "What's she want?"

"None of your business," she retorted.

"How'd you like a good slap? That'd make it my business. Now, what do you want?"

"Ain't nothing to do with her." Wendell leaned forward in his saddle. "We're stopping here to water the horses."

He was going to let her relieve herself, but she knew it was more to assert himself over Dodger than it was for her. This was a good turn, but he was still an outlaw. And if she ever had the chance, she'd make sure he faced justice in a court of law for abducting her.

"I'll ride back a ways." Dodger told them, wheeling his horse. "Don't want nobody sneaking up on us."

As the blackguard started off, Wendell started to call after him but stopped and watched him go, a disgusted frown on his face.

With a glance at Sheila, he dismounted.

"Git now," he said as he helped her get down. "And don't go taking your time, neither."

As soon as her boots touched the ground, her knees buckled slightly. She grabbed hold of the stirrup leather. For a moment, she thought her legs wouldn't hold her weight. She glanced up at Wendell and was surprised by the fleeting look of concern that crossed the hawkish features.

She leaned against her horse's flank and extended her bound wrists toward him. "Would you?"

He frowned at her. "You ain't gonna run away?"

She scoffed and gestured toward the river and the trees surrounding them. "I was raised in New York City. I'm an unarmed woman in a place I've never seen before.

How long would I survive out here if I ran away?"

"That shows good sense."

He pulled a small knife from his boot and cut the rope on her wrists. The blade sliced through the cord like butter. Wendell tossed the rope into the creek, and it disappeared downstream.

"Thank you."

She flexed her elbows and fingers and rubbed the welts where the rope had dug into her skin. Slipping her hands into the arms of the duster draped around her, she took a couple of tentative steps, feeling the blood flow back into her lower extremities.

He led the horses toward the pool of water above the shallows. "Git. We ain't about to be lollygagging around here all day."

"I'm going," she told him, directing her steps toward the brush closer to the river.

"Only to them aspens," he called out. "Don't go no farther."

"All right. All right." Sheila walked, hurried a couple of steps and then walked again to where he was pointing.

She crouched behind the brush in a leaf-lined depression that appeared to be a branch of the creek that only filled during times of flooding. It ran straight down to the river, dropping off near the end.

She pulled up the duster and her skirts. As she relieved herself, she could see the top of a great snarl of fallen timber that the current had piled up at the river's edge. Raising herself slightly, she spied Wendell with the horses by the creek, filling his water flask. The horses were both standing in the pool, drinking.

The earthy smells of evergreen needles and last year's decaying leaves filled her senses. The sound of the waterfall blended with the rush of the river. Her eye was drawn upward to the expanse of blue skies above the bare, tangled branches of the aspens and the silver tips of the spruces.

The world around her seemed to be so finely drawn, so exquisitely sharp in every detail and scent. She chuckled to herself that she should feel this now, at a time when her life was in jeopardy. Perhaps, she thought, it was precisely because of the danger she was facing.

For the first time, she felt the incredible beauty and the allure of this country. It was all so wild and untouched by man, so different from the crowds and the filth of the city.

When she left New York, spring had only begun to touch the neighborhoods of Manhattan. The daffodils were beginning to bloom, yellow and lovely, in the churchyard of the Presbyterian Church across Fifth Avenue from her grandparents' brownstone mansion at the corner of Twelfth Street. But so many of the city's smoke-filled streets were still knee-deep with the muck of a late snow and the endless rain that had followed.

The city was a place filled with self-inflicted problems and dangers. From the Broadway rum palaces to the gin mills of the Bowery to the bucket shops of the Five Points, Manhattan was reeling with drunkenness and crime. Poverty had no place in her family's neighborhood, but a person could see it everywhere if they opened their eyes. The immigrants hawking their wares on the streets. The streetwalkers who would appear at dusk by the wrought iron gates of the parks. The filthy little boys jammed into the chimneys for the monthly cleaning. And the footpads roaming the shadows at night, looking for nobs and swells to prey on, didn't choose that life because they had summer mansions to pay for on Long Island or in Newport.

From what Sheila had seen, Elkhorn and Colorado had its share of lawlessness, to be sure. But at moments like this, with the clean air filling her lungs, with green vistas and shimmering water everywhere, she understood why her father and so many others came here and stayed.

The sound of a horse being reined in near the creek jarred her from her moment of reverie. She shook her head, wondering how she could be so whimsical about things when she was in the clutches of hard, desperate men. She didn't know if she'd survive the day, and here she was ready to paint a picture of it.

"Where is she?" Dodger's voice was brusque and demanding.

"Water your horse. She'll be back in a dang minute."

Sheila raised herself enough to straighten her skirts. She had no desire to spend any more time with Dodger than she needed to.

"Which direction did she go?" There was a hard note in the rogue's tone that made Sheila's blood run cold.

If Wendell answered, she didn't hear it. She peered over the top of the hollow at the two outlaws.

Dodger swung to the ground, and his mount clopped to the creek to drink with the other horses.

Wendell was still crouched by the pool, splashing water on his face. Dodger stood behind him, his eyes scanning the terrain around them. He was obviously searching for her.

"Hear that?" the older man asked, standing up. He was looking back the way they'd come.

"I don't hear nothing."

As Wendell moved past his partner, Sheila saw the gleam of the blade in Dodger's hand. There was no time to shout a warning. There was no time for anything.

The knife slashed across Wendell's throat with practiced precision. The quickness of the move shocked her, and the older man spun toward Dodger, clutching his hands to his neck.

Blood spurted through his fingers and ran down his chest. His eyes were wide, and he staggered backward.

Dodger stood watching, the dripping blade hanging in his hand at his side. There was a smile on his face, as if he were watching a scene playing out on an opera house stage. He had his pistol drawn, in case it was needed.

It wasn't needed. Wendell sank slowly to his knees. His hands fell away from his throat. His head sagged, and he tipped forward onto his face.

Sheila's hand flew to her mouth to stifle a scream. Hot bile scorched her throat, and dizziness staggered her. She dropped to one knee, forcing herself to breathe and think, but anger flashed red in her brain.

Murder. In cold blood. Dodger cut his throat, killing Wendell when his back was to him.

He was despicable. Evil. Inhuman. An animal. But what kind of animal could do such a thing? None. No animal was so vile and conniving and cold.

He'd kill her next. But only after he abused her. She was certain of it. She had no doubt.

She should have shot him in the house when she had the chance.

"Miss Burnett," he called out. "We need to ride. We're waiting."

He thought she was stupid. Or that she hadn't seen what he did. Sheila glanced around her, thinking of escape. She needed to get away.

"Show yourself," Dodger shouted. "We still got a long ride ahead of us."

Hearing the sound of horses approaching, Sheila peeked over the side of the depression through the brush again. Four men entered the clearing by the creek. They didn't dismount.

Dodger wiped the knife on Wendell's coat, slid it into its sheath, and holstered his gun.

"I told you to wait till I signaled," he said coldly. "This fella almost ain't had time to fall on his knife."

The man at the head of the newcomers looked down at the corpse and then swung down from his saddle. "So where is she?"

Sheila recognized him. It was the sheriff from Elkhorn. Sheriff Horner. The man who'd leered disgracefully at her like a common lout.

But he was far worse than that. He was in league with Dodger.

"She's around her somewheres."

The sheriff turned to the other men. "Find her. We can use her."

"Sure can," Dodger replied, laughing at his own dirty joke.

The snake of a lawman stared at him for a long moment as the others climbed down from their horses. Finally, spitting on the ground near Dodger's boot, he turned to his men.

"Search the area. She can't have got too far."

Sheila knew she had to go, and go quickly. Staying low, she moved as fast as she could along the hollow in the direction of the river. She was certain she'd be no safer in Horner's clutches than in Dodger's.

As she got closer to the river, the depression fell away, and she clambered and slid down a short wall of clay and rock to a stream bed of gravel and shallow water. Following it to the end, she reached the tangle of rotten tree trunks and branches. The rushing river surged and splashed up against it.

She looked across the torrent. The opposite bank was so far, and white water was pummeling boulders in the middle. She didn't think she'd survive if she tried to swim across.

Sheila heard Dodger and the sheriff arguing. Their voices were coming closer.

Scrambling through the branches of the waterlogged timber, she climbed over a half-submerged tree trunk and slipped down into the frigid water. She held tight to a dead branch that she feared would snap off at any moment, sending her sailing along the speeding current to certain death.

Sheila had no choice. She lowered herself until only her face was above the surface and prayed that the trunk was enough to hide her.

". . . ain't for you to be doing no deciding," the sheriff snapped. They were standing on the bank directly above her. "I'm running this outfit."

"Seems like I hear that everywhere I turn,

Horner."

"Then you'd best hear it, boy."

As the water pulled at her clothes, Sheila listened, unwilling to breathe.

"Anything you say, Sheriff."

She'd heard Dodger say almost the same thing to Wendell in the exact same tone.

"Dammit," Horner said finally. He shouted to the other searchers. "Forget it. Ain't no point wasting no more time here."

"You're right about that," she heard Dodger say as they moved away. "That prissy bitch won't make it through a night in these mountains."

CHAPTER TWENTY-FOUR

Judge Patterson paced the area behind the desk in his office and listened to Zeke relate the story about the ambush, Caleb Marlowe's intervention on their behalf, and the attack on the itinerant preacher.

His man Fredericks came in again just as the miner was telling about the killing of the cougar, which, as the story was being told, grew to the size of a buffalo. The miner's tale of Marlowe killing the cat with only a knife had held the big man as transfixed as a twelve-year-old at his first girlie show.

Two things ran through the judge's mind. Maybe he did pick the right man to go after the Wells Fargo gang. And second, it was no surprise that Jacob Bell's legendary knife had killed a mountain lion. He should have kept the damned thing.

The judge motioned for Zeke to stop and addressed his man.

"Did you locate the sheriff?"

Fredericks, called Frissy by everyone except the judge, had proven his worth time and time again over the past few years. Huge in proportion to most other men, he was a former head cracker at a brothel in Denver. After killing a patron, Fredericks had come before the judge. Seeing that the man had a brain to go with his muscle, he'd taken him into his personal employ as a bodyguard, an enforcer, and whatever other job needed to be done. He was violent and quick-tempered, but he wasn't a fool. And he followed orders to the letter.

"He ain't at the jail, Judge."

Zeke chuckled. "Today being the Sabbath, maybe Horner's up at the church."

Frissy shook his huge head. "He ain't in town."

Patterson had sent him off for the sheriff after Zeke arrived with two bodies, his wounded partner Everett, and the mauled minister. He wanted Horner to handle the arrangements with the undertaker. "He has to be in town. What about his deputies? What do they say?"

"There's only one of them in town, and I cornered him drinking in the Belle. He says Horner rode out before dawn this morning with three other fellows."

"Rode out?" Patterson barked. "Where to?"

"He didn't kn—"

"*That* worthless sonovabitch didn't ask my permission to go anywhere. He knows my instructions. He's not to leave town without letting me know."

Frissy stood with his hands hanging at his sides, his head tilted, as attentive as a hunting dog waiting for his master's command.

"What else did the deputy say?"

"Nothing. He didn't know nothing more than that."

Patterson was beginning to feel the heat rising under his starched collar. "Did you ask anyone else?"

"I stopped in at the hardware store to see if Lewis had seen him. With his store being close to Rogers's livery, I figured he might have seen something when the sheriff and his men fetched their horses."

"And . . . ?"

"Lewis ain't seen nothing. But his wife had plenty to say."

The judge motioned impatiently for Fredericks to continue.

"Mrs. Lewis says she stopped at Doc Burnett's house this morning. You know, to check on the daughter."

"This had better be relevant," Patterson

warned.

"She's gone missing too. The daughter, that is."

"Now, coming from the East Coast," Zeke put in, "she definitely could be up at the church."

The judge ignored him, and Frissy again shook his head. "She . . . Mrs. Lewis, I mean, says she looked in at Doc's house again at noon. The girl still wasn't there. And when she checked Doc's things, it looks like someone went through his cabinets and took some stuff. Medicine and such."

"Why would Doc's daughter go off with his medicine?"

"Maybe she didn't go off on her own," Zeke suggested.

"What do you mean?"

"Well, Doc's off somewheres. If he's tending to someone, maybe run out of his medicine. So he sends someone after getting his things, and that someone finds the daughter there."

Frissy bobbed his head. "The only thing making sense to me is that the sheriff's gone after Doc Burnett's daughter."

"How would he know the daughter's gone missing? Did Mrs. Lewis tell him?"

"No, Judge. She says I'm the first one she told."

"Did the girl scream bloody murder as they dragged her by the sheriff's office?"

"I don't think so."

Zeke butted in. "But like I said, maybe she didn't get dragged off, at all."

Patterson felt his temper beginning to slip. He waved Zeke off and continued to question Frissy. "Did you speak to Rogers at the livery? Did she take Doc's horse?"

"Malachi ain't around either. Nor his boy, Gabriel. Just some little whelp who said Malachi was out looking for something around town. He wouldn't say what, though. I reckoned it was better not to wait, so I came back here instead."

"You go back to the livery and get some answers," the judge barked. "I want to know what Malachi and his son know. If she took a horse, and when. If anyone was with her. If the sheriff asked about her. Everything. Do you hear me?"

Frissy moved with surprising speed considering his size. The door closed behind him a moment later.

Patterson wasn't happy with all these complications. Nothing was getting accomplished. In fact, the situation was getting worse.

These damned road agents who were robbing the stagecoaches were creating havoc. The governor was getting it with both barrels from Wells Fargo, and the arrogant bastard wasn't being shy about turning the guns on Patterson. And with all he had in the works for this coming summer and the dignitaries who'd be arriving in Elkhorn, he couldn't allow this lawlessness to continue.

The fact that nobody was showing any success in catching these outlaws was as aggravating as it was surprising. Road agents rarely had a brain to speak of. With the right people on their trail, they always got caught. This outfit that had been robbing only the Wells Fargo stages was different. And that was troubling. But now he had Marlowe to take care of them.

His mind turned to the sheriff. What in the blazes was he doing? From the moment he handed Horner the tin star, he didn't trust the man. But they needed someone wearing the badge in Elkhorn. And it was not too comforting that he was the only candidate to present himself.

"Did you see anyone else on your way back to Elkhorn?" he asked Zeke. "Like Sheriff Horner, for instance?"

"No sign of him, Judge. Or anybody else, neither. But you know there's more than one way to get out to Devil's Claw from here . . . if that's where he was heading."

"I know. I know."

It occurred to him that maybe this preacher Zeke spoke of might be of some help. These men went everywhere, saw everything.

"What about this reverend that you found roaming the mountainside?" he asked. "Does he know anything of value?"

"Preacher's full of stories. Couldn't shut him up riding back to Elkhorn. But nothing that'd be any help."

And then there was Caleb Marlowe. The letter he'd promised to send to the governor was sitting in the drawer of his desk. He'd stopped his secretary from sending the thing off until the gunslinger did his part. Patterson wasn't about to use any political capital getting Henry Jordan out of jail until he saw results.

"About Marlowe," he said. He already pretty much had the answer to the question he was asking, but he trusted Zeke's judgment. "What do you think? Does he have it in him to take down this gang of road agents on his own?"

"Don't think I want to be cut out of any of the cash you been paying me, Judge. But whatever you think of Caleb Marlowe and what that man can do . . ." He snorted and reached down for the rolled-up skin on the floor by his chair. "Let me show you the cat he took down all by his self."

CHAPTER TWENTY-FIVE

Once Zeke and Everett and Preacher started back toward Elkhorn with the bodies of the two ambushed men, it didn't take long for Caleb to break camp.

He took the time to pile stones on the corpses of the bushwhackers. He wanted to have a closer look at where they'd kept their horses. That hadn't turned up any sign of the hoofprint he was looking for. The one that he'd seen at the miner Smith's cabin. The one with the gash on the right side of the front shoe.

Preacher told him that the Wells Fargo gang had five men, not including their leader. There had been five gunmen here, and none of the hoofprints had that distinctive mark. Zeke didn't think these fellas were the gang he was looking for, and the evidence seemed to back that. But then, who were they?

As he saddled Pirate and mounted up, Caleb decided to put that question aside. There was no way to find the answer right now, and he had a more important job to do, finding Doc.

Zeke and his men had limited their search to the area where Caleb found them. They hadn't gone through the pass. Caleb had begun his quest knowing he needed to go beyond Devil's Claw.

Preacher told him he'd visited the road agents' camp a number of times. That meant the place had to be on a trail the minister followed. Caleb couldn't simply backtrack along Preacher's route, though. If he did, he could follow the trail for weeks before he happened upon the outlaws' camp. But at least it meant they could be found.

Throughout the morning, his faithful and tireless buckskin carried him toward the narrowest part of the pass beneath Devil's Claw. The entire time, Caleb concentrated on the trail they followed.

It was midday by the time he rode through the shadowed constriction of the pass itself. He remembered it well from his days of riding with Old Jake. With the river to his left, he studied the trail closely. There were tracks, plenty of them; he even spotted the track of Preacher's mule at one point. But there was no sign of the horse ridden by the man Imala had seen taking her husband. The same man who took Doc.

After going through the pass, Caleb rode to the top of a knoll and stopped. There, he sat on his horse and studied the vistas spreading northward before his eyes. In the distance beyond, snowcapped peaks rose above endless ranges and forests and fields and meadows.

This was the wilderness as it had been since the dawn of time. Unmarred. Maybe as it was meant to be. It was a land where a man could hide himself forever.

Almost immediately, the trail took him into a great amphitheater formed by Devil's Claw and another towering peak. Millions upon millions of spruce trees covered the rising land, the unbroken smoothness marred only by scattered groves of budding aspen. Soon the round aspen leaves would open, but now the stands of trees looked like so many moth holes in an evergreen blanket.

Sometime later, he nudged Pirate off the trail and down to the river. As the horse drank, Caleb looked thoughtfully across the flowing water. There were surely more trails there leading from the west. It was worth looking.

A few miles upriver, he found a place where the valley widened and the river flowed around a long bend. The current wasn't as fast here, and he decided this was the place to ford. After wrapping his rifle and gun belt in the bearskin, he urged his horse down the bank and into the water.

The shock of the cold water wasn't unexpected. Caleb gripped the bridle and the saddle with one hand and held the bearskin high with the other. Pirate was a strong swimmer, but halfway across, the remains of a tree a hundred feet long passed close to them, turning and dipping below the surface, only to come up again. The buckskin shied away from it, but the sound of Caleb's voice steadied his nerves and the tree raced by them.

When they reached the far shore, Caleb found a trail that followed the river north. He rode through grassy meadows covered by the pale-blue, star-shaped flowers with the yellow centers that made a fine dye. Entire fields of deep-purple flowers sloped to the river. The trail took him beneath overhanging walls of rock. Caleb and Pirate forded streams of various sizes that flowed through smaller valleys into the river.

Often, Caleb reined the buckskin to a halt. He would listen and put his nose in the light breeze, and then continue on, his eyes everywhere, alert and cautious. Since yesterday, he'd faced an ambush, a rattlesnake, and a cougar attack. He knew from experience that these mountains held many surprises, and a man needed to be ready for them.

Then at the peak of a hill, he spotted the hint of a trail. It snaked along the opposite side of a valley that ran to the south and west, in the general direction of Elkhorn. He nudged his buckskin and made his way across the basin.

As Pirate carried him up the rise on the far side, he found the trail. It was more of a rocky ledge than a trail here, but he turned north, following it. And then he saw it, the first sign.

Any tenderfoot, green as a slip of barley in spring, would have seen it. Caleb dismounted and walked toward it. A broken branch, no thicker than a man's little finger. It hung loose, the inside nearly white, fresh and damp to the touch. It was not the work of a bear or any other animal. It was cut with a knife. There was no doubt it was done intentionally by someone passing by.

Caleb searched the ground. Not far ahead, the trail moved onto softer ground. Hoofprints. And not just two or three. He counted seven riders. Crouching low, he searched among the marks for the one he knew. He studied the prints and sorted them in his mind. Four riders had passed quite recently, perhaps within a couple of hours.

And then he found what he'd hoped for.

Today, earlier than the others, three riders had come through here, as well. And one of them was riding a horse with a shoe bearing the gash he'd been looking for.

Caleb hurried to where he had left Pirate, climbed back up the saddle, and followed the trail. Not far along, he spotted another cut branch. Beneath it, the prints showed the distinctive mark.

The man he wanted had passed this way, and he'd left signs for others to follow.

But why?

CHAPTER TWENTY-SIX

Sheila clung to the branch of the half-submerged tree until she thought her chattering teeth would alert the men to her presence.

Her hands were almost numb as she pulled herself up and over the trunk. Staying low, she crept up the bank of the river until she could see Dodger and the sheriff and the others. They were standing by the pool not far from where Wendell's body lay, still and unmourned.

The men didn't appear to be concerned with her escape any longer. They were talking among themselves. Or rather, the sheriff was talking, and they were all listening. Dodger's back was to Sheila, but she could tell the sheriff was firing questions at him and Dodger was answering.

Suddenly, the discussion appeared to change. She couldn't hear what was being said, but it looked like plans were being laid.

At one point, Dodger sketched something in the soft earth with his knife as the others looked on. The sheriff looked around and gave orders to the other men, pointing to whatever it was Dodger had depicted.

Watching them from the safety of the brush and the riverbank, Sheila waited, hoping they wouldn't search for her again. She didn't know if she could bring herself to go back in the water.

The sheriff straightened up and spat on the ground. He showed not one flicker of interest in Wendell, or in the fact that Dodger had killed him in cold blood.

Sheriff Horner was no good. Certainly no better than Dodger. She'd known it the moment she passed him on the sidewalk in Elkhorn.

He barked a few more orders, finishing with Dodger, and the men started climbing onto their horses.

As the others gathered the extra horses, Wendell's murderer stood over the dead body and turned his gaze in a complete circle. She knew he was looking for her. When he paused, staring in her direction, Sheila's heart began pounding so hard, she was sure he could hear it.

Seconds ticked by, feeling like hours. She didn't dare move.

Finally, Dodger turned his attention to his victim. Shoving Wendell's body over with his foot, he crouched, removed the gun belt, and went through the coat pockets. She guessed he was checking for any valuables.

Sheila didn't realize she'd been holding her breath until Dodger finally stood and swaggered to his horse. He stuffed Wendell's guns into one of his saddlebags and swung up into the saddle.

As the five men rode off, Dodger and the sheriff in the lead, Sheila thought of Wendell's promise about letting her father and her go. None of those words mattered now. The men disappearing along the trail were cutthroats and villains.

She stayed hidden there for a long time, filled with uncertain imaginings of Dodger riding off, doubling back, and catching her. How long she remained crouched behind the brush on the riverbank, she had no idea. But finally, bolstering her courage, she forced herself to move.

The moment she did, her stomach heaved, and she emptied its contents on the ground.

Shock, fear, hurt all welled up inside of her. Her body felt flushed and hot, in spite of her cold, wet clothing. She moved a few feet away, dropped to one knee, and tried to force air into her lungs. Her stomach was empty, but she could not be rid of what tasted like poison in her mouth.

The paralyzing attack of helplessness didn't last long. Slowly, she felt herself growing calmer. The wind stirred the treetops, and she heard the cry of a hawk or an eagle. It came from somewhere far away, reminding her that she was still exposed and vulnerable. She'd been left here on foot, unarmed, unlearned in matters of survival. But she needed to move, or she would surely die.

Sheila forced herself to stand. Moving in a wide arc around Wendell's body, she went to the creek and dropped to her knees. Rinsing her mouth, she drank a little. She rose and shot a quick glance at the road agent's corpse.

Something gnawed at her. She knew very little about him, except that he'd lived the life of an outlaw. He'd robbed stagecoaches, kidnapped her and her father, perhaps even murdered. Nonetheless, Sheila told herself, the Christian thing would be to say a prayer or something over him.

She put one foot in front of the other and walked slowly toward his body.

As she approached, she looked past the blood-soaked ground, past the savaged throat. She kept her gaze on Wendell's face.

281

His eyes were open, and he stared blankly at the patch of sky above the spruces.

With the exception of when her mother died, she'd never seen a dead person before arriving in Colorado. Her eyes had been closed.

Sheila was nine years old when her mother passed. It was summer, and most her family's friends had fled the oven-like city to places where cool sea breezes made the season bearable. Those with loved ones off fighting the Southern rebels could not escape their fears, no matter how far they ran.

Her father couldn't come home to bury his wife. He was away at war. Not fighting, but plying his medical skills. Sheila knew nothing of it at the time, but he was trying to save lives in a bloody place called Groveton, where General Lee and his forces had nearly annihilated the Union's armies.

Before the funeral started, Sheila's grandparents took her into the front parlor where the casket sat open on a table she'd never seen before. The room was filled with the cloying scents of a thousand flowers. Her grandfather, stiff and businesslike as always, walked with her to the open casket. Her grandmother stood back, weeping quietly. Her mother looked at peace, as if she were sleeping. She was wearing a navy-blue, velvet walking dress that she loved. It struck Sheila oddly that they would dress her in that on such a hot day.

She had looked very different from the man lying at her feet now.

Sheila crouched down and closed the man's eyes.

She'd seen Dodger take the revolvers, but it occurred to her that perhaps Wendell had something that could help her. She glanced at his boots, where he kept a knife. She could see the butt of the handle, peeking out. Reaching down, she withdrew it, sheath and all.

"I know you won't mind, Wendell," she murmured. "It's a matter of survival."

Dodger had already gone through Wendell's pockets, but she checked them anyway, hoping she might find something else that might help her, anything that might give her an added ounce of courage as she plunged off into the wilderness. There was nothing.

Sheila started to get up but stopped. She rolled the dead man's body to the side. His coat had pulled when Dodger removed the gun belt. She almost cried out when she saw the derringer tucked into a holster fastened to his waistband.

"Thank you," she said as she took the small weapon.

It was a Remington firearm, and when she broke it open, she saw there were two un-fired bullets in the chambers. She slipped it into the pocket of the duster with his knife.

The derringer wouldn't kill a bear, but she hoped it would be loud enough to at least scare a wild animal away.

She rolled Wendell onto his back and stood. Leaving him like this beside the creek seemed wrong. But what choice did she have? She couldn't bury him. Besides, she thought, she'd probably be dead as well before too long.

Still, she had to do something.

Sheila took his cold, limp hands and dragged him a few steps from the water to a boulder beneath an aspen tree. She was shocked at how heavy he was. She laid his arms at his side, arranging him in what she decided would be a respectable manner.

At the edge of the pool, in a place where the sun warmed the ground, a patch of small, white flowers had just begun to bloom. Although she realized it was a fairly ridiculous gesture for a hard-bitten outlaw and the situation, Sheila picked a small bouquet anyway and placed it on his chest.

Standing back, she addressed him. "I'm

sorry I can't do more for you, Wendell. If there were a minister here, he could say a few words. But I'm the only one to send you off. So I'm just offering up a prayer that you find some forgiveness before you meet your Maker. Amen."

The sheriff and his men had followed them from Elkhorn, and Sheila knew Dodger's plan had been set before they left town. Wendell did kidnap her, thinking she could be used as a pawn against her father, but he agreed to her plea and stopped to let her make water. If he hadn't, she'd be in the grasp of those outlaws right now.

"But before I go, I will tell you this. I'll never forget what you did for me."

Sheila walked away and stood for a moment by the creek. Behind her lay the trail to Elkhorn. She checked the timepiece pinned to her shirt under the vest. It had stopped when she went into the river, but she judged it was somewhere between three and four in the afternoon. They left town before dawn and had ridden almost without stopping. If she tried to go back, she'd never make it by nightfall. She'd be dinner for a pack of wolves, for sure.

Sheila stared the other way, at the trail where Dodger and the sheriff had gone. Wendell told her they were about ten miles

285

from the outlaws' camp. If she followed, she'd be walking directly into the maw of the tiger. At the same time, she'd get to the camp close to sunset.

And she'd be going to where her father was.

The dangers in either direction were real, but she knew what she had to do.

It was possible her father was still needed to keep someone alive. If she approached the camp with caution, maybe . . . though it was a vague and unconvincing *maybe* . . . she could be a help to him. She touched the derringer she'd tucked into her duster.

"I hope you were right about the ten miles," Sheila called back to Wendell as she splashed across the creek.

Chapter Twenty-Seven

The sharp report of a rifle in the distance drew Doc Burnett's gaze to the window. It echoed off a distant ridge, coming back before either he or Lucas moved.

Doc stood and instinctively moved to his patient's side. He realized he couldn't do much to protect her, if needed. Still, she was his responsibility. At the same time, Lucas was on his feet and bounding to the doorway, where he peered out into the golden, late-afternoon sun. His cocked six-shooter was in his hand.

"What was that?" he yelled out.

"Dunno. Jeb's up watching the trail."

Lucas turned to Doc and shot a warning glare at him. "You stay here. Don't move, and don't make no noise. You hear?"

The young outlaw didn't wait to get an answer and slipped out the door.

Doc took a step closer to the door, listening. A spark of hope flared inside him.

Perhaps Wendell and Dodger had been captured when they went to his house in Elkhorn. Perhaps the judge had forced them to tell him where they'd taken Doc. Or perhaps they'd had to make a run for it and a posse had pursued them back to the outlaws' camp.

He was the only doctor in the area, and miners and townsfolk called on him day in and day out. He must have been missed, having been gone for five days. They had to be on the lookout. He could very well imagine the judge directing the sheriff to have someone watch the house. And even if the town officials had done nothing, he believed his friend Caleb Marlowe would be concerned about him.

The thought buoyed his spirits tremendously.

Gunfire erupted, and two shots struck the shack, one piercing the wall on the far side of the doorframe with an explosion of splinters. For a half minute, the shooting continued, with shots being returned from right outside. When it halted, Doc heard muttered curses not far from the open door.

In his mind's eye, Doc envisioned an army of men surrounding the camp. Their sole intention was to rescue him and the wounded passenger.

"What . . . what is it?"

He turned to his patient and found her eyes open. Her lips were dry, her brow covered with sweat. He sat beside her. The fever was worsening.

"Were those gunshots?" she asked. "Tell me. What's happening?"

"I think we're being rescued."

Doc reached under the cot and pulled out the surgical tools he'd stored there. Choosing a scalpel, he slid it into his jacket pocket. He'd do whatever he had to do to help the men coming to free them.

"Rescued?" Her voice was breathless and seemed to border on panic. "Who?"

"I'm hoping it's a posse from Elkhorn."

He moved to the edge of the doorway and peeked out. Lucas had taken shelter behind a cart with a broken wheel that sat akilter beyond a cooking fire. Another outlaw with a rifle was sprawled with his back to a water trough closer to the shack. Both were reloading their weapons, anticipating the next move of the attackers.

"Though I don't have great faith in the town sheriff — the man could kill us by accident — I'd be happy to see a troop of one-armed monkeys out there if they rescued us."

No more shooting. For the moment, all

was quiet, but surely the storm was about to break.

Doc glanced around the shack to see if there was anything they could use to protect themselves from stray shots. He fully expected a hail of bullets to perforate the wood walls any second now. There was very little that could be useful.

The cot groaned, and Doc looked over his shoulder. His patient was trying to sit up.

"No . . . no! You can't be doing that." He hurried to her side and gently pushed her back down. "You're not well enough."

The fever was causing her to act irrationally. He needed to calm her somehow. She needed to feel a sense of confidence that help had arrived. That they were about to be saved.

He only prayed that was true. If he didn't operate on her soon, however, none of this would matter.

"Even if it's the sheriff, he'll recognize me. But it might not be him at all. It could be a friend of mine, Caleb Marlowe. The man is one of the best trackers in the West. He could have organized a posse of his own to come after us. He's a good man. The best shot in the . . ."

Doc realized he was talking too much in his excitement of them being rescued. His words were not doing anything to reassure her. The woman had a death grip on his hand. Her eyes were wide open and wild. And she was obviously trying to get his attention.

"What is it?"

"Where is Lucas?"

He was surprised, but only for an instant, that she would know the outlaw's name. She'd been drifting in an out of consciousness for days. While they had been imprisoned here, Lucas's name had been mentioned a number of times.

"Outside, trying to get himself killed, I'd say."

"No!"

She tried to sit up again, but he stopped her.

"I know this is distressing, but you need to lie quiet. There's nothing we can do right now. The fight is between them. We're safe here." Well, reasonably safe, he thought.

Gunfire started up again. A barrage of bullets was exchanged, and the shooting kept up for a long while. It was relentless. The front wall of the shack was hit a half dozen times with holes opening with a spray of dust and splinters. Doc huddled over his patient, all the while knowing that if he were killed, her chances of survival were nil. Even so, his protective instincts were driving him.

Luckily, none of the bullets struck either of them, but the outlaws were not so fortunate. Over the crackle of gunfire, he heard one of them yelp in pain and curse aloud after being shot.

Doc realized that very few shots were being returned by the road agents. But they were not giving up.

"I have to stop him," she said thickly.

"Stop who?"

"Lucas. Let me go. I have to go out there."

Doc looked into the woman's face and saw tears in her eyes. They filled and then ran off across her temple, disappearing into her hairline.

"Please." She tried to sit up again, but she wasn't strong enough. "Help me up."

"Why are you worried about Lucas?" he asked, unable to comprehend her concern.

"He's my son," she whispered raggedly.

Bits of information began to arrange themselves like chess pieces in his mind. Lucas staying here in the shack constantly. The obvious discomfort as he watched Doc digging the bullet out of her shoulder. The anger over her pain and the insistence on giving her something to relieve it. His blistering words to the two road agents when he sent them off to Elkhorn for the medicine and surgical instruments.

"They've come for me," she said. "Me. And I can't let my boy die."

"For you?" He felt like a simpleton, babbling and repeating her words.

"I'm . . . I'm Mrs. Fields."

Doc stared at her. The name meant nothing to him.

"These men . . . they work for me. I'm the one responsible. I plan the Wells Fargo robberies. I'm the one . . . the one they want. Not him. Not my son. I have to save him."

Doc found himself standing beside the cot. He wasn't aware that he'd risen. His brain was filled with mud. He was slogging through a bog, trying to keep up with what she was telling him. It didn't make sense. How could she be . . . ?

Comprehension dawned in his mind. And with it, every mistaken assumption regarding road agents and outlaws evaporated like morning mist on a woodland lake. She wasn't kidnapped. She wasn't a victim. In barely a moment, this woman — Mrs. Fields — destroyed every image he had regarding what a band of stagecoach robbers looked like.

The gunfight was continuing, but suddenly the sound of pained cursing reached them. Still, shots were being returned by the outlaws.

Hearing it, his patient cried out weakly. She was not about to be held down any longer. She sat up and, with what was clearly a monumental effort, pushed her legs off the cot. The stockinged feet thumped to the floor. She was sitting, but she could go no farther. She hadn't the strength to push up to her feet.

"Wait," he ordered, recovering his bearings. "You wait right there. I'll see what I can do."

Doc tried to think of what he possibly *could* do. He had no idea how he could help this woman's son.

Perhaps if he could communicate with the men who'd laid siege to the camp. Perhaps if he could convince Lucas to drop his weapon and hand himself in.

"You haven't been out of that bed in five days. You're weak and feverish. If you try to get up, you'll just fall and make things worse."

As if they could get worse, he thought.

"You stay put," he ordered again before moving cautiously toward the door.

How could he do anything while bullets continued to fly?

He peered around the doorjamb just as

one of the rescuers' shots found its mark. The road agent by the water trough sat back and then stretched out flat on the ground. Doc glanced quickly at Lucas, who was staring at the body of his partner.

"Throw your weapons down, Lucas," he shouted out at him over the sound of gunfire. "Surrender before it's too late."

The young man's gaze slid to the door of the shack. As he began to shake his head, a bullet struck him, sending him spinning forward to the ground. He writhed in the dirt, clutching his arm, and then shoved himself back up against the cart. Doc saw blood flowing through his fingers.

"Stop shooting," he shouted, waving his hand in the doorway. "I'm Doc Burnett. Stop shooting."

The gunfire slowed and then stopped completely.

"He'll surrender."

A short period of silence followed, and then a voice rang out.

"Stand up, Lucas. And throw your gun out."

Doc was shocked to recognize Dodger's voice. Why the killer was attacking his own gang, he couldn't fathom.

Hope turned to doubt. All the trust he had of being rescued faded. He shrank back from the door.

"Throw your guns out now," Dodger repeated.

Lucas was staring at the shack, his eyes filled with worry. Doc understood this boy so much more clearly now.

"Don't get yourself killed," he murmured to himself, "for her sake."

Lucas sat thinking, his gaze moving from the door to his arm. Finally, he threw the pistols away from the cart.

"Where is Lucas?"

Doc glanced back at his patient and nodded. "He's alive."

She closed her eyes and started crying quietly.

From where he stood, in the shadow of the shack's interior, he watched Dodger, Sheriff Horner, and three armed deputies striding toward them.

Dodger and Sheriff Horner. The last shred of hope that remained in Doc's mind faded.

Of all these outlaws, Dodger had struck him as the most vicious. He was the one who shot the miner outside of town. He was the one who killed the man who wandered into their camp. And here he was, walking with Horner like they were old friends.

And if there was a more ruthless cur than

Gant Horner wearing a sheriff's badge, Doc had yet to meet him.

Chapter Twenty-Eight

"What the devil?" Caleb muttered, eyeing the body across the clearing.

He'd seen his share of dead men left by a trail in his time, but he'd never encountered one like this.

Pirate stamped his foot, not entirely happy to be reined in within sight of the creek ahead. They'd been covering ground quickly for a while, and he was thirsty.

Caleb held him, though, and unfastened the thongs on his twin Colts.

When you found a dead body looking like this one, you didn't want to rush into anything. The last thing you wanted was to walk right into an ambush. He'd had quite enough of that lately.

He scanned the area carefully, looking in every direction. The clearing around the creek and the pool of water by the trail was empty, and he had no sense of anyone lurking nearby. But it didn't hurt to exercise a little more caution than usual.

Caleb sat still, listening intently for anything above the sounds of the creek, the falling water, and the nearby river. Nothing looked or sounded unusual.

Of course, there was *nothing* unusual about a corpse laid out, miles and miles from anywhere, looking like he was waiting for mourners to file by and pay their respects. The guest of honor was even sporting a handsome bouquet of fresh flowers.

And them flowers were fresh. They looked like they hadn't been picked more than a couple of hours ago. He searched around him again. Still nothing out of the ordinary.

"What do you think, Pirate?"

The buckskin snorted, conveying his lack of interest.

"All right, boy." He dismounted. "Go get yourself a drink."

As Pirate wandered off toward the creek, Caleb studied the ground. It wasn't difficult to read the signs. The riders had entered the clearing from the direction he'd come. They were the same seven horses he'd been tracking since he spotted the first cut branch, including the one with the gash in the shoe. They all stopped here, leaving evidence of their presence in the soft ground.

As Caleb moved about the clearing, it all made sense to him. By the creek, the men dismounted, watered the horses. He didn't need to cross the shallows to know they rode out along the trail that way afterward, still moving north along the river.

Caleb stopped by the edge of the creek. A water flask was floating in an eddy. Not far away, the dirt was discolored. He glanced at the body. This was blood from the dead man's severed jugular. More signs of a scuffle. Not that it was much of one. From the marks by the water and the location of blood, he judged the man just finished filling the flask when he had his throat cut from ear to ear. He'd fallen here, and then someone dragged him to his present location and fussed some, making him presentable.

As he turned to take a closer look at the body, Pirate brushed by him and helped himself to the dead man's flowers.

"That ain't right, Pirate." He pushed him out of the way.

Crouching down, he studied the face. Caleb had a good memory for people he'd seen before. This fella was definitely not someone he'd run into in Elkhorn or anywhere else. The throat had been slashed with a single rip of a blade. To cut through all that took a

300

sharp knife and a fairly strong hand. The killer had even wiped the blade off on the victim's coat. Very tidy of him.

There was no sign of any fight that went with the killing. No bloodied knuckles, no mashed nose or bruises of any kind on the sharp features. Everything told Caleb some low-down dog had attacked the fella from behind, and he guessed it was someone he knew.

He once again stared at the way the body was so carefully and respectfully arranged.

Caleb couldn't imagine some outlaw bothering to do such a thing after murdering the man. Unless he wasn't right in the head.

He looked carefully at the drag marks between the creek edge and here. It was among all the men's boots and the marks left by the horses.

"A woman's boot. What do you know!"

Pirate raised his head from the pool where he was drinking but kept his opinion to himself.

The woman wearing those boots was not all that big either. He looked around the area.

"Here," he muttered to himself. "Here is where she dismounted, and she stood talking to someone right here."

He measured the length of the boot print of the man she talked to and went back and compared it with the dead man's boots. It was the same.

"The two of them stood in front of each other." He followed her track toward the river. They led down a dry stream bed right into the river. After scouting along the bank, he saw where she came back out of the river, waited a bit, and then went back to the clearing.

He went back to the body and studied how neatly was arranged.

"Only a woman would do this."

He thought of Sheila Burnett and all her complaining about the dead men at Caleb's ranch. *She* would do something like this.

"No," he said aloud. She was back in Elkhorn. As impulsive as she was, she wouldn't come this far away from the town in the company of a total stranger.

A thought occurred to him. Whoever this woman was, she was riding with the first group. So was this dead fella. She was off by the river when these other riders showed up and did the killing.

On a hunch, Caleb crossed the shallow creek and studied the tracks on the far side.

There they were, clear as bear paws in fresh snow. Those boot prints led north after the other riders.

He whistled for his horse and mounted up. "Damn me, Pirate, if she ain't following those killers on foot."

CHAPTER TWENTY-NINE

"Lucas has been shot in the arm," Doc told his patient.

"Go out to him," Mrs. Fields pleaded.

"I can't right now."

From the shadows, he peered through the doorway. The light was fading, and the darkness was deepening in the surrounding hills. Lucas was surrounded by the men Sheriff Horner had with him. The conversation was not friendly.

"At least he's alive."

"Thank God," she murmured. "What about my other men? Can you see them?"

Doc looked at the outlaw lying dead by the trough. There was no sign of the fellow who'd been up watching for intruders, the one they called Jeb. He guessed he'd been the first to face Horner and the first to die.

He glanced at his patient. "I'd be surprised if any of them have survived."

"They're dead?" Her face clenched with a

pain that had nothing to do with her own bullet wound. "All of them?"

"I wouldn't hold out much hope for them." He peered out, trying to make sense of what they were doing to Lucas.

"Perhaps Wendell and Dodger got away."

"I can't say about Wendell, but Dodger is out there, big as life. He seems to have led Sheriff Horner right to your door."

"Dodger? I shouldn't be surprised." She clutched the blanket. "We only hired him for this last job. He's a nasty young man."

"Well, you're right about that."

"If he's working for the sheriff, he probably turned Wendell in."

Or killed him, Doc thought. Dodger was cold and heartless.

"Poor Wendell. They'll hang him for sure." She sighed bitterly. "I suppose we'll all hang."

The outlaws were asking Lucas questions outside about where the loot was hidden. And they weren't doing it gently. The young man didn't appear to be answering anything.

"I'm not so sure that's what Horner has in mind."

Doc frowned thoughtfully at his patient. As weak and feverish as she was, Mrs. Fields was clearly a well-spoken woman. It still amazed him that she could be the leader of a gang of stagecoach robbers. Be that as it may, if they were to somehow miraculously survive, he needed to know more about her.

"Who knows you're the leader?" he asked.

"Everyone who worked for me. But it was a secret they'd all sworn to keep. And I trusted them. I should say, I trusted all but . . ." The name withered on her lips. "Wendell was supposed to keep a close eye on him."

"Not close enough, I'd reckon."

Doc had known many men in his life like Dodger. They'd swear to anything. But if money was involved, they'd deny they ever made a promise. Men with no sense of honor. They'd kill their brother for a ten-dollar gold piece.

And Dodger would kill for far less. He'd seen it with his own eyes.

They were beating Lucas badly now, kicking and pounding him with the butts of their rifles. Doc knew that as soon as they tired of that sport . . . or killed the boy . . . they'd be coming this way.

He went to her and picked up the bottle containing the last of the morphine and brought it to her lips. "I want you to drink what's left and —"

"I can't." She shook her head, fighting him. "I need to help Lucas. If I talk to them . . . I can't if I'm drugged."

Doc took hold of her arm and looked sternly at her. "That may be the only way you can save him."

"What do you mean?"

He had a thousand questions and no time to ask them.

"Horner has thrown away his badge. From what I'm seeing, he's working for himself. He and Dodger are trying to get Lucas to tell them where you've hidden your stolen money. Does your son know where it is?"

"Only what we took during this last robbery."

"It sounds like they're looking for more than that."

"Everything we've taken from Wells Fargo for the past five years was divided among the men, except for a percentage that I kept and put away. Lucas doesn't know what I did with that money."

The voices outside were getting louder, more insistent.

"How much do they think you're hiding?"

"The men told me that rumors have spread, exaggerating the truth. They say people believe we have a half million or more in gold and paper currency buried somewhere."

Doc's head swam with the number. Even

if she had a fraction of that amount, she'd need an army to protect her.

"I have no interest in your money," he said. "But you need to tell me something of the truth, so I know what to do when I face these men. Otherwise, I don't know how I can protect you and your son."

In spite of her fever, the deep-brown eyes were earnest and the gaze steady. "I trust you, Dr. Burnett."

He nodded. "Is the fortune nearby? Is it hidden somewhere around this camp? Could they drag you around the camp until you showed them where?"

"I haven't a dollar to my name. There's no money or gold left."

He stared at her, not believing what she said. But why should she trust him? "I understand your hesitation, even though you say you trust me."

"I mean what I say. There is no fortune."

Again, she knocked the wind out of him. Questions arose in his mind, but he silenced them. Lucas cried out in pain, and Mrs. Fields's face turned to the door.

"Whether there is or there isn't, these men believe you have that fortune. They want it, and I think they'll do anything to get it."

Certainly, murder was not beyond them.

"I'm asking because if they think they can

beat the truth out of Lucas . . . or you . . . we're in deep — perhaps fatal — trouble. However, if they think the money is somewhere distant and they *need* you to take them there, then we can use that for leverage and force them to keep you both alive."

Dodger's voice lifted above the others outside. "Like I told you, he don't know nothing. It's the mother we gotta squeeze."

Lucas's pained response was muffled, but Doc could hear the note of impassioned pleading.

He had to hurry. Half-baked plans formed in his head.

"Do you understand? If you physically cannot answer their questions, and your survival is questionable, then they need to keep Lucas alive."

She closed her eyes and then shook her head. "But for how long?"

"I don't know. All I'm trying to do right now is to buy us some time." He lifted the bottle to her lips again. "Drink this."

"It doesn't make me sleep. I just drift in a dream somewhere. But over these past few days, I still heard most of what you and my son said to each other."

"Then pretend. Play possum. You have all the symptoms of a dying woman." As she should, he thought, keeping this to himself.

"Giving them any information won't save our skins. Yours, mine, or your son's."

Footsteps were approaching the door.

"Do as I say," he urged her. "Trust me, and we may be able to save your son's life."

The woman nodded, and she drank what was left of the sedative. He pocketed the empty bottle.

"Now close your eyes," he ordered.

Mrs. Fields did as she was told, and barely a second later, men barged into the shack.

"See here, Sheriff," Doc said sharply as he stood to face the man. "I have a wounded woman here."

Horner ignored him and looked past him to Mrs. Fields, lying on the cot. Behind him, Dodger and another man dragged Lucas in and dumped him unceremoniously at Doc's feet. Two other ruffians that he recognized as the sheriff's deputies crowded in as well.

"I'm telling you I won't have you and your men parading through," he said, stepping between Horner and Mrs. Fields.

Horner looked at him, spat on the floor, and cleaned some tobacco juice off his drooping mustache with the back of his hand.

He turned to his men. "You and you, go bring the horses up and bed 'em down in that there corral." As the two men went out, he gestured to the one who'd helped bring Lucas in. "You get out there and keep watch. And drag that carcass off somewheres. I don't want to be tripping over him."

That left only Horner and Dodger in the shack.

Lucas groaned, and Doc immediately knelt beside him, inspecting the extent of the young man's injuries. A bullet was still embedded in the arm, but the bone didn't appear to have shattered. His nose was bent at a bad angle, and his eyes were already swollen shut from the blows delivered to his face. And this was only what he could see. At least he was alive.

"Well, Doc," Horner said over his head. "Glad to find you here."

He pushed to his feet and looked into the man's foul face. "I wish I could say the same."

The sheriff hitched up his trousers. "We come all the way out here to save your hide, and that's the thanks we get?"

"I heard you out there, and the way I see it, you came out here to line your pockets."

"You ain't got no call saying that, Doc. We're here to rescue you and recover stolen property." He spat on the floor again. "But it sounds like you don't trust me."

"I wouldn't trust you to recover a pig's ear from a privy hole."

A dangerous look came into Horner's eye, but Doc was beyond caring about that. He hadn't trusted this man from the first moment he met him.

He scoffed at the tin star on the man's chest. "Don't you think you should throw that thing away if you're done serving the law?"

"What makes you think the judge ain't sent me?"

He motioned to Dodger. "You're standing next to this deranged pup, for one thing."

The young killer took a threatening step toward Doc, but Horner put his arm out, stopping him.

"So you're here. You have your outlaw." Doc gestured to Lucas, lying nearly unconscious at his feet. "What else do you want?"

Horner took a step to the side to look at Mrs. Fields. Doc so hoped the woman was doing a good job pretending to be asleep.

The sheriff turned to Dodger. "He don't know?"

The young outlaw shook his head. "Don't think so."

"I don't know what?" Doc asked.

Horner nodded toward the woman. "You know who she is?"

312

"They told me she was a passenger on the stagecoach. She was wounded when these cowards robbed it."

Horner exchanged a look with Dodger, who was glaring at Doc. He clearly didn't like being called deranged or a coward.

"Did you fetch my surgical instruments from the house?"

"They're outside. How about you and me go out and fetch them together?"

"Never mind that," Horner snapped, asserting his authority. He moved toward the cot. "I need to talk to her."

"This woman is doing very poorly. In fact, she's dying. That's why I sent this one and his friend to Elkhorn for my supplies. If I don't operate, she might not live even two days."

"I don't care if she don't live two minutes. I need to talk to her."

"Why?"

"That ain't your concern."

Doc frowned at the man. "Well, it's not possible. My patient has been enduring tremendous pain, so I gave her all the morphine I had left."

He took the empty bottle from his pocket, showing it to him.

Horner pushed him aside and stood over Mrs. Fields, watching her heavy breathing.

Beads of sweat covered her brow. Her face was flushed. Her fever wasn't something she was faking. Horner reached down and shook her hand. There was no reaction. Doc had to give the woman credit. She showed no signs of awareness at all.

"Wake her."

"I can't, but the dose I gave her will wear off before long. She'll come around soon enough."

"How soon?"

How long would it take before someone came to their rescue? Doc knew he was wishing for the impossible. Mrs. Fields and her gang had been hiding out here for ages, and no one had found them out. In the five days he'd been here, only one poor fellow had wandered through. Other than that, no one had come but these villains, and they were led here by Dodger.

Still, he wasn't about to make it easy for them.

"Maybe by morning. Unless she dies first."

CHAPTER THIRTY

The sun was dropping quickly. Darkness would soon slow him down, but Caleb thought about the woman following the outlaws. She couldn't be too far ahead of him, and he wasn't going to stop until he caught up with her.

These mountains held dangers for anyone, on horse or on foot. The fierce and brutal laws of nature applied here. It was a fact of life. The weak fell by the wayside. The strong — with some luck — survived.

He found signs of her as he rode along. He'd seen her footprints in the mud at the convergence of a stream and the river. The trail of the road agents' horses had turned inland, and her tracks had followed.

As he nudged Pirate along, Caleb could only think of one reason that would drive a woman to tramp so resolutely through the wilderness. It was the will to survive.

The trail skirted a low area that had been

flooded in the spring. Standing water still lay in swampy pools, smelling fetid. Trees, stunted and bent, looked tired, wounded.

A vague, clouded memory came back to him. It was one of his earliest recollections. It was from an afternoon in his childhood. He didn't know how old he was at the time. Two? Three?

He and his mother were on some muddy lane, moving along as fast as she could drag him. Marshes, stinking and populated with snakes and ratlike creatures and snapping turtles that could take a boy's hand off, spread out on either side of the road.

His mother was holding his wrist so tight, it hurt him. He had to run to keep up with her. He was dog-tired, whining at her.

"Where are we going? Carry me."

They'd been hurrying along forever, and she didn't speak. Not a whisper. Not a word to soothe him.

Suddenly, tall, monstrous trees loomed up in front of them, dark and ominous with sharp branches like claws, poised to snatch him.

"No, Mama. Let's go back. I don't like it here."

A gloomy tunnel, bordered by swampy, foul-smelling woods. Clicking, buzzing sounds and ravenous flying creatures. A long, dark-furred animal darted across the road, disappearing into the boggy space between the black trees.

Caleb set his feet, fearful of passing, but his mother pulled him along.

He stumbled in the slippery muck, but she kept him upright, moving forward. The darkness of the woods ahead filled him with cold fear. He didn't want to go.

He glanced up at his mother and found her looking over her shoulder, her eyes peering through the murk. She wasn't afraid of what was ahead. She was terrified of what they'd left behind.

Real or a nightmare, Caleb never forgot. That's how memories went. To this day he didn't know if what he saw that day was real or if it was a slice of some nightmare. His mother never spoke of it. She never allowed him to mention it.

And he understood clearly now what he couldn't grasp then. His mother had to run to survive.

The tragedy was that she'd never been able to run far enough.

Caleb shook off the dark memory and looked ahead. He couldn't change the past. The path in front of him was the only one that mattered.

And somewhere up there, in the fading

light, a lone woman was chasing after some
very bad men.

CHAPTER THIRTY-ONE

Sheila followed the trail, moving as quickly as she could manage. The sun was slanting toward the western ridges, and more than once she questioned her decision about following the sheriff and Dodger and the others.

She worried about what would happen once night fell. Whether she reached the camp or not, she had no plan. And spending the night alone in the wilderness filled her with fears of wild animals. She'd read the stories about wolves so ferocious, they pulled grown men from horseback. And about grizzlies as tall as train cars and strong enough to tear a buffalo apart with one swipe of their razor-sharp claws. And about mountain lions, stealthily stalking and then pouncing on some great animal, bringing down a full-grown elk with a single bound . . . and then toying with the wounded prey as a housecat plays with a mouse. In the end, every story was the same, and it never turned out well for man or buffalo or elk.

The recollections made her walk faster, but the danger didn't change the fact that this was the better choice. The distance was shorter, if nothing else. And her father could be at the end of this journey.

Luckily, the trail didn't branch off very often, and when it did, the tracks of all the horses made it obvious which way they'd gone. She began to have imaginings of herself as a scout.

Not long after leaving the creek, Sheila had stripped off the duster and squeezed as much water from it as she could. She did this with as little slowing of her pace as she could manage and proceeded to wring out the water from the hem of her skirt. It made a difference. After an hour or so of walking, her clothes were still damp, but she was warm from the exertion.

The trail turned inland and moved into the hills at a point where a wide, swift-flowing stream joined the river. She followed the tracks. This was heavier going, since she would climb through a meadow to the top of a ridge, only to see a valley spreading out before her and another steep hill to climb on the other side. She kept going, though.

The path moved along the base of rocky bluffs that rose hundreds of feet in the air. It meandered through dense groves of evergreen. She splashed across creeks and picked her way across rocky fields. Only once did she think she might have lost the trail, but when she reached a muddy stream and saw the hoofprints, she breathed a sigh of relief.

As Sheila walked, she thought of her father. For a long time as she grew up, she'd been angry with him. After all, he'd left her and gone on to adventures that she couldn't share. Her grandmother and her tutors always tried to impress upon her how fortunate she was to have a father at all, never mind one with the presence of mind to leave her where she could grow up safely and be educated according to her place in society. Wasn't it better, they asked her, to be in the greatest city in the world, among decent, civilized people? Did she want to be "stolen by red Indians and raised to be a heathen squaw"?

Sheila knew there were many falsehoods that people in the East believed about natives, but *her* opinions were formed by the letters she received from her father. There was a world out there and people in it that her grandmother knew nothing about. She had never even stood in the same room as an Indian, never mind spoken to one.

Hunger was beginning to gnaw at Sheila, and she wished she had some of those "heathen" skills right now.

In New York, by the time her friends began to marry, Sheila had been thinking for a long time that the world was greater than the one she was raised in. There was far more to life than the endless cycle of social calls and tea parties and concerts and salons. After all, her father had found a place from which he never returned. Colorado. Even the name sounded enticing. She was glad she had come.

How strange that at time like this, when her life hung by a thread, she should think of these things. She only hoped she could keep her wits about her and be strong enough to live through this.

The sun bumped along on the mountains to the west and then slipped down behind them. A glorious glow of colors spread across the blue canvas. Rich hues of red blended with orange, mauve, purple, and blue, fading slowly. But for Sheila, the encroaching gloom now made every tree and boulder look threatening. She began to hear the sounds of night birds and animals, both near and far. The hooting of an owl, the yips and barks that sounded like dogs but that she knew were coyotes.

Sheila walked as fast as she could until the darkness was complete and she was forced to slow her pace. Her courage began to fail. She had difficulty staying on the trail, could barely see it, and then it simply vanished.

She looked up at a sky filled with the brightest stars she'd ever seen and wished she could read them like a mariner on the sea. Squinting to see any sign of man or horse, she crept along, feeling lost. Something large moved in the brush not far from her, and she pulled away. She had to keep going, so she felt her way, Wendell's knife in one hand, his derringer in the other.

Gradually, the star-filled sky began to brighten to the east. The waning moon, like a rescuing angel, edged up over the distant hills. She began to see a little better.

And then she smelled smoke. The scent of beans. A cooking fire.

She climbed a hill, hoping to see a glow cast by the flames. She slipped the derringer into her pocket and scrambled upward through the brush, grabbing hold of branches of scrubby pine trees with her free hand. The slope was rocky and steep.

By the time she'd nearly reached the top,

her breaths were short, and her legs burned from the effort. But the smell of smoke was stronger. She hurried across an open space toward a jumble of huge boulders that topped the hill and cast moon shadows back at her.

When she tripped over something on the ground, the image of Wendell — lying on his back by the creek — flashed across her mind's eye. Before she even landed on her hands and knees in the stones and dirt, she knew what it was. The heavy sack-like presence. The rustle of cloth. It was a man.

Her blood ran cold. Still holding her knife, she rolled and scrabbled back a few feet until her hand touched the thick felt of a hat brim that had fallen to the ground. His hat. She peered at the dark shape on the ground. Whoever it was, she knew he was dead. At that precise moment, the moon rose above the boulders behind her, illuminating the body.

Sheila stood and slowly backed away.

Another victim of Sheriff Horner and Dodger, she had no doubt. She only wondered who he was.

The sound of a shout beyond the boulders cut into her thoughts. It was so close.

Sheila turned and moved through the shadows as noiselessly as if she were one of them. She found a narrow crevice between two boulders, and the flickering light of a fire reflected on the sides. Flattening her body, she slipped between the rocks. On the other side, she found herself on a wide stone ledge that sloped upward.

As she crouched lower, she realized she was still carrying the dead man's hat. She let it drop and edged forward.

The moon glowed on the half dozen ramshackle buildings beneath her. At the far end, a graveyard of discarded wooden equipment of various shapes guarded the open entrance of a mine. One long trough, broken down in places, ran from a small river that glinted with reflections of the shaved white orb in the sky. Hills encircled the camp, giving it a protected, bowl-shaped look. And in front of one of buildings, three men sat around a campfire, talking. One of the voices occasionally rose, arguing some point. By another building, a corral held a dozen horses, and the saddles on the rails gleamed.

She'd made it. Somehow, Sheila had trailed them through the wilderness. She had successfully followed them to their camp. But what now?

There was no sign of her father; she was certain he was not one of the men around the fire. She needed to find him. She prayed he was alive.

As she watched, trying to decide on a plan, a man came from somewhere near the buildings and crossed to the horses. After saddling one of them, he mounted up and rode out of the camp, disappearing into the night.

Sheila knew she couldn't stay where she was. She was not really any safer from animals here than she was on the trail. And if she survived the night, when the morning came, she'd be worse off. At least now, she could use the darkness to her advantage.

She made up her mind. She had to find a way down into that camp then slink through the shadows until she found the building where her father was being held. At the same time, she didn't want to fall into the hands of Dodger and the sheriff. She shuddered at the thought of it.

Somehow, she needed to become invisible. She could not let herself be found.

Sheila heard nothing. She sensed nothing. But when a man's large, rough hand clapped over her mouth, terror fired through her like a lightning bolt.

Chapter Thirty-Two

When Horner and Dodger left the shack, night had been fast approaching, but that was some time ago.

Doc laid a hand on his patient's forehead. It was hot, and the bullet wound in her shoulder was looking more inflamed all the time. As he touched the skin around it, her eyelids flickered and opened for a moment. She made an effort to speak, but she couldn't quite manage it before her eyes closed again.

He looked at Lucas. The sheriff had warned him not to touch the young man lying unconscious by the stove. Doc was afraid that if he went against Horner's orders, it would be worse for the outlaw.

At the sound of someone riding out of the camp, he got up and stood by the open door, looking out at the dark forms silhouetted by the crackling fire. He counted four. They were talking and arguing about their

327

accomplishments in the gun battle. He couldn't tell who was there, or whether the sheriff or Dodger sat among them. He didn't hear their voices.

He didn't know who had ridden off in the darkness, and he couldn't think of a reason why they would go, unless it was to keep watch for intruders.

He scanned the bags and gear piled up near the men, looking for his valise and surgical case, but he couldn't pick them out.

Lucas moaned, and as Doc looked around at him, he felt his anger and frustration growing. It wasn't in him to sit and do nothing while two people were suffering. Horner's callousness was worse than despicable. Even after a battle during the war, most commanders allowed the enemy forces a chance to recover the wounded so they could be tended to.

He looked back out at the men around the fire, wondering what Horner was planning, wondering how it would all end. He didn't have a good feeling about it.

Lucas stirred by the stove and began to regain consciousness. He was clearly in pain, and Doc could no longer refrain from seeing to the injured gunslinger. Going over, he began to work on the young man.

The bullet had lodged itself in the biceps

brachii. Somehow, it hadn't exited cleanly, but it hadn't broken the humerus, either. He was lucky about that, anyway.

As Doc worked, Lucas bore the pain with as much courage as any man could hope to demonstrate.

"Don't let them bastards hurt her," he said through clenched teeth. "Let her die if you got to, Doc, but don't let her suffer."

Mothers and sons, he mused. The relationship between a parent and a child was a complicated one.

If he got through this, the first thing he was going to do was pack a bag, ride to Denver, and board a train for New York. No more letters. No more waiting. He'd surprise her and hold her in his arms, as he should have been doing for too many years.

"What are they doing?" Lucas asked.

Doc continued to work on the battered face of the young man. When he finished cleaning the cuts and the abrasions, he'd need to straighten that nose.

"What's going on out there?" the outlaw repeated, trying to sit up.

Doc leaned back and looked out the door. He couldn't see either Horner or Dodger. "I don't know. They've been gone for a while."

He again turned his attention to the

injured arm. To save it, he'd need to dig the bullet out soon. Dodger said the medical supplies and equipment were outside. He considered going out to fetch his things. To slow the bleeding for now, he grabbed one of the washed bandages, put it over the wound, and wrapped the young man's own bandana tightly around it.

"I got a knife in my boot," Lucas told him. "If you'd stand me on my feet near the door, I can kill one of them when they come back in. Maybe both them. You can grab for their guns and —"

"Hush. Somebody's coming."

Horner strode back into the shack and scoffed at the sight of Doc bent over the wounded man. "No point in that."

"He's bleeding to death."

The sheriff kicked an empty barrel across the floor, where it banged hard against the wall and rolled away.

"I don't *give* a damn," he shouted. "He ain't gonna . . ."

Horner stopped abruptly. He was staring at Mrs. Fields. Doc saw it too. The woman had flinched when he kicked the barrel.

"She's awake."

The sheriff moved to the cot, and Doc got there right after him. The patient's eyes were closed. She said something under her breath and rolled her head from side to side.

"Wake up," Horner poked her on the arm.

"She's hallucinating. It's the fever."

"I say she ain't doing nothing but faking it."

"Feel her forehead. Have you *never* seen a sick person in your entire life?"

Mrs. Fields's face was flushed; her hairline and the collar of her dress were soaked with sweat. Doc laid his hand on her forehead.

"The woman is burning up. No one can fake this, Horner."

The sheriff's hands rested on his pistols, and he kept his eye on her. "When will this stuff you gave her wear off?"

"I told you, maybe tomorrow morning."

"There's gotta be a way you can wake her up sooner."

"There isn't." Doc decided he needed to change things up a little. "Who is she, anyway?"

"I told you before. It ain't your concern."

"Dodger said I don't know something. What is it?"

Horner ignored the question, continuing to stare at her face, waiting for her to flinch or show some hint that she was conscious.

Doc motioned toward Lucas, lying on the floor. "Why are these outlaws . . . and you . . . . so eager for her to get better?"

"She can die, for all I care. But I want to talk to her before she does."

"Why?"

"You really don't know?"

Doc ran a weary hand over his face. He hadn't shaved in days. He'd barely slept. "I reckon she's someone they planned to use to collect ransom. That's why they kidnapped her and brought me to see to her wound. But if you're telling me something different . . ."

"She's Mrs. Fields."

Doc gave him the blankest look he could muster. "Is that supposed to mean something to me?"

"She's the head of this outfit."

Horner was always fond of running his mouth, and Doc decided to keep him going. He wanted to learn more about her, but he also wanted draw the man's attention away from her face.

"That's impossible."

"And she's sitting on her loot, Doc. A fortune in loot."

"What are you talking about?"

Horner shot him a look of superiority. "I'm talking about what I know from a drifter up north. Said he rode with her gang. 'Course, I don't believe that. The fool also claimed that he rode with Quantrill, the

James boys, and even Dirty Dave Ruda-baugh. He was a lazy, lying sumbitch. Dead now. He threw down on me in a card game, and I gunned him down like the filthy dog he was. But I'd known about the Fields gang for a long time, and what he said fit."

"Well, I've never heard of the Fields gang."

"That's cuz they got themselves going out in Montana." He nodded at Mrs. Fields. "This one's husband got into a beef with some Wells Fargo men in the gold fields out there. They done killed him and her son . . . her older son."

He spat on the floor and looked at Lucas.

"That right, boy?" When the young outlaw said nothing, the sheriff strode over and kicked him in the arm. "This one's her other boy."

Lucas was writhing from the pain, and Doc instinctively took a step toward him. The young gun warned him off with a look.

"And this fortune you think she's sitting on came from her husband?"

Horner walked back to the cot, looking at Doc like he was the village idiot. "Hell, no. With her husband and boy dead, she wants revenge. She starts her own gang, hitting Wells Fargo stages."

Doc shook his head. "I believe someone has sold you a bill of goods, Horner. There is no way this woman, at her age, could be a stagecoach robber."

The sheriff glanced down at her once more and then strutted toward the door. "Don't matter what you believe, sawbones. It's the truth. Fifty robberies from California to Colorado. Maybe more. And that's a lot of money stashed up here somewheres."

Doc shook his head. "What makes you think *this* gang is the same one?"

"I've been trailing after them for a while. Me and a dozen other men all over the West. But it weren't till my man Dodger got picked up by these folks as a hired gun. That there was my way in, and here I am."

Horner stood by the door and looked out. "Why not take them in to face justice in Elkhorn? If you're so sure, there must be a good reward out for her and her gang."

"I ain't looking to take no scanty-ass pittance of a reward when there's thousands to be got here."

"Thousands?"

"*Hundreds* of thousands."

Doc scoffed. "How could one person have so much? She had a gang to split the stolen property with."

"Dodger says she takes the lion's share after each robbery and divvies up the rest."

Doc recalled her words earlier. *I haven't a*

dollar to my name.

"I figure she's hiding her take close by," Horner told him.

"And you think she'll tell you where it is?"

"She will cuz I have her son. And she ain't gonna sit still while he gets skinned alive in front of her eyes."

"What kind of a brute . . . ?" Doc reined in his temper. "I don't believe you'd do such a thing."

"Oh, I ain't doing it, Doc. You are."

He took a step backward. "I'll be damned before I do."

"Then damned you'll be." The sheriff grinned maliciously. "Cuz you'll be breaking out your skinning knives as soon as Dodger comes back . . . with your daughter."

"My daughter?" Doc's stomach dropped. Anger roared in, replacing his shock. He could tear Horner's throat out . . . but what if he was telling the truth? "But she's —"

"The lovely Miss Sheila Burnett come in on the Wednesday stagecoach from Denver. And she was in Elkhorn until this very morning. Dodger and the man you sent for your surgical things found her in your house and decided she was too pretty to leave behind."

The doctor felt the blood drain from his

head, and a cold, sick feeling gripped his stomach. His hand went into his pocket and closed around the handle of the scalpel. He'd kill these bastards. But before they died, he'd make them suffer far more than anything they could imagine.

"If you *touch* my daughter, if there is one hair —"

"Shut it, Doc. That don't mean nothing to me. Dodger is the one bringing her here, and believe me, he's keen as mustard to keep her."

"If he hurts her in any way, I'll kill him and then I'll kill you."

"I'm quaking in my boots, Doc." Horner laughed. "But I'll tell you what. I ain't unreasonable. Maybe we can come to an understanding, you and me."

He spat on the floor again.

"But while we wait, you go ahead and start sharpening them knives."

CHAPTER THIRTY-THREE

Caleb held his hand firmly over her mouth. The last thing he wanted was to frighten Doc's daughter, but he didn't want to alert whoever was down in that camp.

He didn't expect the warmest of greetings, but the knife flashing toward his face didn't exactly say, *Mighty glad you happened by, Marlowe.*

Catching her wrist, he stopped the blade about an inch from his eye.

He pulled his hand from Sheila Burnett's mouth, still holding her knife hand with the other, and she spun away. As she turned, her other hand was diving into the pocket of the duster for something else.

"Hold on there," he ordered in a low voice.

A derringer appeared, and he managed to get his hand around it before the thing went off and she put a hole in his hide.

Her eyes were flashing fire in the moonlight, and she looked fiercer than that cougar he faced earlier today.

Thankfully, she recognized him immediately, and her mouth dropped open.

"Marlowe!" she exclaimed as he let go of her.

"Keep your . . ." His words were cut off as she threw herself at him, wrapping her arms around his waist. Her face was pressed against his chest, and he could feel the butt of the knife and the little pistol against his back. He didn't know if she was going to accidentally stab him or shoot him.

"Keep your voice down, Miss Burnett," he said in a gruff whisper.

Before Caleb could say anything more, or even pat her on the back to comfort her, she jumped away from him with the speed of a bobcat.

He looked over the edge at the camp and the men around the fire. They were far enough away that her outcry hadn't drawn their attention.

"You're here," she whispered. "I can't believe my luck."

"Never mind that." He nodded to the derringer that was waving in his general direction. "Why don't you let me hold that cannon of yours before you put a bullet in me and let them boys down there know we're here."

"There's no need, Mr. Marlowe." She slipped the pistol back into her pocket. Pulling a leather sheath from the other, she slid the knife in and pocketed that as well.

"All right. Then why don't you tell me what the devil you're doing out here?"

She was wearing her father's duster, buttoned up all the way to the throat. At the bottom, a skirt protruded, as well as the boots that left the prints he'd been tracking. Her hair was hanging down her back in a thick braid, and a wide-brimmed hat was lying on the ground.

She shook her head. "I barely know where to start."

"Hold on, miss." He put a hand on her arm and had her crouch down next to him as he peered down at the camp. It was plenty dark out, but he didn't want that moon reflecting anything that would make them a target. Reaching back, he picked up the hat and put it on her head. "Try to keep your face in shadow. It's mighty bright out here."

He'd seen a woman climbing the hill. Before he spotted her, he'd been smelling smoke, and he knew he was close to a camp. So he tied Pirate off the trail and followed her up here. He'd been damned surprised, though, to find that the woman he was tracking was Sheila Burnett.

"Honestly, I never thought anyone would come after me. Come after *us*." She was frowning. "I thought I'd die here, right here on this rock. After everything that's happened, I'd never get to my father. That vile sheriff would kill him down there, and no one would ever know what happened to us."

"Horner is here?" Caleb wondered what the hell he was doing here and what he was up to. The judge said he was keeping the sheriff in Elkhorn.

"He came today." She looked over the edge. "He's down there now. But he's not a good lawman. He's only wearing that badge to . . . to . . . I don't know *why* he's wearing it. But I can tell you, he's no better than the ones who have my father. He doesn't care that men kill each other in cold blood."

This came as no shock to Caleb.

She was staring at one of the shacks. "I haven't seen my father yet, but I'm praying he's still alive."

"Before we figure out what we need to do, Miss Burnett, why don't you start at the beginning and tell me how you got here?"

"Sheila. Please call me Sheila. I've been

through too much today to deal with formality."

"Fine, Sheila. How'd you get here?"

"It started this morning. Actually, it was before dawn. I woke up to hear two people downstairs in my father's house, going through his things."

"Let me guess. You went down there and confronted them."

She jabbed her elbow into a rib still sore from his wrestling match with that cougar.

"Give me more credit, Mr. Marlowe."

He didn't know why he should. She'd come out to his ranch in the middle of the night, trailing after a half dozen rustlers. But he decided this wasn't the time to rile her. She was right. She'd been through the wringer today, and he wanted the story.

"Go on."

"One of the men must have heard me. He came up and found me. Then the second one came up, and they tricked me into going downstairs with them. They said my father sent them, which I suppose was technically true. They were in Elkhorn to refill my father's medicine bottles and bring his surgical case back with them. When they had everything, they forced me to go along."

"Did you know them?"

She shook her head.

"Was the sheriff one of them?" he asked.

"No. One of them was a man named Wendell. The other was called Dodger."

At the miner's cabin, Imala had mentioned Dodger's name. These had to be the same two who forced Smith to go and get Doc.

"Was Dodger young and big?" he asked. "A nasty sorta fella?"

"Nasty? He's a heartless killer and a pig. I was terrified what he'd do to me without Wendell there."

"I take it that was Wendell laid out by a creek a ways back?"

"You found him."

Her eyes welled up, glistening. Caleb saw a surprising mix of sadness and pity flit across her face. It set him back some. Then her lips thinned, and her face hardened a little.

"Dodger killed him," she said in a voice like ice. "He stood behind Wendell and cut his throat. When Sheriff Horner arrived only a minute or so later, I saw that Dodger was working with him. He was leading the sheriff out here."

She faced the camp, and Caleb saw the derringer appear in her hand. "Oh, how I would enjoy seeing him get a taste of his own poison."

342

He didn't think he'd mention it while she was holding that gun, but Miss Sheila Burnett of the New York Spencers had changed quite a bit since giving him hell about dead rustlers.

"How come the sheriff and them other fellas didn't get you at the creek?"

"I was out of sight, attending to private business. That was when Dodger murdered him. I just hid until they all rode off."

"That was a brave thing, hiding that way. And smart."

She shivered. "Wolves and bears are far less frightening than Dodger and the rest."

"Why follow them, then?"

"Wendell had said it was about ten miles to this camp. It was much farther to Elkhorn. I found they hadn't taken his gun and knife, so I decided to try to find my way here. I thought perhaps my father could use my help. But once I got here, I wasn't sure what to do next. And then you arrived."

Caleb thought about what it meant, Horner being out here. There was always a chance that the sheriff was doing what he was paid to do — stopping these Wells Fargo robberies. And it was possible that he somehow got this Dodger fella to turn on his own gang and lead him out here. Horner would be within his rights to overlook the killing of outlaws like Wendell and the man on the hill here. But Caleb knew Horner, and nothing smelled right about any of this. And from the way the judge spoke, he didn't trust the sheriff either.

Even so, he'd need to be sure what Horner was up to. And Caleb was glad Doc's daughter had showed enough sense not to walk right into that camp.

He stole a glance at her profile. Sheila was wearing the look of a soldier ready to go into battle. She had more of her father in her than he thought.

She pointed to the only shack they looked to be using. Light was spilling out the open door, and smoke was coming from a stovepipe. "I think that's where my father is being kept . . . and maybe the passenger who was injured in the stagecoach robbery."

"How many were with Horner?"

"Three armed men and Dodger."

He looked down into the camp. He hadn't seen anyone go in or out of that shack since he got here. Caleb counted three men around the fire. They looked like Horner's deputies. And if his eyes weren't deceiving him, there was a lifeless body stretched out over by a water trough.

"I tripped over a dead man on the other side of these boulders. This is his hat." She tapped the brim.

"Saw him. He ain't gonna be needing it."

Preacher mentioned five gang members plus the leader of the outfit. There were at least that many horses in the corral.

He looked around at the surrounding hills, wondering whether they might have posted another guard to watch for trouble. If they had, he was sure to be as dead as this one.

"Anyone left the camp since you got here?"

"One person rode out just before you scared the daylights out of me. I couldn't see who it was, but he went that way."

If Caleb had come a few minutes later, he would have run head-on into the fella.

He was willing to wager that the Wells Fargo gang was all dead, with the exception of the one Sheila saw leaving. And the chances were that man was Dodger, because if Horner was up to something — and Caleb's instincts said he was — then the sheriff was not about to let any of the other gang members go free.

He thought for a moment and then decided.

"This is the plan," he told her. "Whoever's in that shack — and I'm guessing it's Horner and the gang leader, at least — I want to get them out in the open. If I don't, as soon as the bullets start flying, they could use your father as a hostage."

She nodded. "So how are we going to do it?"

"There ain't no *we*. You'll stay here and hide. And whatever happens, don't let nobody see you. If it all goes bad, my horse, Pirate, is down at the bottom of the hill that you come up. As soon as it's light enough, you ride —"

"No, Mr. Marlowe," she said with an edge sharp enough to cut stone. "That's my father down there. I intend to help. Now, you can give me a job to do, or I'll have to think of how I can make myself useful."

One stubborn woman, Caleb thought. Well, there wasn't time for arguing with her.

As he looked into her determined face, it struck him that maybe she had a right to be. The woman had been through hell in one day. Kidnapping. Witnessing a murder. Tramping ten miles at least through unfamiliar wilderness. Smart enough to find this place and smart enough not to get caught by killers.

Surviving all of that took more than just luck.

"All right. I have a job for you. But you have to follow it every step of the way."

"Absolutely. I'm excellent at following directions."

Caleb doubted it, but he was willing to give it a try.

CHAPTER THIRTY-FOUR

As Caleb and Sheila started back toward his horse, a chill breeze began to pick up, and above them, across the vast expanse of star-studded blackness, ragged plumes of clouds moved quickly in a procession. Shadows raced across far-off peaks, and the distant cry of a wolf was answered by another, even more distant.

Caleb steered wide around the corpse at the top of the hill, and he turned to see how Sheila was doing. It was difficult to determine with the wide brim of the hat putting her face in shadow. But her footsteps were quick and sure, and she didn't lag behind. They moved carefully down the rocky hillside, holding branches of scrub pine.

The skies had been so clear over the past week or so, but Caleb thought that any added shadow could be a help to them. They needed to use the darkness. Surprise would be their greatest advantage.

They reached the place where he'd tethered his mount. Taking his Winchester from its scabbard, he hesitated and then turned to Sheila.

"You ever shot a gun?" he asked, keeping his voice low.

"Many times. I used to go target shooting all the time in New York."

He reached into one of the saddlebags and pulled a pistol out of the holster of a rolled gun belt. The short-barreled Colt Gunfighter had belonged to one of the bushwhackers who ambushed Zeke and Everett and the others. He held it up, and the barrel gleamed like silver fire in the moonlight.

"I'll trade you this gun for the one in your duster. That toy would be lucky to hit a barn door ten feet away."

He waited as she dug the derringer out of her pocket.

"I don't want you shooting anything unless you have to," he said as they exchanged weapons. "But I want you to have it for your protection."

She slipped it into the duster.

"Now, let's go do what we planned."

The two skirted the hill, following the trail leading into the camp. When they reached the clearing, Caleb led her into the deep shadows of an abandoned shack. Silently, they crept up until he could see the entire camp.

Before the Wells Fargo road agents took it for their own, the place had been a mining camp. The layout resembled a large, elongated horseshoe, with the trail entering at the left side of the heel. At the top-most point in the shoe, the abandoned gold mine gaped like the open maw of a long-dead giant.

Amid piles of gravel and dust in the center of the camp, derelict carts, barrels, rocker boxes, and cradles, long toms, and broken wheelbarrows had been dragged out and dumped and left to decay. The winter snows and the rains and the summer suns had clearly done their work, and remains of former industry lay scattered and broken. Caleb supposed they would have provided fuel for fires if the mine had continued to produce, but his thoughts now dwelled on how they could be used for cover in the upcoming fight.

A long sluicing trough, broken now in four or five places, stretched from the front of the mine to a wide creek that ran behind the buildings opposite, where Caleb crouched with Sheila. Halfway down the untidy row of buildings on their left, the makeshift corral held the small herd of horses. That was where he would position Doc's daughter. Hopefully, out of harm's way.

Almost directly across from the corral, perhaps fifty yards or so, the sheriff's men sat jawing around the fire. Their rifles were visible, propped up and handy for use, should the need arise. Beyond the men and the fire, he could see the open door of the shack where Sheila thought her father was being held. Lamplight still glowed from inside, and wisps of smoke drifted from the stovepipe.

To the right of the occupied shack, two burned-out buildings stood together. Charred corner posts and black roof joists, sitting askew where they'd fallen, were all that remained. Next to them, another shack had fared slightly better. Only the roof had collapsed, and the walls still stood, silvery in the moonlight. From there, at the open heel of the horseshoe, the pine-covered hill led upward to the ledge where he found Sheila.

Caleb had his plan set in his mind.

Then, just as he started to draw back, a figure appeared in the door of the shack, silhouetted by the light behind him. It was Horner, talking to someone inside, standing and holding on to his lapels like the Lord

Mayor and looking like the cock of the roost.

Caleb gestured for her to go to the left. They moved together behind the buildings, staying low and keeping to the shadows when they could. It took only a few moments to reach the building behind the corral.

He left her at a corner where she could see the mine entrance and the place where a pile of gravel partially hid the long trough. That was where she was to remain until she saw him move into position there and signal to her.

Caleb moved quickly from the back of one building to the next. When he reached the last one — a dilapidated storehouse for hay and grain — he peered across at the men around the fire. They were still lounging. The doorway of the shack was empty, and the sheriff was nowhere to be seen.

Keeping the discarded equipment and the gravel piles between him and Horner's men, he reached his designated place. Quietly, he cocked his Winchester.

He had very little doubt that the sheriff was here for his own benefit. What Horner wanted had nothing to do his sworn duty. Still, he needed to be absolutely sure. Caleb hoped his plan would give him the answer and that Doc and his daughter would not suffer for it.

He took off his hat and waved it to the side where Sheila could see it. Just as he did, a cloud drifted in front of the moon, casting the camp in shadow. He glanced up at the sky, cursing under his breath.

The plan was for her to scream loud and clear and draw the sheriff out of the shack and his deputies into the open area. Where Caleb was situated, he would have clear shooting straight down into the heel of the horseshoe, avoiding both the corral where Sheila was located and the shack where Doc was. But all the planning in the world wouldn't matter if he couldn't signal her.

He frowned, waiting impatiently for the cloud to pass.

One of the men at the fire stood, stretched, and started for the corral. Caleb wasn't about to risk him stumbling into Sheila.

When the deputy got halfway across, Caleb stood and got him in his sights. The man was only about eighty yards away, and Caleb could have taken him down with a rock.

"Well," he muttered. "The best damn schemes of mice and men . . ."

Before he could squeeze the trigger, the moon reappeared. Sheila must have been able to see him clearly, standing with his rifle at his shoulder, because the shriek she let out could have curdled milk. And she kept it up, riling the horses something fierce.

The deputy in the center of the camp stopped dead in his tracks, but the other two were on their feet in an instant. They grabbed their rifles and started for the corral. The man in the lead drew his pistol and ran toward the horses.

That was when the sheriff himself finally came out of the shack, his pistols drawn.

Caleb waited until Horner got out beyond the campfire before shouting, "Stop right there, boys!"

They all froze, their heads swiveling as one toward him.

"It's me, Sheriff," he called out. "Caleb Marlowe. The judge sent me out here, so that puts us on the same —"

Horner's Remingtons were spitting fire before Caleb could finish. And Horner was moving his fat carcass back toward the shack as quick as he could go.

"Kill that sumbitch!" he was shouting at his deputies as he ran.

That was all Caleb needed to hear.

He swung his Winchester toward the man closest to the corral. He was running hard and firing on the run. Caleb's rifle barked, and the deputy took one more step before pitching forward into the dirt.

Dropping down behind the gravel pile, he levered in another cartridge and looked back at the sheriff. Horner had nearly made it to the doorway of the shack. *Damn.* Caleb couldn't afford to shoot and miss. Not with Doc inside.

As the sheriff was about to reach the building, though, the door slammed shut, and Horner — still firing in Caleb's direction — didn't see it until it was too late. He bounced off the door and landed on his ass.

The sound of crackling gunfire filled the camp. Bullets thunked into the gravel dust and the trough and whizzed past him. He sidestepped, swinging the rifle toward the two men raining down bullets on him. They'd quickly taken cover, one behind a rubble pile and the other behind a stack of barrels. Caleb fired a volley at each of them and glanced over at the shack. The door was still shut, but there was no sign of the sheriff. He'd disappeared.

Caleb moved quickly along the trough toward an upended cart. He wanted to get to a better angle on the gunman behind the barrels. Before he could reach the cart, one of the shooters' bullets struck Caleb's Winchester square above the trigger, behind the loading gate.

355

At first, Caleb thought he'd taken the bullet in his hand. The rifle was knocked from his hand, and he dropped to one knee, clutching his wrist as the pain flashed up his arm and into his head.

The deputies were not letting up, and the shots continued to thud into the trough and the ground around him. If he stayed there, he was a dead man.

He dove for cover, drawing his left side Colt. Holding his numbed right hand up, he saw there was no blood, no hole, and all the fingers were accounted for. But the pain in his arm was bad.

As he lay there, trying to breathe and clear his head, he knew it was futile to think that the feeling in his hand might come back. It didn't change the fact that he had to take these two. If he didn't, Doc's and Sheila's lives were over.

The deputies were calling to each other, planning their move. Caleb glanced around the edge of the cart and saw the deputies running on an angle away from each other. They planned to catch him in the crossfire.

Caleb stood and took aim at one of them. At seventy yards in the dark, hitting a moving target would be a tough shot. One thing he was sure of, though: his left hand was as good as his right. The ball struck the man in the chest, putting him down. He writhed and shuddered in the dirt for only a moment then lay still.

He swung the Colt toward the other deputy. Seeing his partner fall, the man veered off, heading instead for the corral. He spun and ran, firing shot after shot.

Caleb was not about to let him reach either Sheila or those horses. He squeezed the trigger twice, hitting him with the second shot. The bullet knocked the man's head askew and sent him hatless off to the Promised Land.

Caleb swept his gaze toward the left, searching out the sheriff. This was not over.

After hitting the door, Horner had disappeared. The only place he could have gone, however, was into the shadows behind the row of buildings. Back there, the wide creek washed along the base of the hills. Caleb could see the thick, dark evergreens covering the hillside with a thousand places to hide.

His right arm was completely numb now, and it hung loose at his side. If he was going to go after Horner — and he was going to do exactly that — Caleb couldn't have the damn thing flopping around. After putting his pistol down, he reached across, drew his other Colt, and pouched the iron on his left hip. Carefully, he slid his injured hand into the right holster.

He heard the crunch of gravel on his left, and turned to see Horner step out of the shadows. His Remington was leveled on Caleb.

"Ain't this something?" the sheriff sneered. "It'll be a fine thing, crowing about how I outdrew Caleb Marlowe."

"Did you, snake?"

Horner raised his pistol just a whisker before firing. That was all Caleb needed. Lightning never struck with the speed that his left hand moved.

Both pistols fired almost simultaneously, but only one bullet found its mark. Horner's head snapped back, then righted itself. The round hole in the center of the sheriff's forehead, an inch above the bridge of his nose, trickled blood, but Caleb knew the man had bigger troubles where the bullet left the back of his skull.

The sheriff's body sagged, his hands dropped, and he collapsed backward onto the ground.

Caleb walked over and looked down at him. A little tobacco juice dribbled from the corner of Horner's mouth into his drooping mustache. And as Caleb watched, the life faded from the man's eyes.

CHAPTER THIRTY-FIVE

Doc Burnett pulled open the door and rubbed the bruised shoulder he'd used barricading it against the sheriff. Beyond the campfire, a cowboy in a duster and a wide-brimmed hat was coming across the open space and stopping to look at each dead man.

Caleb strode up, pistol still in hand, and Doc greeted him like the hero he was.

"Damn me, Marlowe, but I knew you'd come. Somehow, I knew it."

"Ain't nobody else in there to worry about, Doc?"

He glanced back at the open door. "Well, that's complicated. But the short answer is that you don't need to be worried. I'm sure as hell glad you're here, Marlowe."

As Doc thanked Caleb, he tried to shake the cowboy's hand, but Caleb's right arm was hanging loose at his side. He gestured toward it questioningly.

"Got the feeling knocked out of it when one of them knotheads got lucky and hit my rifle. Busted the damn thing. A good rifle too."

"Let me look at it."

"Ain't nothing, Doc," Caleb said, grudgingly submitting to a cursory examination.

Nothing appeared to be broken. The impact of the bullet striking the rifle had numbed the limb, but he was certain the feeling would soon return, and he told Caleb so.

When the cowboy coming from the corral reached them, she threw off her hat, and Doc forgot about Caleb, his arm, the sheriff, the outlaws, and everything else in the universe.

"Sheila," he croaked, his throat tight.

Her face lit up, and there was no hesitation as she ran toward him. The pages of time flipped backward. Doc was once again the tired but happy father, coming up the front steps after visiting with a patient. And she was that little girl in the doorway, delighted that he was home.

"Papa."

His arms closed around her. He held on to her as she held on to him. She was safe, he kept telling himself. *Safe!* When Horner told him they had Sheila, the pain that had clawed at his insides was far worse than death.

Doc would have done anything they asked him to do in return for her safety. He couldn't allow her to be hurt. Even as he told himself that, however, he'd known in his heart that both Horner and Dodger were evil men. Whatever promise they made was sure to be a lie.

He couldn't believe it. His daughter was here, a bit worn and tired, but she was alive. And they couldn't harm her. She was out of their reach.

They held each other for a long time, and Doc was not ashamed of the tears coursing down his cheeks. His heart was about to melt.

Suddenly, she pulled away from him, wiped her own tears away, and then looked at the open door of the shack.

She shot a glance at Caleb. "Dodger. He's not one of the dead men."

He was standing a few feet away, discreetly focusing on reloading his pistols. Not an easy task with one functioning hand.

"Do you know anything about a fella named Dodger?" Caleb asked Doc.

"He's one of the road agents, but he was working for Horner. He rode out a while ago." Doc gazed at his daughter. "He was going back to look for you."

Caleb holstered his pistols and motioned toward the shack. "You two stay inside. I'll take a look around."

Doc ushered his daughter in. Lucas was sitting beside his mother and holding her hand. Other than a quick look in their direction, the gunslinger didn't say anything more. He was very pale, and Doc was surprised he was even upright. Mrs. Fields's eyes were closed.

"Let me look at you."

He sat Sheila on a barrel by the stove and dragged another over for himself. He cupped her chin with one hand and gazed into her face. How many years had it been since he'd last seen her? Six, seven, eight? His mind was too slow to recall. She was no longer a child but a young woman in the prime of life.

"I'm sorry I didn't write to you and say I was coming to Elkhorn," she told him, taking his hands and holding them in her lap.

"I'm sorry I sent those fellows to the house in the middle of the night." Horner had tormented him with the story Dodger had related to him about finding her there. He had so many questions for her, but the most pressing ones had to do with her safety. "Did they hurt you? Were you . . . ?"

"No, Papa. I'm fine. Tired from that journey. And damp from going into a river. And still a bit stunned by it all. I can't believe everything that has happened, but I'm fine. More important, you're safe and well. I was so worried."

Her voice was strong, and Doc hoped she was telling the truth. "The two that went to get my things, were they . . . were they rough with you?"

She held his gaze. "One of them, Wendell, was actually decent with me. Before he was murdered, he was watchful and protective, in a way. I was able to escape when Dodger killed him."

He wanted to hear the whole story. How she came to be in Elkhorn. How she escaped. How she and Caleb connected. Doc owed his friend a great deal.

But just then, Caleb came into the shack, eyeing Lucas warily. "Who's this, Doc?"

Lucas struggled to his feet, but he was unable to stand straight.

"This is Lucas Fields," Doc explained quickly. "He and his mother are the last of the outlaw gang. And the only weapon on them was this."

He handed him the knife the outlaw had hidden in his boot.

"Dodger dead?" Lucas asked.

Caleb ignored the question, glancing down at Mrs. Fields as Doc continued.

"Dodger was in league with Horner. And he was worse than any of them."

"Not *was,* Doc." Caleb flexed his hand and winced. He must have been starting to get the feeling back in it. "Far as I know, Dodger could be up in one of these hills right now, waiting to get a shot at us. Can't tell from down here, though. I have to go look around some."

Doc motioned to the mother and son. "These two need to be operated on. He's been shot and beaten by the sheriff and his men. Her situation is more critical."

"I ain't going far," his friend replied. "I don't want to leave you alone here."

He started to go out then stopped and nodded toward Mrs. Fields. "The woman is running this outfit? I heard the leader of the gang was some former war hero who had a bone to pick with Wells Fargo."

Doc was glad Caleb knew something of their history. "It's a long story, my friend. But I'm sure Lucas will be happy to answer all your questions while I operate on his mother."

Lucas frowned but nodded.

"And right now, I need to find my surgical case and valise."

Sheila jumped up. "I saw them by the fire. I'll get them."

She started going out, but Caleb grabbed her arm. "I'll get Doc's things. It ain't safe out there with that Dodger fella on the loose."

Sheila took the Colt six-shooter out of her pocket and waved it at him. "No worries, Mr. Marlowe. I'm armed."

Pushing past him, she went out the door. Doc looked in surprise at Caleb. "She's changed a great deal in the past few years."

"Past few years?" Caleb scoffed. "This past *week*."

Waving Doc off, he went out after her.

CHAPTER THIRTY-SIX

Lucas Fields was staring into the fire. "I don't think you need to worry much about Dodger."

Caleb studied him. The road agent's face was pale, and he'd obviously taken a pretty good beating, but he was trying to tough it out. He'd done what he was told and been polite to Doc and Sheila. He certainly was not the killer that Caleb had expected to find when he left Elkhorn. Lucas was more like the way the preacher described this gang of outlaws. And he kept frowning anxiously at the shack where his mother was being operated on.

Caleb stretched and flexed his sore arm again. This had been a full day, starting with that tussle with the cougar.

Once Doc went to work on Mrs. Fields, with Sheila at his side helping him, Caleb had gone out to bring Pirate in. He'd climbed the hill to that ledge overlooking the camp and the trail. When he looked down on the camp, the moon was setting, and he decided it was too far for a clear shot with the breeze that had picked up. Piling some rocks on the dead outlaw up there, he retraced his steps to Pirate. After riding the buckskin back to camp, Caleb fed him, watered him, and left him in the corral.

Dead men were scattered hither and yon, so he took out one of the other horses. Throwing a rope around each of the bodies, he dragged them off to where the sheriff lay next to a gravel pile. He lined them up and covered them with stone and dust, thinking that was more than Horner would have done for him and Doc and Sheila. After gathering up all the weapons and stacking them together, Caleb put their horses in the corral and came back to the fire.

He sat with his back to the shack, a Winchester '73 that had formerly belonged to one of the deputies across his lap. He'd seen no sign of Dodger, but if the gunslinger came riding into the camp, unaware that there had been a fight, he'd be ready for him.

"What makes you think Dodger won't come back?" he asked Lucas.

"I think he'll smell trouble and hightail it.

I've seen the way he handles himself, and he ain't one to face trouble on his own or head-on. He thinks he's smart, but he needs someone else telling him what to do. Don't get me wrong, though. If he's got a grudge, he'll gladly shoot you in the back."

Caleb thought of the man he'd found by the stream with his throat cut. Wendell. He was attacked from behind. And how appropriate that Dodger should work for Horner. Another backstabber.

"If he thinks there's trouble waiting for him here, where do you think he'll go?" He was still a killer, and Caleb wouldn't mind bringing him in to face justice.

"North, probably. He already got what he was owed after this last robbery. He'll look for another outfit to join up with."

Doc already told him Mrs. Fields would need some time to recuperate before she could move again. If she survived the operation.

Caleb glanced across the open space at the place where the trail came into the camp. If the killer didn't stumble in here unawares tonight or tomorrow, he'd feel a little easier about believing Lucas was right.

"You know all this, but you kept him on in your gang. Why?"

"Not kept him on. He was new to our

outfit. We'd lost a gun, and we thought it best to bring on somebody for the one last stage we wanted to hit."

Lucas moved slightly, holding his arm gingerly. Blood had soaked through the bandana wrapped around it.

"Ma had a bad feeling about him as soon as she met him, but we didn't listen to her. She did the planning. Me and Wendell ran the men. He was gonna keep an eye on Dodger."

"From what I heard, your outfit never was big on gunning down drivers and stagecoach guards. Dodger is a killer."

"I know that now. By the time we figured out we shouldn't have hired him on, the bodies were dropping."

Caleb hesitated. He had something he needed to find out. "The miner they took to get Doc from town. What happened to him?"

The young man stared into the fire. "Friend of yours?"

"It makes no difference. Did you kill him?"

"Not me. Not Wendell neither. Dodger shot him when they were bringing Doc up to the camp. It was all his doing. Doc can tell you."

Caleb thought about the miner's wife. He

owed Imala an answer. He knew she was plenty capable of living alone. Still, he worried about the trouble she could butt up against coming to Elkhorn on her own to sell her things.

"What happened to his body?"

"They left him where he fell," Lucas said. "Wendell said out on the Denver road somewhere. I'm really sorry about that. I'm sorry about them two dead Wells Fargo men too. That ain't our way."

Caleb was still trying to figure out what kind of people these were. Before he could ask another question, Lucas put in one of his own.

"Who was this sheriff? He was wearing a badge, but he was definitely working for himself."

"Grat Horner."

"Was he the sheriff in Elkhorn, or are you?" He nodded toward the tin star on Caleb's shirt.

"He was sheriff. But you're right about him working for himself. I don't think he planned on going back there."

Lucas started to say something but stopped. Caleb wondered what it was. Instead, the outlaw rubbed dried blood from the corner of his swollen mouth and touched his broken nose.

"From what I heard them say tonight," Lucas continued, "he and Dodger went way back. There's no way Horner could have found his way out here if that rat didn't lead him to us."

Caleb didn't want to sit out here all night and talk about Dodger and Horner, but there was one question that burned on his tongue.

"Where's your father?"

"Dead and buried out in Montana. Alongside my brother."

When Preacher told Caleb about them, he mentioned no names. He also said nothing about this being a family outfit. He only talked about the father.

"I'm listening."

Lucas peered toward the door of the shack. "Why do you want to know?"

"I was hired to come up here and bust up your gang. I'm supposed to bring you all in. But I don't think the authorities in Elkhorn know a woman is running this outfit."

Or if they knew, they weren't telling. He thought of Preacher again and how insistent he was that Caleb knew these were not bad people.

"Why do you want to know?" he asked again. "Why do you care?"

"Curious, I guess. I want to know whose

371

necks I'm sticking in a hangman's noose."

Lucas shrugged. "If I tell you what you wanna know, how about you take *me* back and leave her to go her way?"

The young man was willing to die to save his mother. Lucas didn't have many chips to bargain with, but Caleb's respect for him grew, anyway.

"Well, let's just see."

"Do you know anything about us?"

"Only what I heard from a tough old fella who calls himself Preacher."

Lucas brightened at first, obviously remembering the man, but suspicion immediately darkened his face. "He didn't show you the way out here, did he?"

"I asked him, but he wouldn't say."

"I didn't think so." A smile tugged on his mouth. "But I don't know why I'm complaining. If it weren't for you gunning us out of this, that sheriff would have killed me and my mother, and Doc too. There wouldn't have been no trial and no hanging."

"I'm still waiting."

"I'll tell you everything," Lucas replied. "But don't forget, you promised only to take me in."

He scoffed. "I ain't made no promises."

"I know. But a man can hope."

372

Caleb took notice of the sadness in the way he said the words. Lucas was begging for his mother's life. The young outlaw looked again at the light spilling out of the shack before turning to Caleb.

"The preacher told you something of my pa?"

"Said he was a brave fella who ran into trouble with some Wells Fargo men out in the gold fields."

"And did he tell you that he took his wife and children with him out to Montana?"

"He said nothing about family."

"Well, it was four of us children out there. And it wasn't just prospecting, though he did that too. He bought himself some land for a ranch and sent for Ma and us to go out there right after he was settled."

The muscles in the young man's jaw tightened as he tried to keep a hold on his emotions.

"When those Wells Fargo agents came out to the ranch, it was the middle of the night, and they came with a gang of gunmen carrying torches. My pa and my brother were shot down before a word was spoken. I was only twelve then. But what we never talk about outside of family is that my two younger sisters died that night too."

Caleb felt sick, not wanting to imagine

373

what might have happened. Whatever it was, the husband and three children belonging to the woman in that shack had been murdered.

"After killing my father and brother, them animals went after the rest of us. They couldn't find us. My ma and me were out in the fields beyond the barn. My sisters must've gone to hide in the root cellar. When the bastards set fire to the house, me and my ma couldn't get my sisters out."

Lucas covered his eyes with his hand, and Caleb looked away. He knew what it was like to lose everyone you care for overnight. But he locked down his own childhood memories, burying them deep in the back of his mind.

The sighing of the evergreens in the soft night wind and the crackle of the fire were the only sounds, and he doubted they offered much comfort. No words could soothe a grief like that.

They sat in silence for a few moments. Finally, the high-pitched yelp of a coyote close by in the hills came to them, and then the distant answering note of a trailing mate. It roused Caleb, and he stood up.

"I got things to do," he said.

"Tell me what I can do to help," Lucas replied.

"You can wait inside with Doc."

The two of them went to the door of the shack. Doc turned his head to them. He was working on the woman's shoulder, and Sheila was holding the lamp for him.

"I'm leaving him here." Caleb motioned to the young man. "Do you want me to tie him?"

"Don't need to. Leave him be," Doc told him. "I know he won't go anywhere, nor will he do us any harm. He and his mother are the last two left of his family. He won't do anything to hurt her chances."

"I'll sit over here, Doc," Lucas said, going to a barrel by the stove. "Out of your way."

Caleb carried his rifle and crossed the open space to walk down the trail. It was very dark now, for the moon had set, but his eyes adjusted quickly. He climbed to the ledge where he'd see and hear anyone riding toward the camp.

He settled in and thought about what Lucas told him. He and his mother had embarked on a life built on avenging the loss of their family.

Caleb recalled something his own father liked to say: *Vengeance is mine, I will repay, says the Lord.* Losing a father and brother and sisters is a heavy load for anyone to carry.

Vengeance.

Over the years, there were many times when Caleb thought about his father using those words . . . but the old man used them for the wrong reasons.

He didn't want to think about that now. He almost never liked to think about it. One thing he knew, though — one thing he could never forget — when he was a young fella himself, vengeance drove him to do things that changed his life.

The sky was brightening in the east when he saw Doc and Sheila come out of the shack. Caleb went down the hill and followed the trail around to the camp. By the time he reached the fire, Doc was sitting and stirring beans in a pot, and Sheila was dozing off near her father, a blanket wrapped around her.

Caleb joined them, sitting where he could watch for any visitors.

Doc looked at him and grumbled, "I've been in there so long, I forgot what the air smells like and what the sky looks like."

"How are your patients?"

"The wound was festering, and I needed to excise more flesh inside. She didn't die while I was cutting into the wound, so that's a good thing. And the bullet is out of Lucas's arm. I believe he'll do just fine."

376

"Are they awake?"

The doctor shook his head. "They're sedated. They'll be sleeping it off for a while. The longer, the better."

"You think they'll live?"

"Lucas will. But the mother . . . ?" Doc paused and pondered his answer. "Time will tell. She's struggling. But I've done all I can."

Doc then told him everything that had happened. What he said about the killing of Smith supported what Lucas told Caleb. And Doc shared everything Horner told him about the rumors of the fortune as well as what Mrs. Fields had to say about it.

They lapsed into silence, a group of exhausted people, and Caleb thought about it all.

Then, as the dawn light broke over the mountains, his own past again edged into his mind. The hard things that happened to a family were not always the work of torch-bearing gunmen who rode up in the middle of the night.

There were secrets about Caleb's life that no one knew. Things he'd done that were far worse than anything the sleeping mother and son in that shack had done. He ran a tired hand down his face, trying to make sense of the argument being waged between his brain and his gut.

Doc broke into his thoughts. "I see you're wearing a tin star. So the judge asked you to come after us?"

Caleb glanced at Sheila. "Patterson and I struck a deal. But I would have come after you anyway."

Sheila remained silent, her back straightening visibly. Her blue eyes spit fire at him. He had no doubt that she was thinking of the night at his ranch. She'd been right to worry about her father, and he was wrong. But the argument was between the two of them, and there was no reason to get Doc involved.

"So what were the judge's orders?" Doc asked.

Caleb nodded toward the shack. "He wants these stagecoach robberies to stop. Feels it's giving Elkhorn an undesirable reputation. Of course, he wants the strongboxes back, and he'll want those two to stand trial."

"And you are prepared to give him everything he wants?"

Caleb looked steadily at his friend. Doc was not a very subtle fella. When they played chess, he would almost always come right at him. Caleb knew he didn't give a damn about the first two things. He was asking about what would happen to his two patients.

Caleb pulled his hat off and ran a hand through his hair. He could make do without the reward money. But there was still the deal he'd made to get his partner out of jail. Without Henry Jordan joining him soon to run the ranch, there was not much point in sticking around Elkhorn.

"Before I know the answer to that, Doc, I reckon there's a question or two I'd like to ask Mrs. Fields."

CHAPTER THIRTY-SEVEN

Caleb leaned against the tall boulders on the lookout ledge and watched the red-gold sun fit itself down between two peaks. Up in the hills to the south of the camp, some bird was watching, as well, and whistling the notes of its melancholy song.

Once the sun disappeared, the air began to cool quickly. The breeze picked up, sweeping through the bluffs and mountainsides and ravines, sighing softly through the pines. And twilight gradually began to give way to night.

He glanced down at the old mining camp lying in deepening shadow below him. At the far end, where the graves of dead men looked like a neatly ordered garden plot, the wind stirred the dust and lifted it into a tight, whirling cloud, before it all spread out and faded like a ghost at dawn.

Caleb expelled a deep breath through puffed cheeks. They'd been here two full days since the shootout, and he was restless to get going. He had a job to do, getting everyone back to Elkhorn. But until Doc said his patient was ready to travel, they weren't going anywhere. Still, Caleb wasn't built for sitting for too long. The urge to get moving had been nipping at him all day, and it wasn't letting up.

Maybe it was also this place, he thought, looking down at the camp. Dead gray shacks, some burned out, some collapsed in on themselves. The piles of gravel. The busted, discarded tools and conveyances of a played-out mine scattered everywhere. Even outlaws that made it their hideout were now mostly dead and gone.

Whatever it was, until they got back on the trail, it was his job to keep these folks safe.

In the hills beyond the creek, a family of foxes started yipping and barking, and it made him think of his dog. This was the time of day when he especially missed Bear.

Caleb didn't much like going to town too often and staggering back brandy sick. Bear was all the company he needed. He never complained or rattled on about nonsense. He was smart as a whip, but, try as Caleb might, he couldn't get that dog to play chess worth a damn. Still, Bear kept an eye on things and on his master, and that boy had an unbeatable nose for sniffing out danger.

What Caleb had smelled for the past hour was fresh stewed rabbit, beans, and hot biscuits, and his stomach was rumbling. Doc had said, all casual, that they could do with something other than beans and dry biscuits. So Caleb put out some snares yesterday and skinned four fat cottontails today.

Just then, Sheila Burnett came out of the shack. She was wearing the hat and the duster she seemed to have become attached to, and she walked with the sure step of a confident woman. Since arriving here, he'd realized she had a great many of her father's qualities in her. She was hardy, despite being a city-bred woman. She seemed to be able to adjust to whatever the frontier life threw at her. She even had a sense of humor, but she wasn't always willing to let it show.

She stooped over the fire, filled a plate, poured coffee into a cup, and started across the camp toward the trail.

Before she'd gone too far, Lucas Fields appeared in the doorway, looking across the camp at Sheila's departing back. His arm was in a sling, and he was obviously still hurt from the beating, but he walked to the fire and managed to sit. A moment later, he lit a cigarette and sat smoking.

He seemed to be improving, but Caleb didn't have to worry about his whereabouts. The young gunslick never moved too far from his mother's side.

Mrs. Fields was another story. Doc wasn't sure whether she would live or not. The fever was still high and didn't show any signs of breaking. If she died, Caleb figured that'd be the time Lucas would make a run for it.

So far, the outlaw had been right about Dodger. Over the past two days, Caleb had kept watching for the killer to reappear. He'd searched the surrounding hills, but he could find no trace of the backstabber. With any luck, he'd gone off to find trouble somewhere else.

Caleb's instincts were telling him something different, though. Doc had shared with him everything that Mrs. Fields and Horner said about the fortune she'd supposedly stashed away. Lucas didn't seem to know anything about it, but Caleb guessed Dodger knew everything that the sheriff knew. And that was a lot of money to walk away from.

However, there'd been no sign of him and no sign of Zeke and his posse either. Caleb guessed he was probably still searching that area around Devil's Claw pass. Getting from there to here would be no easy task, and he didn't expect to see Zeke or anyone else from Elkhorn. This abandoned mining camp was a good hideout, and he understood why it had gone undiscovered for so long.

Before long, Sheila came around the boulders onto the wide ledge, and they exchanged greetings.

"Getting dark fast," she noted, handing him his supper.

"Much obliged for the food. My stomach was about ready to drag me right over the edge and make straight for that fire."

She smiled and gazed down at the camp. Lamplight was beginning to glow in the shack door.

"Can I sit a minute?"

"Sure."

Caleb ate as he watched her settle down. She sat cross-legged, half facing him so that she could see the camp at the same time. She took off her hat and laid it beside her, smoothing her hair back with both hands. She was a very pretty woman, and — whatever he thought of her before — she was a damn sight prettier now. From the furrowed brow, he knew something was troubling her.

So he waited until she was ready to get to it.

"Do you think Dodger might have gone for good?" she asked finally.

She'd been through a great deal, and he knew the possibility of Dodger showing up was wearing on her. For these past two days, she'd stayed pretty close to her father, but she wasn't one to be kept under anyone's thumb. Caleb had already seen that. In fact, she was much tougher than he'd initially given her credit for.

Even so, he had a strong feeling that once all this trouble was behind them and they were back in Elkhorn, she'd be more than ready to go back to her normal life in the East.

"Gone for good?" Caleb shook his head slowly. "Sooner or later, he'll show his face. The question is whether he'll come at us alone or get himself a gang of gunslingers to back his play."

She pursed her full lips and looked off into the shadowy mountains.

"I agree. That's why I cleaned and re-loaded all the guns you collected from the outlaws."

He cocked an eyebrow at her.

"I do know how to care for a gun, Mr. Marlowe. I told you, I went shooting quite often in New York."

"That ain't it."

"No? Well, if you're worrying about Lucas having access to them, you needn't trouble yourself. My father is keeping an eye on him and on the guns." She hesitated. "Not that I think he would do anything to hurt us, considering his mother's condition."

What he was going to say was that he could barely taste gun oil in the stewed rabbit at all, but he decided to hold off teasing her. Those two lines in her forehead were still there.

"How is she?" he asked instead.

She shrugged. "No change, really. My father says if the fever breaks tonight, she has a chance. If it doesn't, we might be digging a grave for her tomorrow."

He had to admit, he liked the matter-of-factness of how she spoke. He studied her as once again she stared down at the camp. The thick braid was gone. Her long, brown hair fell in waves to her waist. She had a scratch along her jaw along with a smudge of dirt on her cheek, and the duster she wore looked like she'd been driving cattle through the dust of New Mexico. She didn't seem to be bothered by any of it.

Caleb reminded himself that her acceptance of everything was probably because she knew this frontier living was only temporary. With all she'd been through, Sheila would have stories to tell back in New York that would make her friends stare with shock and admiration.

"It's been really good having a chance to spend time with my father. He sees me as a grown woman. I haven't always felt that in the wording of his letters."

Caleb focused on his plate of food.

"I've been able to help him, and I've seen the look of respect in his eyes."

In spite of the situation they were still dealing with, Caleb didn't think he'd seen Doc this happy since he'd met him.

"And thank you for not telling him about my coming out to your ranch that first night. I know now it was a foolish thing to do."

Caleb touched the brim of his hat. "Your secret is safe with me."

"But I was right. Wasn't I?" Her blue eyes sparkled, and he read mischief in them. "I mean, about asking you to go after him."

"Based on what I knew then, my answer was justified."

"Justified or not, I was right. Admit it, Mr. Marlowe."

"Only if you admit that I was right shooting them rustlers who came after me and my cattle."

"But you shot them dead. Every single one of them."

He put the empty tin plated on the ground and leaned toward her, frowning. "We ain't really gonna have this conversation again. After everything you've gone through?"

She took a deep breath, glaring at him and ready to go at it one more time. Then she paused. "No. You're correct. We *are* done with that conversation."

"Good, cuz you ain't in New York no more."

"I definitely am not."

"But you'll be able to return to the safety of that life soon enough. And then you can just forget about everything that happened here."

She looked at him like he'd just told her she could fly to the moon. "The dangers in New York are different from what you face here, but the city is no safer than the frontier."

"I can't say nothing about that, but I'd wager you're better protected there."

"One can build a fortress to live in anywhere, Mr. Marlowe, but that is not the life I'm looking for. In fact, you should know, I'm not going back. I'm staying in Elkhorn."

She blurted out the last words, and Caleb

388

watched her full lips thin and the furrows deepen in her forehead. Her chin jutted slightly, and she looked ready to fight this out.

Caleb wasn't the one to fight with, however. "Talked to your father about it?"

"Not yet." Her features softened, and she looked for a moment like a lost child. "You're his friend. You probably know him better than I do. Do you think he'll object to me staying?"

Caleb knew nothing about father-daughter relationships, but this woman was looking pretty damn vulnerable right now. When it came right down to it, though, Doc was his friend. Who was Caleb to say anything about his daughter's future? Hell, he and Sheila were closer in age than he'd like to admit.

Still, he knew he'd object if she were his daughter. No matter what she thought, frontier life was hard and dangerous, especially for women. That is, women who weren't raised to it. This past week was proof of it. She survived the perils she faced, but she'd also been lucky. He'd face a hungry grizzly before he'd say that to her, though.

"I'm sure Doc only wants what's best for you."

"And who's to know what's best for me?" The fighter was back. "My father? My grandfather in New York? You?"

"Don't come at me with your claws out. You asked a question. I answered."

"Is that so? How old were *you* when you left your parents' home, Mr. Marlowe?"

"We ain't talking about me." Her question took him by surprise. "But I see what you're doing."

"What am I doing?"

"You want someone so you can practice the argument you know you're gonna have with your father." He shook his head. "Sorry, Miss Burnett. I'm the wrong person for it."

"I think you're the *right* person for it." She was not quitting.

"And why is that?"

"Because you're a man. The only man out here that I can talk to about this before I speak to my father."

"Go practice on Lucas."

"What does he know about my father? Or me?" She made a face that said she was appalled he would even suggest such a thing.

"Well, it don't set well with me, Doc being my fr—"

"He needs me." She was going to have this conversation with him. Period. "I lost my mother at the age of nine. Since then, my father has been alone. Don't you agree that I should come and live with him now that I'm a grown woman? He's not married. He has no one to look after him, and I'm his only daughter. It's my duty!"

The only way to avoid getting dragged into this was for Caleb to pick her up and throw her off this ledge. And she'd still be jawing at him all the way down.

He took a deep breath. "Miss Burnett, are you doing this for him or for you?"

"For both of us."

He held her gaze. "For him, or for you?"

She paused before answering. When she did, her voice was no more than a whisper. "For me. I *need* to stay. I can't go back to New York. The life I had there ended when I left."

Caleb was surprised by her reply and — he hated to admit it — curious what had happened in New York. But that was none of his business, he told himself.

"You tell Doc *that,* Sheila. He'll want to know why, but you'll see. It'll all turn out fine."

The smile on her face blossomed like a morning glory on a summer day. "You think so?"

Caleb shouldn't have done it, but his

fingers had a mind of their own. He reached out and wiped that smudge of dirt off her cheek. Damn, but she had the softest skin. Her eyes opened wide, and suddenly his buckskin breeches got mighty tight.

"I do. Now get. You might want to have that conversation with your father sooner than later."

Sheila jumped to her feet and disappeared into the darkness like a flash.

Caleb shook his head at the thoughts that had rushed into his mind. All he'd been doing was talking and admiring her smile and her skin and how damn pretty she was. And kissing her wasn't the only thing he was thinking about.

"No," he said out loud. A man would be a low-down dirty dog to mess around with his friend's daughter. It just wasn't done.

When he got back to town, the first thing he was gonna do was make a long-overdue visit to one of them girls at the Belle Saloon.

Hearing her coming back, Caleb turned to look at her. He'd need to apologize. But before he could say a word, he froze. It was Doc's daughter, but she wasn't alone. The man behind her was young and big, and the smirk on his face was nothing if not nasty. And the look in Sheila's face told him exactly who the man was.

"Weren't that touching? I damn near started bawling over here."

Dodger was holding his pistol to Sheila's temple and using her as shield.

"And I'm much obliged to you, Miss Burnett, for distracting Marlowe like you done."

CHAPTER THIRTY-EIGHT

"Raise them hands up nice and high."

As Caleb raised them, he looked steadily at the gunslick.

There was no doubt who he was facing, and there was something familiar about him. Beneath the brown, wide-brimmed hat, the face was round and boyish. He could have been sixteen or twenty-five; it was difficult to tell. Gunslingers just kept getting younger, he thought. But that didn't mean they'd live to see thirty.

This one wouldn't.

Just as Imala had described him at the cabin she shared with her dead husband, Dodger was wearing a dark-brown coat and a dark bandana. His black vest was worn and missing buttons. The tan wool pants he wore tucked into his scuffed boots were filthy. He had a second Remington holstered on his right hip that matched the one pointed at Sheila's head.

She'd lost her hat, and Dodger had a grip on her hair that he used to give her a good jerk, just as a reminder for her that he was there.

This burly gunslinger was not making a very good first impression on Caleb.

"Now lower your right hand and ease that nice, shiny Colt out and lay it on the ground. And if your finger decides to go anywhere near that trigger, I'm gonna blow this pretty little thing's brains all over this rock. And I know that ain't something you wanna see happen."

"Don't do it." Sheila's eyes met Caleb's. "He'll kill both of us anyway. And if you think you're doing me a favor keeping me alive . . . think again."

"Shut up," Dodger said, yanking on her hair.

Caleb did as he was told.

"Now the other one. And remember to move real slow."

As he laid the second revolver on the ground, something about this fella tugged at a memory. It was something about the voice.

"Do I know you?" he asked.

Dodger smirked. "I'm the man who's gonna put you in the ground."

"We'll wait and see how that plays out."

He shook his head. "But we ain't met before?"

"You really don't know me?"

Caleb wracked his memory. "I can't recollect, but there's something."

"I'm Dodger Clanton."

A face popped fleetingly into the back of his brain but didn't take hold. "You famous, Dodger Clanton?"

"How about this name . . . Jack Clanton?"

Jack Clanton. Caleb reached back to see if he could catch the image of that face. The memory darted by like a swallow in April, so quick that it was gone before he even got a good look. Then, it set down in a nest on the wall of his brain, and Caleb threw a net over it.

"Jack Clanton," he said.

It all pieced together like a nine-patch quilt. And that quilt had blood on it.

Jack Clanton was a drunken bruiser of a ranch hand who thought he was the meanest, toughest, quickest gunslinger south of the Badlands.

One night, while Caleb was playing nursemaid to a couple of touring dignitaries and delivering them up to Cheyenne City in Wyoming, Clanton and a few of his friends rode in to raise hell in Greeley. And raise it they did. They started in one saloon, where after a few hours of drinking, they got into an argument at a poker table. The fight that followed involved about thirty fellas and nearly wrecked the bar. From there, his pals went on to another saloon with less dramatic but similar results.

Jack Clanton and one of the boys, however, decided that a visit to a brothel just off Maple Street was in order. It was a place Jack had visited before, and the whore he was interested in still couldn't hear out of one ear because of him batting her around. She wanted no part of him. Instead of leaving, Clanton and his pal beat the hell out of the bouncer. And then Clanton decided that the woman needed a beating as well.

Caleb arrived back in town in time to drag the filthy dog out of the brothel without anybody getting killed, which was a miracle in itself. Clanton did have a few bruises himself, however, by the time Caleb got him stowed in the Greeley jail. But at least he was breathing. If there was one thing he couldn't stomach, it was a big man laying his hands on people who couldn't defend themselves. He never could sit still for that.

The next morning, the madam running that brothel didn't want to press charges. Bad for business, she said. The woman he beat up knew what would come of the trouble if she pushed it. He'd get thirty days, if that, and then he'd come looking for her.

So the end result was that Caleb had to turn him loose about noon, whereupon Clanton went down to a saloon he hadn't wrecked, drank up some courage, and came back to the jail with his six-shooters loaded and loose in his holsters.

It was sheer luck that Caleb had been sitting out front when Jack Clanton came walking up the street with his friends mouthing off and goading him the whole way. The fool called him out. He wanted blood for being "humiliated," and Caleb couldn't talk him down. The man threw down, and that was that. Clanton lay in the dust, his own blood draining away in the street.

Curiously enough, Jack Clanton had been working on the same ranch as Grat Horner. Like a patchwork quilt.

And now his boy was following in his old man's footsteps.

"I remember," Caleb said. "You sound just like your pappy."

"Well, this is the last voice you're gonna hear."

Caleb nodded at Sheila. "She don't have nothing to do with this. Why don't you let her go, and we'll settle this. You and me."

"She's been getting at me since I first saw her in Elkhorn. The business I got with her is separate. Though it's more pleasure than business."

Dodger released her hair and grabbed her around the waist. Even if Caleb were able to get to his guns, the outlaw was using her as a shield.

"Never mind her. You plan on killing me out of revenge for your old man?"

"I've been looking forward to this ever since you shot him in the back going out of that jail."

"That's what you think?" Caleb scoffed. "Jack Clanton came looking for me. And he wouldn't be reasoned with."

"That's a lie. I heard it all from them ranch hands that saw it."

"I don't know what they told you, but if I shot him going out of that jail, there ain't no way I would've stayed sheriff up there after that." Caleb held his gaze. "And when I went riding out to that ranch on other business a month or so later, why didn't those ranch hands call me on it? I'll tell you why. Cuz it ain't true."

"You're a coward and a damn liar."

"That so?" Caleb spat on the ground. "I don't shoot men in the back, like your friend Grat Horner. And I don't creep up and cut their throats from behind neither. Ain't that the way Wendell got it?"

"Wendell was a pain in my ass. Always pushing me. Knocking me down in front of other people." Dodger jerked Sheila off-balance but kept the Remington pointed at her head. "He got what he had coming."

"I say you're a low-down coward and a bully, just like your old man. He got a real thrill out of beating women."

Caleb didn't look, but he saw Sheila's hand slip into the pocket of her duster.

Dodger's eyes grew wide, and the smirk was gone. "Don't you talk shit."

"I'd wager he beat your own mama, ain't that right?"

The killer's mouth was twitching, pulling to the side. "He never done nothing. My pa —"

"A man like that, always trying to puff himself up. Always thinking that beating on his wife or his children would make him a man."

"Shut up. My pa was a real man."

"Your pa was a stupid, low-life weasel and yellow-bellied, to boot. Just like you."

Dodger stared, unable to say a word.

"If you're waiting for Horner to tell you what to do now, little boy, you're gonna have to ask him in Hell. Cuz that's where he is, and that's where you're heading."

"I don't need *nobody* to tell me that you're the one gonna die," Dodger rasped, white with fury.

"You're forgetting about the Code of the Gunslinger, Dodger," he said coolly.

As the gunslinger began to turn the muzzle of his six-shooter from Sheila's temple toward Caleb, he hesitated. "What code?"

The moment he paused, Sheila's hand flared out to the side. An instant later, she drove the blade of her knife deep into the outlaw's thigh and pitched herself forward, grabbing for his gun hand.

Dodger let out a shriek of pain and outrage.

Jake Bell's knife came out of Caleb's boot and flashed through the Colorado night, burying itself to the hilt in Dodger's chest.

The outlaw's mouth dropped open in shock, and he gaped at the handle. He reached up and grasped it with his free hand. Unsure of whether to pull it out or not, he looked straight at Caleb, hatred in his eyes.

With Sheila still hanging on to his wrist, Dodger reached for the other Remington, still pouched at his hip.

His pistol cleared leather and was coming

401

up fast. But not fast enough.

Caleb snatched one of his Colts from his feet and, with a single movement, blasted Dodger between the eyes, sending a red mist into the mountain air behind him.

The outlaw dropped backward, his burly body thudding as he hit the ground. He never twitched, never moved.

The sound of the gunshot echoed off the hills and peaks, like thunder in a receding storm, slowly subsiding.

Caleb walked over, drew his knife from Dodger's chest, cleaned it off, and slid it back into his boot. Taking Sheila's knife out of the dead outlaw's leg, he wiped it on the man's coat and turned to her.

She was sitting close to the edge, holding Dodger's revolver, staring at her foe. When Caleb held out his hand to her, she took it and got to her feet.

"I saw you put your hand in that pocket, and I was wondering if you were still packing that pistol I gave you." He looked at the knife before offering it to her. "Wendell's?"

She nodded and took it from him.

"Well, that's sorta fitting, don't you think?" he asked.

Sheila gazed at it for a moment, slipped it into her pocket, and threw her arms around his neck.

They stood there together, and Caleb felt her body shivering. It was only natural. They'd been in a tight spot. She'd claimed that the streets of New York City were dangerous, but he doubted she'd ever faced anything like this.

She drew back a little and looked straight into his eyes. "Thank you. You saved my life."

"You did real well. Couldn't have done it without you."

Sheila pressed a kiss on his cheek and backed out of his arms. She turned, took a couple of steps, and frowned down at Dodger's dead body.

"I'm glad you killed him." She glanced over her shoulder at him. "If you hadn't, I would have done it myself."

Without another word, she started back along the boulders and disappeared. Watching her go, Caleb thought that maybe Sheila Burnett was tough enough for frontier life, after all.

CHAPTER THIRTY-NINE

Early the next morning, Doc sent Sheila to fetch Caleb, who was drinking coffee by the campfire, keeping an eye on Lucas, and trying to decide what he wanted to do with the boy and his mother.

Sheila told him that the fever had broken, and Mrs. Fields was awake. The woman was weak, but Caleb could speak to her if he promised not to wear her out.

By rights, he knew he shouldn't be thinking about it at all. He should simply truss them up and haul them back to Elkhorn to face justice. They were stagecoach robbers and accessories to murder, even if he believed Lucas and the stories Zeke and Preacher told about them.

If he did take them back to face the judge, however, Elkhorn would be having a mother and son hanging. That was the punishment for murder. No matter how he thought of the Fields gang, two men were dead in the

404

last stagecoach robbery. And there were no witnesses who could testify Dodger had actually been the one who killed them.

A hanging like that would sure as hell draw a crowd.

It would be an interesting trial, though. From the talks he'd been having with Lucas and the one Doc had with the mother, those two would be testifying under oath that they alone were to blame. Neither one wanted the other to be dancing for the hangman.

Sheila stayed outside the shack with Lucas while Caleb and Doc spoke to the patient.

Mrs. Fields knew what was going on. Doc had filled her in with what had happened while she'd been unconscious. Caleb guessed that the flush in her cheeks was not all caused by fever. She'd lost men she was responsible for, and the future for herself and her son wasn't looking all that rosy either. She had to be feeling sadness, anger, worry, desperation.

Doc introduced him and told her what Caleb had been sent to do. He also told her that her son had confessed to their past crimes, where they came from, and what they'd been doing since her husband was killed.

She spoke directly to Caleb. Her voice was

not strong, but she was clearly a bright woman.

"If Lucas has told you anything that makes him look responsible for all that has happened, it's a lie. I'm the leader of this gang. I'm the one responsible for the robberies of the Wells Fargo stages. I'll swear that he never participated in any holdup. He just arrived here after I was wounded. I'll swear to that on my husband's grave. I'm the one who should be punished for those crimes."

She paused, trying to catch her breath. She was growing paler, but she still clung to a hope of saving her son's life.

"Lucas admits he was part of the gang," Caleb told her.

"He's only seventeen. He was a child when I got started. For all the years I've been robbing those villains, I kept him away. And he did what I told him to do."

Caleb had no doubt this was all a lie, but he understood her fierce determination to save her child.

"Ma'am, I ain't no lawyer or judge or jury. But in this last robbery, you were sitting inside that stagecoach. Your blood was left on that seat. So there's no way you can take responsibility for shooting the driver and the guard riding shotgun. They'll hang you for robbing those stagecoaches, but murder is the most serious of everything that you've done. And Lucas was outside holding a gun."

"It wasn't him." She closed her eyes, and long lashes lay on the pale cheeks. "That was Dodger, acting against orders."

"So you say. But your word ain't gonna be good enough. I seriously doubt Judge Patterson will believe you. And I know them Wells Fargo men chirping in the governor's ear in Denver will be calling for your head . . . and for your son's."

She tried to sit, and Doc helped her, propping her up with a folded blanket behind her back. Caleb didn't know what she looked like before being shot, but right now she seemed shrunken and spent, a frail slip of a woman. Her right arm was bound in a sling.

"I've already told you what I'll tell the judge and jury, Mr. Marlowe. I will take the blame, and I'll say whatever needs to be said. I won't have my son wrongfully accused. But would you like to hear the whole story?"

Despite the days she'd spent in this cot, her eyes were clear when they met his, and her voice was growing stronger. There was a hard edge to it, but Caleb also took notice of the motherly tone of command. Right then, he understood how she ran the tough men who worked for her, minded her orders, and remained devoted to her. How many men were capable of disrespecting and ignoring their mothers? She had a quality in her manner that made any half-decent man sit straight and listen.

"I'd like to hear the whole story . . . if it's the truth."

She nodded with satisfaction. "I want you to forget, just for a moment, this last robbery on the Denver road and those poor dead men. I want to tell you exactly how we've conducted our business for the past five years."

"I'm listening."

As she shifted her weight, trying get comfortable, she gasped and clutched her shoulder. Whatever color remained in her face drained away now. It took her a few moments to recover, and Caleb waited. Doc was watching her carefully.

"For each robbery," she said when she could continue, "I'd choose one of my men to take the lead. That person would wear a long duster and a flour sack over his head. We'd cut holes for eyes, and he'd wear a special derby."

This was why there was no description of

the faces of this gang, Caleb thought. There was no possible way for anyone to describe them.

"My man would jump out from behind a large boulder or tree on whatever route we'd chosen for the robbery. He'd wave his shotgun at the driver."

"Why would they stop? Why didn't they run him down or shoot him dead?"

"Because at that very moment our other men were hiding in the brush or behind trees or boulders at the side of the road. We chose our spots carefully. My men would have their rifles pointed at the driver, and the weapons would be conspicuous, even if my men weren't. When we started our campaign against Wells Fargo, we made it even more daunting. We'd use carved pieces of wood painted to look like rifles, wedged into the brush. We made it look like there were dozens of us."

"Go on."

"My man would tell them to throw down the strongbox."

"And they always did."

"If the stage driver hesitated at all, my man would yell out and instruct the group in the bushes. Something like, 'Give him the solid volley, boys.' Or some words to that effect. Once or twice, we had to shoot into the air to get their attention, but never once did we wound a driver or a guard or a passenger."

To be a stagecoach driver on these dangerous roads, men took their lives in their hands. Caleb understood that seeing rifle barrels pointed at them from the bushes would seal the deal. A driver would gladly throw down a strongbox if he thought it would help him live to see another day.

"Very quickly, word got around. Five years we robbed Wells Fargo, and no one was ever shot. Not one drop of blood shed. They always did what they were told, and no one got hurt. During one robbery, a woman passenger even stepped out to voluntarily surrender her purse, but our man declined, saying that we only wanted the Wells Fargo box."

This was starting to sound like some fanciful Robin Hood tale. But there *was* blood.

"You lost a man in a recent robbery," Caleb asked. "What happened?"

"Jeb's older brother was the one picked to step in front of the stagecoach. After the driver dropped the strongbox to the ground, the stage guard shot him."

Mrs. Fields's face sank. She was obviously still upset at the memory.

"What happened then?"

"He was hit, but we thought it wasn't serious. My men started shooting to scare them, and the driver whipped up his team. We only found out later that he was badly wounded. He died within the hour."

She used her left hand to rub her forehead.

"That's when Dodger joined your outfit?" Doc asked.

She nodded. "We should have quit right them. Ended it. But as a group, we decided on one final holdup. To do that, Wendell felt we needed another gun, so he rode to Denver. That's where he found him."

Caleb glanced at the place where the bullet had struck the woman. "Why were you inside the stagecoach for this last robbery?"

"My gang was breaking up. I planned to ride the coach to Elkhorn and make arrangements for going on to California. There would be no reason to suspect me. What was taken in this robbery was to be divided amongst the men. I wanted no share. Once my son was done, he was to go Elkhorn. The others were to split up and go east or north. From here, Lucas and I would travel west and never look back."

"Were there other passengers in the coach?" Doc asked.

"I was the only one."

411

"What went wrong?" Caleb already knew who was killed, but he wanted to hear how it happened from her pale lips.

"*Everything* went wrong. Wendell went out into the road, and the stagecoach stopped. The driver was ready to throw down the strongbox, but Dodger stepped out of hiding. There was no reason for it. I'd like to think panic hit him, but whatever possessed him, he started shooting."

"Who shot you?" Doc asked.

"It had to be Dodger. I don't believe any of the others fired a shot." Her brown eyes looked up at the doctor. "I don't recall what happened afterward. They carried me here somehow. When I opened my eyes, you were tending to my wound."

It all made sense to Caleb. Dodger had been hired by Horner to become part of this gang. They were after the loot accumulated during the years of holding up stagecoaches. Horner may even have taken the job of sheriff in Elkhorn for that reason. It was possible that shooting Mrs. Fields was an accident, but Dodger may have thought Lucas knew where this treasure was hidden. No way to know what was going on in that killer's head.

"You don't need to tell us what you've done with all the money you took in those robberies over the years," Doc said. "But you said you haven't a dollar to your name. You told me straight out that there's no money or gold left. I'd like to know why you told me that . . . unless you were lying."

"I wasn't lying," she asserted as vehemently as she could manage. "I sold my husband's claim and our ranch in Montana. I used that money to buy some land for a new ranch south of San Francisco. That's where I planned to settle."

"And the rest?" Doc asked.

Mrs. Fields paused, looking from Doc's face to Caleb's. She looked like she was trying to choose her next words carefully.

"The rest went to charity," she said finally.

"What charity?" they asked at the same time.

"When my husband went to war, I almost lost him. A great many other women did lose their husbands. That money has been going to two widows' funds, one in Pennsylvania and one in Virginia. They help war widows and their children, women who may have lost everything in that fighting. Lost their men. Lost their future. I lost my own husband and all my children except for Lucas to a company of gunmen in a single night. Mourning my family was one thing.

Trying to survive was quite another."

Mrs. Fields's attention turned to Caleb next.

"I can give you the names of the directors of those two charities. They can tell you how much money I've sent them over the past five years. And they can tell you the good it's done."

Caleb stood and went to the door of the shack and looked out at the remains of the deserted mining camp and at the hills and mountains beyond. Laws were made in cities like Denver and Washington, and the people who made the laws mostly lived in them places. Out here, it was a rough and violent country. The laws from back East didn't always work, and the truly guilty never felt the hand of justice.

Wells Fargo's hired men were responsible for four deaths in the Fields family. Over five years, she had — without bloodshed — exacted what she felt they were due. Because of Horner, blood was spilled, and two men were dead at Dodger's hand. Now, the killers themselves had paid the price.

And who came out ahead? Caleb thought. Widows.

Frontier justice. It was rough, and maybe not what the judge was looking for, but sometimes life had a way of working things out.

CHAPTER FORTY

Two days later, Caleb and Doc and Sheila got on the trail back to Elkhorn.

The horses, tied in a line behind them, carried the strongboxes with the cash and letters and certificates they'd contained, as well as the weapons that had belonged to the outlaws, the sheriff, and his men.

The weather was clear, and the morning sun was bright in the sky. The trail, hills, and valleys held no mystery for Caleb now. Many of the same dangers existed, but he was traveling over familiar ground. The last time he'd come this way, however, his attention had been focused on tracking outlaws and killers. Today, he could simply breathe the cool mountain air and revel in the endless forests, the power of the river, and the majesty of the soaring peaks.

"Do you think everything she told us was the truth?" Doc asked, interrupting his thoughts.

They had only an hour or so of easy riding left till they reached the Denver road, and Devil's Claw loomed behind them.

"It would be easy enough to write to those charities. I could do it, if you like," Sheila offered. Her father had told her in confidence everything about Mrs. Fields.

Doc agreed. "Yes, that part of it is verifiable. But what about giving up the life of a road agent and settling down in California?"

Caleb knew Doc had begun to develop a friendship with the mother and son as they both recuperated. He shot a questioning look at his friend. "I thought you trusted her."

"I do. But how can a woman with her quickness and drive settle on a ranch after all she's done? It certainly will be a relatively quiet life."

"You should have asked her," Sheila told him. "I am certain Mrs. Fields has plans, even if she didn't share them. I think she's a woman who knows exactly how to put her abilities to use."

Caleb sensed that Sheila's comment to her father had as much to do with her own future plans. The night she'd intended to speak to him, she was interrupted by Dodger's appearance. Since then, she'd had no chance to tell him what she wanted to do with her life. Or rather, what she didn't want to do.

Doc turned to him again. "Have you decided what you're going to say to the judge when we get to Elkhorn?"

"Nearly."

After talking to Mrs. Fields, Caleb decided that he wasn't going to take the mother and son back to Elkhorn. They were mending nicely, according to Doc. She was even up and moving about a little. So he left them at the mining camp after getting their promise that, when she was ready to travel, they'd go to Denver. From there, they'd board a train for California. And that their days as road agents were behind them.

"You'd better decide soon," Doc said. "Because we need to have the same story."

Caleb's instincts told him Mrs. Fields was telling the truth about what had happened to her family in Montana, how she'd approached getting her revenge, and what she'd done with the money.

Who was he to throw stones at a woman who promised to change her life and start herself and her son down a new road? He didn't see that hanging them would do much good. They wanted to start over, and he wasn't going to stand in their way.

Hell, he'd done it himself.

When they reached the Denver road, Doc pointed to a group of riders approaching from the direction of Elkhorn. Even from a distance Caleb immediately recognized the hairy, boar-like figure in gray at the head of the others.

Doc seemed to recognize him too. "Isn't that Zeke, the miner who works for Judge Patterson on occasion?"

"The very man."

"We still haven't worked out a suitable story, Caleb."

"We'll be all right, Doc."

The judge's hired man was genuinely happy to see them — especially Caleb.

"We've been searching the hills for two days. Yesterday, we decided to take a look west of the river. Didn't see no sign of you. And now, here you are, coming back with Doc and his daughter, saving them all on your own."

"That's not all he's done." Doc motioned to the strongboxes and the string of horses.

The man's eyes lit up. He rode past them and inspected the box and the cache of weapons.

"What happened? I want to hear the whole dang thing." He tipped his hat at Sheila. "Pardon my language, miss."

"Before I start, anybody missing the

sheriff in town?"

"Horner disappeared the day Doc's daughter went missing." He tilted his head toward Sheila. "He and three of his men lit out, not saying a word to nobody. The judge was fit to be tied. I don't think he's feeling too good about our two-bit lawman right now. I told him the polecat probably weren't up to no good."

"You were right. He wasn't."

Caleb exchanged a look with Doc. He now knew exactly the story they'd be telling.

"Horner was in cahoots with one of the members of that gang, a fella named Dodger Clanton. They were the ones that took Miss Burnett here, and that outlaw left a trail for the sheriff. Horner was after these strongboxes, so him and his men followed and shot up the road agents' hideaway. It was an old mining camp way out beyond Devil's Claw."

Zeke stared at the doctor and his daughter. "You're lucky he didn't kill you both. He wouldn't have let you go, knowing what he was up to."

"We owe our lives to Marlowe," Doc said. "He arrived while Horner was about ready to kill us both. And then he put an end to their thieving lives."

Zeke's eyes widened and looked at the horses. "So Horner and his no-account deputies are dead?"

"They're all dead."

The miner scratched at his whiskers. "What about that passenger in the stagecoach?"

Doc cut in. "That passenger was actually a member of the gang, wounded during the holdup. That was why they came for me." He shook his head. "That outlaw will never be robbing another stage."

Caleb nodded his head soberly. "That gang is finished."

"And you brought back the strongboxes."

"Leave it to Marlowe to handle everything right," Doc told Zeke and his men.

"We searched that hideout for any more loot, but there wasn't nothing," Caleb said. "This was all of it."

"Dang, but we got another story to tell!" Zeke patted Caleb on the back. "This yarn is even better than you taking on that cougar with your bare hands out by Devil's Claw."

"What cougar?" Doc and Sheila asked, turning to him simultaneously.

Caleb shrugged. "Zeke will be happy to tell you all about it."

There were two bits of unfinished business sitting heavy on him. The first was letting Imala know that Smith was dead. The second was the letter he'd been carrying in his saddlebag since the dying rustler gave it to him to send to his mother.

He addressed Doc and Sheila. "How about if you two ride back with Zeke and his men to Elkhorn? Take the strongboxes back and all these horses and guns with you. I got one stop out here I need to make."

"What do you need to do?" Doc asked.

"I'm gonna pay a visit to that miner's wife and let her know about her husband."

"He's dead too?" Zeke asked.

"Doc saw the whole thing," Caleb said. "Dodger Clanton shot and killed Smith in cold blood."

"He shouldn't have died, the poor fellow." Doc shook his head sadly, looking at his friend. "I didn't know he had a wife."

As Caleb untethered the string of horses from his own mount and handed the rope to Zeke, he asked him to let Patterson know what had happened.

"The judge is gonna be real happy about what you've done. Last time I saw him, he didn't sound too dang keen about how wild and dangerous the newspapers would make Elkhorn look," Zeke told him. "Yep, he's gonna be a happy man. I don't know if he told you, but he has big plans for this here eclipse that's gonna be darkening the sky this summer. All manner of dignitaries are gonna be traipsing into town to watch it from here. All these stagecoach robberies was definitely upsetting his plans."

The most important thing Caleb cared about was having the judge live up to his promise of getting Henry out of jail. But he'd have to stop in and see the man himself about that.

Just as he was getting ready to leave the group, Sheila nudged her horse up next to him.

"May I come with you to the miner's cabin?"

"Why?"

"Because you're taking this woman news of her dead husband. Sometimes it's better to have another woman present in these situations."

Caleb looked at her doubtfully. "Smith's wife ain't one of your New York —"

"I know. But I'd still like to come."

He looked at Doc, who shrugged, mouthing, *Take her.*

"Fine," he said, turning his horse in the direction of Imala's cabin.

She rode beside him in silence for a while, then asked, "Will you tell me something about Mrs. Smith?"

"What do you wanna know?"

"Anything. Her name. Her age. Whether they have any children."

"I will . . . if you'll tell me why you're coming along with me instead of getting back to your father's house in Elkhorn. I'd have thought a bath and some clean clothes and a decent meal might have been a mite more appealing."

She looked steadily at him. "I'm coming because if I'm going to live out here, my father needs to know that I can fit in. That I can belong in this community. That I have at least one friend. I thought, why not start with a widow who might possibly use some company?"

"First of all, this woman lives a couple of hours outside of Elkhorn. You ain't exactly gonna be neighbors." He shook his head and held Sheila's gaze. "Second of all, however you're picturing Mrs. Smith, she ain't it. She ain't a helpless widow any more than Mrs. Fields. Smith's wife don't need no saving. She can live her life perfectly fine without friends. And I have a strong suspicion that might be her wish entirely."

"I won't be a bother. That came out wrong. I meant no disrespect to her. It's just that I have to start somewhere. And I thought, why not today?"

"Well, we'll just see."

She had her father's heart, and Caleb knew she meant well. Knowing Doc didn't give a damn whether someone was white or not, he guessed Sheila would know how to behave. Still, he had to tell her. "The miner's wife is named Imala. They ain't got no children that I know about. And she's from the Arapaho people."

"A native woman! That's wonderful." Sheila's face lit up.

"Why is it wonderful?"

"Maybe, if we *do* become friends, she'll teach me a few things about surviving on the frontier."

ACKNOWLEDGMENTS

We'd like to thank Christa Soulé Desír, an editor without peer. And our profound gratitude goes out to the entire team over at Soucebooks for getting behind Caleb Marlowe and his adventures.

We'd also like to thank our true-blue agent, Jill Marsal of Marsal Lyon Literary Agency.

To our readers, whose encouragement and support fuels our writing, thank you.

Finally, a huge thank-you to our family, who are always there for us when we emerge, beastlike, from the cave.

ACKNOWLEDGMENTS

We'd like to thank Christa Soule Desir, an editor without peer. And our profound gratitude goes out to the entire team over at Sourcebooks for getting behind Caleb Nair's... and his adventures.

We'd also like to thank our time-bite agent, Bill Marsal of Marsal Lyon Literary Agency.

To our readers, whose encouragement and support make our writing, thank you.

Finally, a huge thank-you to our family, who are always there for us when we emerge, batlike, from the cave.

ABOUT THE AUTHOR

Nik James is the pen name for Nikoo and Jim McGoldrick. The two embarked on a marriage of minds decades ago. Since then, they've been around the world.

Twenty-five years ago, they began writing what some critics have referred to as "Northerns" — stories in which the fictional setting and story have a functioning system of justice in place. These were the McGoldricks' early historical, British-set novels. From there, they created a dozen "Easterns" — stories in which the system in place is corrupted by the "bad apple" on the inside. These were the Jan Coffey contemporary thrillers. Continuing their literary journey, they traveled into the world of "Southerns" — stories in which the system itself seems stacked against the hero. This sojourn included the authors' late historicals, also British-set.

Their journey has now taken them to the

place they belong, to the fictional world of "Westerns," where there is no viable system of justice in place, no law and order . . . except that which the strong, independent hero can impose. It is a world where Caleb Marlowe, the protagonist of their new series, lives by a code that pits him against the ruthless greed and murderous ambition of landowners and railroad barons as well as the powerful natural forces of the American frontier. Drawn to the chaos in which men and women must carve out a place for themselves, the authorial team of Nik James has finally come home.

If you enjoyed *High Country Justice*, be sure to tell a friend . . . and leave a review somewhere.

And stop by for a visit at our website nikjamesauthor.com. We'll have a pot of coffee on.

The employees of Thorndike Press hope you have enjoyed this Large Print book. All our Thorndike, Wheeler, and Kennebec Large Print titles are designed for easy reading, and all our books are made to last. Other Thorndike Press Large Print books are available at your library, through selected bookstores, or directly from us.

For information about titles, please call:
  (800) 223-1244

or visit our website at:
  gale.com/thorndike

To share your comments, please write:
  Publisher
  Thorndike Press
  10 Water St., Suite 310
  Waterville, ME 04901